Tidings of Murder and Woe

AN ANNA NOLAN MYSTERY

CATHY SPENCER

Comely
Press

Published by Comely Press
www.comelypress.com

ISBN 978-1-926486-02-4
eISBN 978-1-926486-03-1

To the university colleagues I've worked with over the decades.

At least no one ever got murdered.

Other titles in the Anna Nolan series:
Framed For Murder, Book 1
(Winner of the 2014 Bony Blythe Mystery Award)
Town Haunts, Book 2

Also by Cathy Spencer:
The Dating Do-Over
The Affairs of Harriet Walters, Spinster
Tall Tales Twin-Pack, Mysteries
Tall Tales Twin-Pack, Science Fiction and Fantasy

Connect online with Cathy Spencer:
Subscribe to her blog at
http://cmspencer.blogspot.ca
Like her Facebook page at
https://www.facebook.com/CathySpencerAuthor

My thanks to Constable Riley Babott, Public Affairs/Media Relations Unit, Calgary Police Services for answering my questions about Calgary police procedures, and to fellow-author and Emergency Room physician, Tom Combs, for providing information about poisonings and toxicology testing. If there are any errors in this story, the fault is mine. My gratitude to John Mitchell for helping to make my cover gorgeous. I'm also grateful for the input of my discriminating beta readers, Elise Bédard, Ann Pappert, Diana Patterson, and Debbie Welland, and to my always patient editor, Kate Spencer. It takes a village to publish a book.

1

"I hope you haven't got any plans for lunch."

Anna looked up from her desk to see her boss, Dr. Magdalena Lewis, standing in the office doorway. Magdalena was the chair of the Kinesiology Department at Calgary's Chinook University. The regal blond looked perfectly turned out, as usual, in a red-and-black wool jacket and black pencil skirt.

"Why? What's up?"

"Julia Moreland wants to vet the candidates for the Robert Moreland Scholarship over lunch at her house. With you."

Anna's eyes widened. "You're kidding. Why would she want to see me instead of you? I'm just the administrative assistant."

"She mentioned that she wants to meet, and I quote, 'the assistant who sounds so capable over the phone.' More likely, however, she's read about the two murder investigations in Crane this past year and wants to meet the woman who almost died in both of them. Victoria would think that was fun." Anna noted a touch of sarcasm in Magdalena's voice.

"Are you sure you don't want to go?" Anna asked. "I'm in the middle of the verification report for the spring course schedule, and Scheduling wants it by the end of the week. Besides, I'm hardly dressed to have lunch with the CEO of Westmore Resources."

Magdalena perused Anna's green-and-white striped t-shirt, black corduroy trousers, and black flats. "You'll do. If the sponsor of a $5,000.00 scholarship wants to meet you, you go. Besides, her cook is excellent. I'm sure you'll enjoy the meal. Last year's meeting only took an hour and a half, by the way, so you should have no difficulty in returning in time for the department meeting at three." The toe of one of Magdalena's red crocodile pumps started to tap impatiently on the floor, and Anna took the hint.

"No problem. I'll have lunch with Mrs. Moreland and see you at the meeting at three."

"Excellent." Magdalena retreated to her office across the hall while Anna sighed and returned to her spreadsheet.

Two hours later, Anna was waiting in the foyer of Julia Moreland's mansion on an acreage just south of Calgary. She had carefully wiped the snow from her boots on the outdoor mat, but was conscious of a puddle spreading on the pristine grey-and-white marble floor beneath her. She looked up as she heard the sound of heels coming toward her down the hall. A young woman with flawless coffee-coloured skin, prominent cheekbones, and designer pink-and-silver eyeglasses appeared. She smiled coolly as she offered Anna her hand.

"Ms. Nolan? I'm Latona Taylor, Julia Moreland's personal assistant. A pleasure to meet you."

Anna returned the smile as she shook the young woman's hand. "How do you do?"

"Very well, thank you. Julia is waiting for you in the dining room. Please follow me."

As Anna hurried after Latona, she admired the hall's graceful columned arches and the colourful glass sculptures suspended from the ceiling. "Such a lovely house," she said. "I bet you enjoy working here. It sure beats the university."

"Yes, it is beautiful," Latona replied over her shoulder. She paused outside an open doorway. "The dining room is right through there. Enjoy your lunch."

Anna nodded her thanks and walked into the room. She hesitated before a gleaming mahogany table with eight chairs sitting on an Indian carpet of soft blues and greys. There were two place settings at the far end of the table, next to a crackling fire in an open, marble hearth. She recognized Julia Moreland sitting at one of the places. Julia, wearing a pair of black-framed reading glasses, was studying some paperwork. She looked up seconds after Anna's arrival, however, and removed her glasses.

"Anna, thanks for joining me on such short notice." Julia's smile was warm and welcoming as she patted the chair beside her. "Come and sit next to me."

Anna studied her hostess while hastening across the room. Julia wore her silvery hair short and spiky, and her blue silk tunic matched her sparkling eyes. Anna knew that Julia had to be at least sixty, but the effects of aging were difficult to detect on her heart-shaped face.

"I'm delighted to be here, Mrs. Moreland. I saw the newspaper spread on your home in the *Calgary Record* last summer. I'd have paid money for a tour."

Julia laughed. "Really? Well there's no charge today, plus we're throwing in a free lunch. And please call me Julia." She offered her right hand with its glowing, square-cut emerald ring. Julia's clasp was firm. Anna liked that in a woman. She placed her tote on the floor and slid into a chair at the second place setting.

A middle-aged woman dressed in a sleeveless black tunic and slacks entered the room carrying two bowls. She marched up to the table and placed the bowls carefully on the gilded charger plates before Julia and Anna.

"What have you got for us today, Nicolette?" Julia asked.

"Sweet potato and red pepper soup." Nicolette waited next to the table with her hands clasped over her stomach.

Julia turned to Anna. "You'll like this. It's creamy with a touch of heat." She watched as Anna carried a spoonful to her lips and sipped.

"You're right. It's delicious," Anna said. The cook nodded and left the room.

"I hope you don't mind looking at the scholarship applications while we eat?" Julia asked. "Magdalena asked me to choose the winner before the end of exams. That's a week from tomorrow, correct?"

"That's right."

"I have some pressing business to take care of over the next few days, so why don't you help me make the decision right now?"

Anna nodded. "I'd be happy to." Putting down her spoon, she ducked to retrieve the files from her tote before laying them on the table next to Julia's bowl.

"The scholarship committee has already screened the applicants based on academic achievement and financial need," Anna said. "These applications are from the top six students."

Julia nodded, fixed her glasses on her nose, and opened the top file. Her hand absent-mindedly ferried soup to her mouth as she flipped through the pages. Anna was just swallowing her last mouthful when Julia looked up.

"This group is an improvement over last year's candidates." Julia pointed at the pile. "At least this bunch can spell."

Anna's mouth curled into a smile while Julia pulled out two files and set the others aside.

"If it were up to Robert, he would choose the boy who plays hockey." She tapped the top application with her finger. "Robert loved to play hockey when he was a boy. It was because of your department's sports research, and because Chinook University was Robert's alma mater, that he decided to endow the scholarship for the Kinesiology Department in the first place."

Julia laid the file on the table and held up the second. "But this young woman's average is two points higher, and I'm impressed that she wants do a master's degree on bone loss resulting from spinal injury. I have a friend who broke her back in a motorcycle accident twenty years ago and has been confined to a wheelchair ever since. It would be lovely to think that something could be done to rehabilitate patients like my friend someday." Julia laid the second file on the table. "Who do you think I should choose?"

While she waited for Anna's answer, Nicolette returned to the room. She set two plates of what looked like a meat and bean stew with a side of corn before the women and removed their soup dishes. Anna waited until Nicolette had left the room before responding.

"I'm afraid I'm out of my depth when it comes to academic evaluation. Maybe you should call Magdalena for her opinion?"

Julia shook her head. "If I do, I'll just get a lot of hot air about test percentiles and academic aspirations. I want to know who these kids *are*. I bet you've seen them around your office, though."

"Sure. The kids are in and out all the time, dropping off assignments, picking up essays, and making appointments to see Magdalena." Julia nodded encouragingly, and Anna shrugged. "Okay, here's what I think. When Jessica, the girl who wants to study spinal cord rehabilitation, comes into my office, she always helps herself to my stapler and pens without asking. I know that it's a small thing, but it's rude, you know? Nick, on the other hand — the hockey player studying sports kinesiology — always apologizes whenever he hands in a late assignment. Not that he's habitually late, you understand, but a couple of the professors set an exact deadline, like 3:00 p.m., on the day their assignments are due. If the kids are even a few minutes late, I'm supposed to stamp their papers with tomorrow's date. Then they get docked five percent of their grade." Julia nodded. "So if Nick's a few minutes late, I laugh and tell him that he should apologize to his prof, not to me, and then I stamp his assignment with today's date."

Julia smiled. "I understand. Nick's polite, and Jessica's presumptuous."

"Exactly."

"Done!" Julia slapped the two files back onto the pile. "Good manners triumph over academic achievement. Nick gets the scholarship." She picked up her fork. "Now, let's enjoy Nicolette's pork and duck cassoulet. It's a real stick-to-your-ribs kind of dish, and perfect for today's cold weather."

Anna sniffed the delicious, garlicky aroma steaming up from her plate and tasted the food. It was so good that she closed her eyes as she chewed.

"To change the topic, I hear that you were the top suspect in your ex-husband's murder case last spring," Julia said.

Anna's eyes sprang open. "Excuse me?"

"So, I'm curious. What's it like to be the focus of a murder investigation?"

Anna groaned inwardly. She should have known that Magdalena would be right; she always was. After being intimately involved with two murder investigations in less than a year, Anna still felt shell-shocked. After all, the last murder had just happened five weeks ago, right before Halloween. She was sputtering, trying to think of a way to change the subject, when Julia's assistant hurried into the room waving an envelope. Anna took one look at Latona's tense face and knew that something was gravely wrong.

Julia looked up. "Yes?"

"It's another one," the young woman said, halting beside the table and handing the envelope to Julia. Anna peeked at it sideways and saw "Julia Moreland" spelled out in black block letters cut from a newspaper or a magazine.

Julia grimaced. She picked up her butter knife and slit the envelope open. Gingerly removing a single sheet of folded paper, she flicked it open and studied the contents. Anna was unable to read the message, but saw that it was spelled out in the same cut-out letters.

"What should we do?" Latona asked. "Do you want to call the police this time?"

"What?" Julia returned her attention to her assistant. She refolded the message and slid it back into the envelope. "This is getting to be a nuisance. I think we may have to involve the police this time." She tossed the envelope onto the table and glanced at Anna.

"Will you excuse me?"

Julia rose from her chair while Anna gaped up at her. "I hate to cut our lunch short, especially when you were about to tell me about your ex-husband's murder, but I have some urgent business to attend to."

Anna half-rose, but Julia waved her back down.

"No, please don't let me interrupt your lunch. Nicolette will be angry if at least one of us doesn't enjoy her food. I only wish . . ." Julia paused to think. "I don't suppose you're free tomorrow night?"

Anna was startled. "What's tomorrow? Thursday?"

Julia nodded. "November 29th."

"No, I don't have any plans," Anna said warily.

"Good. Do you think you might like to come to my Christmas party?"

"What, here?"

"No, at the Vandesand Hotel in Calgary."

"Wow!"

Anna felt tempted. The Vandesand was a private hotel with notoriously-expensive rates. She had always wanted to have lunch there — maybe even peek into a guest room — but had never splurged on their gourmet menu.

Julia half-smiled. "Yes, it's a very nice hotel, especially the ballroom. The party's my annual bash for the oil company bigwigs, plus some friends and family. I'd love for you to come. We could continue our conversation about your ex-husband's murder there."

Anna frowned. Not only did she not want to discuss the murder with Julia, but she knew she'd feel uncomfortable at the party.

"I'd feel out of place. I wouldn't know a soul."

"That won't be a problem. Latona can arrange for you to sit at Warren and Magdalena's table."

Anna stared at her. Did Julia mean *her* Magdalena?

"Didn't you know that my stepson is dating your boss?"

Anna shook her head.

"I'm not surprised. Magdalena is practically a clam when it comes to discussing her private life. She and Warren have been seeing each other for months. So, can I count on you? We usually have a good time. It's one of the perks of being the second-richest oil company in Canada."

Anna hesitated. She had read about the glamorous Moreland Christmas parties in the *Calgary Record*, but had never imagined attending one.

"I just happen to have a new dress," she murmured, weakening. Oh, what the heck. She'd never get the chance to attend an extravaganza like this again.

"Thanks, I'd love to come."

"Great. The party starts at seven. I can't wait to see Magdalena's face when you show up at her table." Julia glanced at Latona, and her smile faded. "I'll see you tomorrow, Anna. Business before pleasure, I'm afraid." She nodded at her assistant, and the two women exited the room.

Anna picked up her fork and thoughtfully ate another mouthful of cassoulet. It really was delicious. Too bad that Julia's meal had been interrupted. Latona certainly had seemed upset about the note, whatever it said. Anna's eyes strayed to the envelope next to the files. Julia had neglected to take it with her. Maybe it wasn't such a big deal after all.

Anna looked back at her plate and tried the sweet corn flecked with red pepper. Hmm, was that a hint of maple syrup she tasted?

Her eyes strayed to the envelope again. She nudged it until she could read the letters the right-side up. The only reason someone composed a message with cut-out letters was to avoid having his or her handwriting identified. That indicated criminal intent.

Anna knew that curiosity was her downfall. It had gotten her into trouble plenty of times. Just this once, she should mind her own business. She drummed her fingers on the table. Still, what harm would a peek do? No one would ever know. She snatched up the envelope, took out the sheet, and read the message. It said: "Holding the press conference on Monday could be hazardous to your continued existence."

Shoot! Anna refolded the note, shoved it back into the envelope, and dropped it hastily onto the table. Who was sending Julia death threats? And what was this about a press conference on Monday?

Fumbling for her napkin, she wiped her mouth, bent to retrieve her bag, and stuffed the files into it. Time to go. She didn't want to be anywhere near this kind of trouble again. No sir! Julia was rich and she had three sons, or two sons and a stepson. She could have all the help she needed. She was probably calling the chief of police right this minute, as a matter of fact.

Damn, now she wished she hadn't accepted the Christmas party invitation. It would be best to stay away from Julia and her friends. But Anna couldn't risk Magdalena's wrath by not turning up for the party and possibly jeopardizing the scholarship.

Springing from her chair, Anna was making a beeline for the door when Nicolette returned with two plates of fruit tart.

"Where are you going? Where's Julia?" the cook demanded.

Pausing, Anna said, "Julia got called away unexpectedly on business. I'm so sorry to rush out on you like this, but I've got to get back to work. The cassoulet was delicious, by the way, and the soup was to die for. I mean, it was really terrific." Anna coloured and clutched her bag to her chest. The threat of death was making her as jumpy as a cat.

Nicolette frowned. "Are you all right?"

"Sure. So, I guess I'll see you at the Christmas party tomorrow night. Should be fun, eh?" Without waiting for a response, Anna bolted from the room, leaving Nicolette shaking her head and staring down at the dessert.

2

Anna sighed. She was the only person at the table without a date, and her dinner companions had abandoned her as soon as the music had started. She cupped her chin in her hand and watched the dancers. The orchestra was playing a cha-cha, and her toe tapped in time to the throbbing beat. She felt conspicuous sitting alone. It reminded her too much of being a wallflower at high school dances.

"Would you care to dance?" a cultured male voice inquired.

Anna peered up into Rick Moreland's face. Blue eyes, dimples, sunny smile. This blond Adonis was the answer to her prayers.

"I'd love to," she replied eagerly. Rick drew back her chair and escorted her to the floor, where he demonstrated his proficiency at the cha-cha. Anna wiggled her hips and tried to keep up with his footwork.

"You're really good," she said.

Rick nodded. "Mother would be pleased that the ballroom dance lessons she foisted on my brother and me weren't wasted. I'm Rick Moreland, by the way."

"I know." Anna had seen pictures of him climbing out of sports cars while escorting models to the trendiest hot spots. "Your mother made you and your brother take dance lessons?" Just then Julia danced by in the arms of the

Calgary Symphony general manager, a diamond art deco pin glittering on her shoulder. She smiled, and Rick waved back.

"Every Saturday morning for half a year when I was twelve. It was sheer torture."

Anna smiled in sympathy. "Well, thank you for rescuing me, anyway. I was having flashbacks to sitting alone at high school dances."

"A woman as beautiful and graceful as you was never a wallflower."

"Oh, it's true." She looked up into Rick's eyes. "But I think you flatter me, sir."

Rick swung her past a lofty Christmas tree resplendent with blue and silver decorations. "I wouldn't say that." A moment later, he asked, "So, how do you know Mother?"

"I'm the administrative assistant for the Kinesiology Department at Chinook University. I helped your mother choose the winner of your father's scholarship."

"That makes Warren's girlfriend your boss, doesn't it?" Anna waited as he sashayed around her and pulled her back into his arms.

"That's right."

"Magdalena's quite a lady. I think Warren's finally met his match."

"What do you mean?"

Rick grinned. "Let's just say that the women who pursue my brothers and me aren't generally the brainy, career-woman type. But Magdalena's got brains as well as beauty. She's a class act, as my mother would say."

The number finished, the couples separating to applaud. Rick drew Anna's hand through his arm and escorted her back to her table.

"Well, I'm grateful that you came. It was a pleasure to dance with you . . ."

"Anna Nolan. You're welcome, Rick."

He bowed, held out her chair, and waited for Anna to sink into it before departing. She watched him leave, appreciating the rear view of a well-built man in a finely-tailored tuxedo.

"Enjoy dancing with my stepbrother?"

Anna jumped as Warren and Magdalena sat down beside her. She felt a little heated from her recent exercise, but Magdalena looked as poised and cool as ever.

"Very much. He's an excellent dancer."

"It must run in the family." Magdalena's eyes gleamed as she gazed into Warren's eyes.

They looked happy together. Good on you, Magdalena. Out loud, Anna asked, "Are your other stepbrother and his wife here, too?"

"They're here somewhere." Warren craned to look around the room. "There they are, at the table in the back corner. Julia likes to spread family members around so that we can help entertain her guests."

Anna turned to look. She spotted Kevin Moreland, Julia's elder son, at the table Warren had indicated. Kevin had the same sunny blond good looks as Rick, but was a couple of years older and carrying a few extra pounds. He was scanning the room, looking bored, while his wife, Lauren, a dark-haired beauty with almond-shaped eyes, was talking animatedly with a middle-aged man in a tight-fitting tux. Lauren rested her hand on the man's shoulder and laughed. Her companion took advantage of the diversion to stare at her ample cleavage.

"Well, if you'll excuse me, I'm going to go powder my nose," Anna said, turning back to Magdalena and Warren. The couple were engrossed in each other, however, and didn't seem to hear her. Anna smiled and rose. She would leave them to enjoy themselves alone for a while. Exiting the ballroom, she strolled down the lushly-carpeted hall past a room labelled "The Library Lounge." The door was ajar, and she overheard the clatter of crockery and a female voice. It was Julia's. She was probably in a private meeting with someone. Apparently business never stops when you're a CEO, even at parties.

Something caught Anna's eye on the carpet at the far side of the door. She bent down for a closer look. For heaven's sake, it was Julia's diamond pin. Anna snatched it up. It was beautiful, a round circle of diamonds with a sapphire-encrusted arrow piercing the centre. Julia mustn't have realized it was missing, or she'd be out searching for it.

Anna hesitated outside the door. She heard Julia say something in a low, intense voice, and a man's angry response. What should she do? She didn't want to interrupt, particularly if Julia were embroiled in an argument, but a missing diamond pin was a big deal. Taking a deep breath, Anna knocked on the door.

"Yes? What is it?" Julia called.

Anna stuck her head around the door. The room was dark except for the glow of a lamp between two high-backed, leather chairs. Julia was leaning forward toward Anna, while the other person was swallowed up by his chair with his back to Anna.

"I'm sorry to disturb you," Anna said, "but I found your pin on the floor in the hall."

"What?" Julia's hand leapt to her shoulder. "I had no idea it had fallen off. Thank you, Anna." She rose and nodded at the person in the chair. "That's all I have to say on the matter. Excuse me."

Anna stepped back as Julia emerged from the room. In the light of the hall, the older woman's face was pale. She glanced at Anna.

"I'll have to ask the jeweller to take a look at the clasp.

I always have trouble with it. Would you mind coming to the ladies' room to pin it back on for me?"

"I'd be happy to." Anna followed Julia into the ladies' room, where the older woman watched in the mirror as Anna pinned the brooch to her shoulder.

"A little higher, please. It doesn't quite catch the light down there. That's better." Julia's eyes met Anna's, and she grinned. "If you've got it, flaunt it, right?"

"You bet." Anna turned to look at Julia's reflection. "Not that you need diamonds to catch people's attention. You look spectacular in that dress, by the way." Julia still had great curves, which the clinging, navy-blue velvet evening gown accentuated.

"You should have seen me in my twenties. I was only twenty-three when I met Robert, back when he was still married to his first wife." The smile faded as Julia stared. "I wish he were here with me now. It's no fun handling the company on my own these days." She glanced at Anna. "I may not have always been the nicest woman in the world, but I've worked damned hard for my two businesses. It's time for my sons to step up to the plate. I'm only sixty, you know. Still young enough to enjoy myself."

"I'd never know you were a day over fifty," Anna said, wondering if Julia were a bit intoxicated. Something must have prompted this confession.

One of the guests from the Christmas party walked into the washroom, letting in a blast of dance music. Julia winked.

"Come on. Let's go find ourselves a couple of good-looking men to dance with."

"Just give me a minute, and I'll be right with you," Anna replied, hurrying to a stall.

Five minutes later, the two women strolled arm-in-arm back into the ballroom and paused at Anna's table. Warren and Magdalena were still sitting with their heads close together, deep in conversation. Anna admired how her boss's aristocratic, cool blond looks contrasted with Warren's wavy black hair and bottomless dark eyes. Julia rested her hands on her stepson's shoulders, and he stiffened.

"Get me a drink from the bar, will you, Warren?"

He tore his gaze away from Magdalena to look up. "Sure. The usual?"

"Yes, please. A Lagavulin."

He glanced at Anna and Magdalena. "Ladies, can I get you anything?"

"I'm happy with champagne," Magdalena said, raising a half-full glass.

"Could I have an orange juice, please?" Anna wasn't much of a drinker, and she had to drive home later.

Warren smiled with amusement. "Certainly. Be right back."

Anna and Julia sat down on either side of Magdalena, who studied Julia. The older woman ignored her gaze to look around the room.

"Hail, hail, the gang's all here," she murmured.

"I recognize most of Calgary's social and cultural illuminati, but not everyone else," Magdalena said.

"Illuminati?" Julia smirked as she peered sideways at Magdalena, but Anna's boss stared back at her impassively. Julia sighed. "Let's see. There's the board of directors from Westmore, and the CEOs from the other oil companies. Oliver Sumpter, my president at Golden Farm Fertilizer, and his wife, Beatrix. The people from my charities. The mayor, the chief of police — Robert always said to stay on the good side of the police — our MLA and MP. You recognize the president of Chinook University, of course. Assorted significant others. And one or two new friends." She smiled at Anna before gesturing at the crowd dancing on the floor, mingling at the tables, and lining up in front of the bar. "It doesn't take long to fill a ballroom."

A mature woman in a gold taffeta gown with a ruby pendant dangling between her breasts squeezed Julia's shoulder. "Wonderful party as usual, dear."

"I'm glad you're enjoying yourself, Vera. See you at the art gallery opening next week." The woman's escort nodded, and the couple strolled away.

"It must be difficult, putting together a function like this," Magdalena said, but Julia shrugged.

"My assistant did most of the work. I just gave her the guest list. I'm too busy these days to get involved with party preparations. Did Warren tell you that I'm holding a press conference on Monday?"

"Yes. He's very curious to hear what it's all about."

Julia turned away. "Just a little housekeeping business, really. My sons and the board of directors have been pestering me all week to find out what it's about, but I've had to keep this one to myself. I'm going to Banff to relax for the weekend first, though. I'm headed there right after the party." She looked at Magdalena. "Tell Warren not to worry. I'm taking care of things."

"Tell Warren not to worry about what?" he asked, placing Julia's scotch at her elbow on the table. His face was impassive.

"Thanks. I sure can use this." She raised the glass to her lips and sipped. Shivering, Julia took another sip while Warren handed Anna her orange juice. "My press conference on Monday."

"Right. We're all wondering what that's about." Warren sat down beside his stepmother, but she sprang to her feet.

"Never mind, you'll all know soon enough. I just

spotted David Krale. He looks so much better since he got rid of Edward, that ingrate." They all looked to where an attractive young man was swaying with a sexy redhead on the dance floor. "Poor David. Luci's wasting her time with him. I'm going to cut in and save him. See you all later." Julia grinned before sweeping through the couples on the dance floor. .

Warren shook his head. "My stepmother is one fine hell-raiser." He moved over to sit back beside Magdalena as Anna leaned toward him.

"So, what about this press conference Julia's talking about. Are you worried?"

Magdalena's eyebrow arched as she stared at Anna. "It's all right," Warren said, resting a hand on Magdalena's arm. "I don't mind talking about it." He looked past her at Anna. "I don't have a clue what the press conference is about. I can only guess."

Anna ignored her boss's disapproval. How often did she get a chance to pick the brains of the VP and chief financial officer of a big oil company? She had a little windfall to invest. Maybe she should buy some Westmore shares?

"So, what's your best guess?"

Warren leaned back in his chair to consider. "I think that Julia is going to announce her retirement."

Anna nodded. "That makes sense. She did say something about wanting to enjoy herself more. If she retires, does that mean you automatically become the CEO?"

Warren shrugged. "I don't know. Maybe. I've been with the company long enough. Nineteen years. But Kevin's been with Westmore for eight years, and Rick for six. And you never know what Julia's up to. She might want one of them to take over."

"Can she just say who gets to be CEO?"

"Technically, no. The way my father set up the company, not only do the shareholders elect the board of directors, but they also vote for the CEO. However, since Julia holds fifty-one percent of the shares, she's actually the one who decides."

"And she's been the CEO since your father died?"

"That's right." Warren was about to say more when Magdalena interrupted him.

"Let's not talk shop, Warren. How often do we get a chance to dance? Dance with me." She rose and held out her hands.

Warren took hold of both hands before turning to Anna. "Sorry to abandon you."

"That's all right. I wasn't planning to stay much longer. I've got work in the morning, and my boss doesn't like it if I'm late." She winked at Magdalena.

"Personally, I wouldn't mind if you weren't there until noon, Cinderella, but I've got a meeting with the dean at nine."

"And Bryan's students' take-home exam is due tomorrow, so they'll be dropping them off with me all day. You know how anxious the kids get if they have to leave exams in the drop box rather than handing them to me personally. I'll be there bright and early at eight-thirty."

"Make it nine. Students are never in before then." Magdalena drifted off to the dance floor with Warren while Anna stared after her. Hoo boy, was that the champagne talking? Her boss was usually such a stickler when it came to office hours. Maybe Anna should keep a bottle of champagne in her desk drawer if it was going to have such a mellowing effect on Magdalena.

Deciding to stay for another ten minutes, Anna settled back in her chair and hummed along with the Christmas music, watching the other guests swirl around the dance floor in their elegant gowns and tuxedos. Which is why she had such a good view when Julia Moreland collapsed.

3

"Hello, this is Charles Tremaine."

"How's it going, hot stuff?" Anna curled up on the bed beside her phone, preparing herself for a long chat.

"Anna! I was just thinking that you and Ben must be finishing dinner right about now. Every Friday night, like clockwork. How are you, love?"

"Ben's already gone home. He's worn out from writing exams, plus he has to work tomorrow, so he's making an early night of it. My son is growing wise in his old age."

"That's good to hear, but you didn't answer my question. How are you doing?"

"Can't get one past you. I guess that's why you made sergeant. How's the murder case going, by the way?"

"Anna."

She sighed. She had been torn about calling Charlie, wanting so much to hear the sound of his voice, but not wanting to bother him about Julia. He couldn't get away for a visit even if he wanted to, what with his work on the Swift Current murder. Besides, she'd be seeing him for Christmas in just three weeks.

"Well, there's been some trouble," she said.

"Tell me."

Anna explained about Julia Moreland and the Christmas party. "I was watching Julia dance with a young man named David Krale when she stumbled. I saw David take her arm and speak to her, but Julia didn't respond. She just stared into space as if she hadn't heard him. Then she collapsed and had some kind of seizure. It was horrible. I tried to go to her, but David called for help and a bunch of people surrounded them. One of the guests was a doctor, so he started working on her right away. The chief of police was at the party, and he must have called for help because an EMS team showed up with the police in a matter of minutes. They took Julia away on a stretcher. Last I heard, she's in the hospital, and they're not sure she's going to make it."

"That's too bad. Did Mrs. Moreland have a history of health problems?"

"I don't know. But the police must have thought something was fishy because they rounded up all us guests and took us for questioning to the Westwinds Investigative Services building in a city bus."

"That must have gone over like a lead balloon."

"Most of the guests were cooperative, but a few complained. They didn't like getting dragged into a police investigation. When we got to Westwinds, we had to wait our turn for a detective. Our interviews were videotaped, so it was a lot more high tech than when I was questioned at the Crane RCMP station last spring."

"The small town RCMP detachments don't have the budget that Calgary Police Services has. Who interviewed you?"

"A Detective Sandra Soo."

"I don't know her."

"Let me tell you, she was all business when I saw her. She was very interested in an argument I overheard between Julia and a man at the party. They were in a private lounge off the ballroom."

"What did you hear?"

"Well, Julia said, in this really intense voice, 'It's too late. There's nothing you can say to change my mind,' and the man said something like, 'I've done all you asked. I provided you with the names. You've got to help me.' But I didn't see who he was. The room they were in wasn't very bright, and the man was sitting with his back to me. I had to interrupt them because Julia had dropped a diamond brooch in the hall, and I wanted to return it to her."

"Would you recognize the man's voice again?"

"Detective Soo asked me that, too. I don't know. I'd never heard his voice before. Anyway, I gave the detective my contact information, and she let me go. By the time I got home, it was two o'clock in the morning. I made it into work by nine, but I wasn't much good for anything. Magdalena must have been kept up as late as I was, but she seemed as fresh as a daisy at work. Sometimes I wonder if she's really human."

"Magdalena was at the party, too?"

"Yes. She's dating Julia's step-son, Warren."

"How long has that been going on? You haven't mentioned it before."

"Apparently for several months. I didn't know about it until this week. Julia told me about it at our lunch meeting."

"Your boss has always been something of a dark horse. But I'm sorry you had such an unpleasant experience on top of everything else you've been through this year. You're not feeling nervous again, are you?"

"No. The problem I had before was just a bit of a delayed reaction to what happened at Halloween. I'm fine now. I just wish things could get back to normal."

"I feel badly that I can't come see you, but we're at a crucial point in collecting evidence for the trial. I wish you'd have taken Magdalena's offer for some time off, though."

"But it was right in the middle of term and we were too busy. Besides, I wanted to save up all my vacation time to see you at Christmas. Two whole weeks. We haven't had that much time together since the summer."

"I know, and I'm really looking forward to it. Still, couldn't you take a few days off when exams are over and come visit me in Swift Current? It would take your mind off things."

"Detective Soo wouldn't be pleased. She said she wants me to be available for questioning."

"Oh." There was silence on the line.

"Don't worry, Charlie, I've already told her everything I know. It's not like I have a connection with the family or anything. I just met Julia two days ago. Oh, I must be losing it. I forgot to tell you about the threatening note Julia received when I having lunch with her." She told Tremaine how Latona had brought the note to Julia, and how Julia had left it on the table, wording her tale to make it sound as if the note had been left lying open where just anyone could have seen it. Even so, there was a pause when Anna finished. After a few seconds, she couldn't stand the silence any longer.

"Come on, you would have read it, too."

Tremaine sighed. "Maybe. I don't you suppose you could have ignored it. Did you tell Detective Soo about the note?"

"Sure. Besides, she'd already heard about it from Latona and wanted me to corroborate the details. Latona is Julia's personal assistant. Poor girl, she looked so upset when Julia took sick at the party."

"Hmm. Sounds like there may be something in that. Well, at least it's unlikely that you'll have anything more to do with the investigation."

Anna nodded. "That's what I said. I was just at the wrong place at the wrong time."

Tremaine chuckled. "That's the story of your life. That's how I ended up investigating you for your ex-husband's murder last spring."

Anna frowned at the phone. "Okay, I've had some bad luck this year, but things are going to get better. The term's almost over, and we'll be together for Christmas before we know it."

"Keep a good thought, love."

Saturday night, the doorbell chimed. It was late, going on midnight. A light switched on in the bedroom at the top of the stairs. Moments later, the bedroom door opened onto the hall and Magdalena, tying the sash on her silk robe, trotted down the stairs and padded quickly to the front door. She switched on the light in the vestibule, glanced through the peep hole, and opened the door. Warren Moreland was standing on the porch. He looked exhausted and had a day's worth of dark stubble on his face.

"I hope it's not too late," he said.

"Come in." Magdalena waited for him to trudge past her into the foyer before shutting the door.

"It's over. Julia's gone," he mumbled.

Magdalena pulled him into her arms. "I'm so sorry," she whispered. They stood clasped together for a long moment, her white-blond hair cascading over his shoulder as they pressed their heads together.

Magdalena pulled away to peer into his face. "Did you have a chance to say goodbye?"

Warren shook his head. "No. The last time I saw her was Thursday night when they were wheeling her into Emergency."

"Come and sit down. You look exhausted. I bet you could use a drink."

Magdalena walked ahead of him into the living room, where she switched on a lamp before continuing to the sideboard in the dining area. Sliding one door open, she removed a port glass before retrieving a bottle from the other side. When she returned to Warren, he was standing next to the floor-to-ceiling window in the space behind the couch. He accepted the drink with a half-smile and took a sip. Magdalena wrapped her arms around his waist, and they gazed out the window at the reservoir, the city lights reflecting on the still, dark water.

"Did they tell you the cause of her illness?" Magdalena asked.

He looked at her over his shoulder. "When the boys and I first arrived at Emergency, the doctor asked us lots of questions, like did Julia have a seizure disorder, was she diabetic, or was she taking anti-depressants or using recreational drugs? Later, when it was over, he said there were symptoms he couldn't explain, like dilated pupils and delirium. Ultimately, he wasn't sure what she had died of." Warren rubbed his eyes. "Did Detective Soo question you after the party?"

"Yes."

"She was at the hospital this evening when the doctor gave us the bad news. She said that the Medical Examiner's Office will be doing an autopsy tomorrow, but that they'll have to wait for the toxicology report to come back from an RCMP forensics lab in Ottawa. Normally, it would take a few weeks, but the Calgary police chief will be pushing to get the results back sooner. He and Julia were friends, you know."

"It all sounds very frustrating, not knowing why she died and having to wait."

Warren nodded. "It is. I can't believe she's gone. Rick and Kevin took it pretty hard, by the way. Especially Rick. He was her baby."

"What about you?"

Warren turned to gaze back out the window. "It's so unreal. Julia was never a mother to me, even though I was only eight when she and Dad got married. She wasn't that kind of woman. At least, she wasn't very affectionate with Kevin and me. Still, she was a large part of my life. I feel as though I've lost a hand or a foot." Magdalena squeezed his arm to show that she understood before moving away to sit on the couch.

"What will you do about Westmore?"

Warren followed to sit next to her. "I've called a special meeting for Monday morning. The boys and I will be attending with Jack Upton, the chairman of the board, and Oliver Sumpter, the president of Golden Farm Fertilizer. That was Julia's father's company before it passed to her. We need to do some quick damage control before rumours start circulating about Julia's death. It will be all over the papers by Monday."

Magdalena laid her head on his shoulder. Warren put his drink down on the coffee table and wrapped her in his arms.

"Sorry to be going on like this, Maggie. I know that you didn't care for Julia much. Do you want me to leave so that you can get some sleep?"

Magdalena shook her head. "I respected her, Warren, even though I didn't like her very much. I was the object of her jokes too often for us to be friends. I'm sure she thought I was priggish."

He gazed into her eyes as he slipped his hand into her robe. "You're not."

With their faces only inches apart, Magdalena said, "Please stay."

4

Anna hurried into the department mail and photocopy room at twenty minutes to nine on Monday morning to put Dr. Bryan Carmichael's take-home exams into his mailbox. Bryan, a muscular young professor with a shaved head, was crouched over the photocopier, muttering angrily as he opened the door, played with the levers, and finally ripped a sheet of paper off a roller.

"Morning, Bryan. I've got your exams," Anna said, struggling to stuff them into the too-small space.

"Damned piece of junk," he muttered, slamming the copier door. He turned to the second machine, placed his originals in the automatic feeder, and punched in the number of copies. Dr. Loulia Georgiou-Bates, known as "Lou" around the Kinesiology Department, rushed into the room just as the copier started spewing out pages and stapling them together. She read the error message on the first machine, frowned, and glanced over at Bryan. He was innocently reading the week's cafeteria menu on the bulletin board.

"You going to be long, Bryan? I've got an exam at nine." She shoved a short, brown curl behind her ear.

"Sorry, I've got an exam at nine, too."

Lou turned to Anna. "Anna, help! I can never get these paper jams cleared."

Sighing as she bustled around the work table, Anna bent over the first machine. She opened the door, flipped a toggle, and removed a sheet of paper from the duplexer. Pushing the door shut, she waited for the error message to clear, but a new message indicated a problem in another area. She re-opened the door, knelt down, and began painstakingly removing a scrap of accordion-folded paper from one of the rollers.

"You know, if you sent your printing to Document Services ahead of time, you wouldn't have these last-minute headaches," she murmured.

"Yeah, yeah," Lou said, folding her arms over her chest. Anna dug the last bit of paper out with her fingernail, stood, and bumped the door shut with her hip. The copier sprang back to life and began pumping out pages. Lou removed a stapled set from the growing pile.

"Bryan, this is your exam. You're hogging both machines," she howled.

"Just cancel it," he said as the second copier stapled his last set of exams together. Grabbing his printing, he jogged out of the room. Lou flung a final "hog!" after him as Anna cancelled his printing job, pulled the sheets from the machine, and flung them into the shredding bin.

"It's all yours," she said.

Lou fed her originals hastily into the copier as Anna hurried out the door. She had to get an urgent purchase order into the outgoing mail before Alice Cobb, the campus mailperson, arrived at nine-twenty to pick it up. Scurrying into her office, Anna grabbed an interoffice envelope and scribbled the correct contact name and location on the front. She was trying to remember where she'd put the purchase order when Magdalena stepped into the room.

"Good morning, Anna. I'd like to see the student evaluations, please."

Anna nodded, rolled her chair backward into the file cabinet with a bang, and opened the bottom drawer. Heaving out a pile of documents, she said, "They're not all here yet. We're still missing four."

Magdalena frowned. "Have you contacted Planning about that? Surely the evaluations should all be back by now."

Anna shook her head. "At this time of year, Planning's top priority is scanning the exams. I can call Darcy, if you like, but she won't be able to get the evaluations here any faster."

"Please do. This tardiness is unacceptable."

Anna refrained from rolling her eyes while handing the pile to her boss. "They're in alphabetical order by professor's surname."

"Thank you." Magdalena whirled and strode out the door.

Anna heard a "Whoops!" and an "Excuse me" before Alice popped into the office. She was carrying a bundle of envelopes and a small box, which she deposited into Anna's in-tray.

"Alice," Anna said. "I didn't hear the mail cart coming down the hall. Can you wait for just one second?"

"Sure. No rush."

Now all Anna had to do was find the purchase order. She banged the file drawer shut, rolled back to her desk, and reached for the chair's signature file. Aha, it was still inside!

Alice sat on the edge of Anna's desk as she waited.

"How was your weekend?" She picked up her single, long grey braid and began fiddling with it.

"Crazy." Anna jammed the purchase order into the envelope and wrapped the string around the button to seal it. "Did you hear about Julia Moreland?" She handed Alice the envelope.

"I think I heard something about her on the radio on the way into work this morning. Wasn't she the lady in charge of Westmore Resources?"

Anna nodded. "She died at her Christmas party Thursday night. Magdalena and I were both there. Me, because I worked with Julia on our scholarship applications, and Magdalena, because she's dating Julia's stepson, Warren."

"Wow," Alice said, her eyes widening. "Magdalena's dating a Moreland? Though I'm not surprised that she'd be dating a bigwig like him. Doesn't her family have money?"

"Yes. They have some sort of investment business back in Toronto. Magdalena led a privileged life when she was a girl. She even attended the National Ballet School. She might have become a principal dancer if she hadn't injured her knee. That's when she decided to study kinesiology and pursue a university-teaching career."

"What a shame," Alice said. "She has such great presence. I bet she'd have made a terrific ballerina."

"I was too tall," Magdalena said from the doorway.

Alice sprang to her feet and grabbed Anna's envelope. "Sorry to hold you up. See you later." She nodded to Magdalena and fled down the hall, the rumble of the mail cart vanishing in the distance.

Anna coloured. "Sorry to be talking about your personal life."

Magdalena shrugged. "That's ancient history." She returned the pile of evaluations to Anna, who put them away. When Anna rolled back to her desk, however, Magdalena was still there, picking at a loose thread on the sleeve of her jacket.

"I haven't had a chance to say that I'm sorry about Julia's death," Anna said. "I heard about it on the news this morning. Julia and I had a good time at lunch on

Wednesday. It was kind of her to invite me to her Christmas party, too." She paused, but Magdalena said nothing. "If you don't mind my asking, how's Warren doing? He seemed like such a nice man at the party. Is he okay?"

Magdalena accepted Anna's condolences with a nod. "It's difficult for him and the family right now. Not only because they lost Julia, but because she died in such a public manner. The family intends to make a statement about her death at the press conference she had planned for today."

"That's right. Julia told me about the press conference. Did they ever find out what she was going to announce?"

"The family still doesn't know. They're meeting this morning to discuss it."

Warren strode into the Westmore company boardroom with his secretary, Helen, trotting at his heels. Kevin and Rick were already seated at the table. Kevin was dressed in a suit and tie, while Rick was wearing jeans and a t-shirt. His eyes were blood-shot, and he needed a shave. Across the table from them sat Oliver Sumpter, president of Golden Farm Fertilizer. He was tall and slightly stooped with a full-head of silvery hair. Jack Upton, chairman of the board for Westmore, was seated at the head of the table. He was a bulldog of a man, short and broad with a thick neck. He tugged impatiently at his necktie to loosen the knot.

Helen, Warren's secretary, a mature woman with cropped blond hair, paused to close the boardroom door before sitting next to him and opening her laptop.

"Thanks for coming on such short notice, everyone," Warren said. "We need to release a statement concerning Julia's death to the press today."

"Warren, before we get busy on that, I'd like to express my condolences to you and your brothers on your mother's passing," Oliver said. His face looked earnest as he spoke. "I worked with Julia for nineteen years, and she was both a savvy businesswoman and a fine lady. The flag is flying at half-mast at Golden Farm Fertilizer today in her honour."

"Thank you, Oliver," Warren said. "Much appreciated." Rick nodded, looking up from the table top, while Kevin rolled his eyes.

"Have we found out what Mother was planning to announce at the press conference today?" Kevin asked.

"No," Warren replied. "We've invited Latona, Julia's personal assistant, to see if she can enlighten us. She should be here any minute."

"I want to know what's happening with the police investigation," Jack Upton said. "It's shocking. I've heard all kinds of rumours, even that Julia died of poisoning."

"Well, Jack, I'm sorry to say that we don't know yet." The older man slumped in his chair. "The Medical Examiner's Office performed an autopsy, but they won't get the toxicology report back for several days. Our hands are tied until then." Warren glanced at his half-brothers for support. Rick was staring into space while Kevin gazed back at him, his mouth pressed into a tight line. Oliver shook his head, his eyes mournful.

"Who's in charge of the investigation?" Jack asked.

"A Detective Sandra Soo. She was at the hospital on Saturday to talk to us about the autopsy."

"A female detective?" Jack asked. "Is she any good?"

"She spoke to me the day Mother died," Rick said. "She seemed to know what she was doing."

Warren nodded. "I've asked around about her. Her credentials are good. She was with Homicide for five years and Organized Crime three years before that."

There was a knock at the door and Latona entered carrying a briefcase. She hesitated on seeing all the men staring at her. Warren rose to greet her.

"Good to see you, Latona. I think you know everyone?"

The young woman checked all the faces in turn before glancing back at Warren. "Yes."

"Please take a seat," Warren said, indicating the chair beside his own. "As you know, we'll be meeting with the press at noon today."

Latona nodded as she slipped into the chair, her poise returning. "Julia's press conference."

"We want to know what Julia was planning to announce."

Latona folded her hands in her lap. "I'm afraid I don't know," she said in a quiet voice.

"What?" Kevin asked. The other men also seemed startled while Warren's secretary calmly continued taking notes on her computer.

Latona met Warren's gaze. "Julia didn't share that information with me."

"What the hell?" Kevin said. "Mother was holding a press conference and her own secretary doesn't know what it was about? Didn't you help her with her speech?"

Latona shook her head, her cheeks flushing. "No. Julia composed her own announcement. No communications concerning the press conference went through me, aside from my initial contact with the press. Julia told me that she didn't need my help this time, that the Christmas party would be enough to keep me busy."

"Was that normal procedure, young lady?" Jack asked.

"No," Latona replied. "Usually I briefed the media about the announcement ahead of time, so I was surprised when Julia didn't provide me with any information. But she insisted on total secrecy for this one."

"Was she working on anything special at the time?" Warren asked. "Did she ask for certain files, or drop hints about anything?"

Latona shook her head. "Nothing out of the ordinary. Just the regular monthly company reports, but she always read those."

"Did she seem worried about anything?" Warren asked.

Latona considered for a moment. "She did seem more serious than usual lately, not laughing and joking around as much. And she stayed late in her office several times. There were even a few evenings when I left before she did. But she seemed more like herself last week. I think she was looking forward to the party and to going away to Banff for the weekend."

"Did she intend to meet anyone there?" Warren asked.

"I don't think so. I wasn't asked to contact anyone or to make a second hotel reservation. Julia did say something about holing up in her suite and ordering room service and massages."

Warren leaned back in his chair and tapped his fingers against his chin. "I see."

"When Detective Soo talked to me about Mother's collapse, she asked if I knew about some anonymous notes that Mother had received," Rick said. "It was the first I'd heard of them. Do you know anything about that, Latona?"

The other men looked up in surprise. "You didn't tell me about any notes," Warren said to Rick, an edge in his voice.

"There was so much going on with the police and with Mother in the hospital, I forgot about it," Rick protested.

They all turned to Latona, who opened her briefcase to remove a single sheet of paper. She studied it for a moment before responding.

"There were two anonymous notes. The first one came two weeks ago, just after I contacted the media about the press conference. I found it in the mailbox with the regular post. The envelope was addressed to 'Julia Moreland' in letters cut out from a newspaper or magazine. There was a message inside composed of more cut-out letters. The message said: 'No news is good news. Keep your mouth shut.' The second note came last Wednesday. It was left in the mailbox again. I brought it to Julia when she was having lunch with Anna Nolan, Dr. Lewis's assistant."

Kevin and Rick turned to look at Warren.

"Go on, Latona. What did that note say?" Warren asked.

"It said: 'Holding the press conference on Monday could be hazardous to your continued existence.'"

Warren frowned. "What did Julia do after she read the notes?"

"The first time, she tore it in pieces and tossed them in the garbage. I asked her if I should call the police, but she said not to worry, that it was just a prank. The second note she took more seriously. She told me that she was going to call the police, although I didn't actually hear her make the call. I saved that note and gave it to the police the day after the party."

"Julia should have cancelled the press conference," Oliver said with a solemn face. "If she had listened to those notes, she might still be with us today." Kevin glared at the older man and shook his head.

"What was Julia playing at?" Jack asked.

"Is there anything else you can think of that might be useful?" Warren asked Latona.

The young woman shook her head as she looked down at her lap. "I'm sorry."

Nodding, Warren rose from his chair. "We appreciate your help today, Latona. Thanks for coming."

Latona stood up beside him, her face composed. They shook hands and she left.

Warren paused to glance down at his secretary. "That will be all for now, Helen." The secretary nodded, closed her laptop, and exited the room.

"What do you think we should do?" Warren asked Jack.

"I think we should comb Julia's office for anything useful before the police beat us to it," the chairman said. "It'll be only so long before they get a search warrant."

"I agree. I'll go over to the house this afternoon, after we meet with the press."

"I'll go with you," Jack said. "It will look better if there are two of us. We want everything to appear open and above-board."

"Good idea," Warren replied. "Now, about the press release. I don't think we can avoid saying that Julia's death is currently under police investigation — that's public knowledge — and that the cause of death is unconfirmed. But we don't want anyone getting panicky before we know what happened. If there are any questions concerning Julia's original reason for calling the press conference, I think we should say that she was going to make a personal announcement, which her death has now negated."

"Well done, my boy," Oliver said with an approving nod. "That will deflect curiosity away from the companies."

"But you don't know that Mother's announcement was going to be personal," Rick said. "People will start to wonder. You'll be opening up her life to all kinds of speculation."

"I don't like this any better than you, Rick," Warren said, "but with Julia keeping the announcement a secret, she's left us little choice. She always got a kick out of stirring up the hornet's nest. Now it's come back to sting her."

"That's a lousy thing to say. Someone's just murdered her," Rick said.

"We don't know that for sure," Warren replied.

Rick snorted. "She didn't die of natural causes. She was only sixty and healthy as a horse. And what about the anonymous notes?"

"Could have been a crackpot," Jack said. "Might have even been a coincidence."

Rick glared at him before turning to Kevin. "What have you got to say, big brother? You've been awfully quiet."

Kevin frowned. "I have to agree with Warren. We can't help what people think."

"Of course you agree with Warren," Rick sneered. "Stick to the company line. Be a good boy."

"Shut up, Rick," Kevin snarled.

Rick turned back to Warren. "You wouldn't be doing this if you cared about Mother's memory."

Warren gave him a level glance. "Right now, I care more about father's legacy. I'm doing my best, as the senior vice president and chief financial officer, to see that we come out of this alive. I'm sorry that you're not happy with my decision, but it's the best I can do until the police tell us more. Unless you have an objection, Jack?"

The chairman shook his head. "I don't like causing speculation about Julia, not one little bit, but I agree that our hands are tied until the police find out what happened. We don't want negative talk about Westmore or Golden Farm. Julia wouldn't have liked it."

"You're a real pair of shits," Rick hissed. He stormed out of the room, flinging the boardroom door open so hard that it crashed against the wall, before stomping away down the hall. Warren stared after him and sighed.

Jack checked his watch. "We still have an hour before the press conference. Let's go find some coffee. I could really use some."

5

Warren went after Rick to calm him down. By the time the press conference began, Rick was dressed in a suit and tie and shaved. The conference was being held in the Westmore Resources' amphitheatre, a large hall in the office tower where the annual meetings were held. The three brothers stood shoulder-to-shoulder on the stage, with Oliver Sumpter and Jack Upton flanking them. As senior vice president, Warren made the announcement about Julia's death and then paused to allow the media representatives to ask questions.

"Warren, what about the rumours of foul play surrounding Mrs. Moreland's death?" one of the reporters called.

"We won't know anything for certain until the police get the autopsy results."

There was an excited buzz of conversation.

"Is it true that Mrs. Moreland intended to spend the weekend in Banff after her Christmas party?" a reporter from a national newspaper shouted.

"Yes."

"Why? What was she running away from?"

"No comment."

"Was she hiding? Was she afraid for her life?"

"No comment."

"Mrs. Moreland originally arranged this press conference to make an announcement. What was she going to say?"

Warren felt Rick stiffen.

"2012 has been a banner year for Westmore Resources," Warren said, leaning toward the microphone stand before him. "As part of Westmore's stewardship program, Julia wished to share this good fortune with Calgary's underprivileged. She believed that want is felt most keenly during the holiday season when everyone should be able to gather around the family table in a spirit of thankfulness. Unfortunately, Julia Moreland is not with us today to make the announcement herself, but she was going to donate $100,000.00 to Calgary's food banks just in time for the holidays. Of course, Westmore will honour her intention. Let's show our appreciation for Julia's generosity."

Warren caught Jack Upton's grimace out of the corner of his eye as the members of the press burst into spontaneous applause. It didn't matter. The company's coffers could afford it, and the $100,000.00 price tag was worth it to quell the negative impact of Julia's death, not to mention a fracture in the family.

Rick grinned, and he patted Warren on the back. A picture of the three brothers, smiling and with their arms around each other, made the front pages of all the national newspapers that day.

Warren, Rick, Kevin, and Kevin's wife, Lauren, met at the lawyer's office at two o'clock on Wednesday afternoon for the reading of Julia's will. Rick frowned when he saw that Kevin had brought Lauren, but if he felt that she was butting in where she wasn't wanted, he kept his mouth shut.

The four were shown into a private meeting room, where they sat at a round glass table and drank tea until Julia's lawyer, Tobias Rapp, joined them ten minutes late for their appointment. He was a trim, handsome man in his mid-thirties with a goatee and a gold stud in one ear. The three men rose to shake hands with him while Lauren smiled from her chair.

"You're not like any lawyer I've ever seen," she said. "I'm Lauren Moreland, Kevin's wife." She held out her hand, and Tobias took it with a smile.

"I'll take that as a compliment. Happy to meet you, Mrs. Moreland. Please, gentlemen, take a seat."

Tobias sat in the chair next to Warren and opened the file folder he had brought with him. A thick pile of papers was clipped together inside. Folding his hands on top of them, the lawyer said, "You have my deepest sympathy on the passing of your mother. I was shocked to hear of her death. She was in my office just three weeks ago to update her will."

Warren took the news quietly, while his two step-brothers exchanged an anxious glance.

"That's quite a coincidence," Kevin remarked.

"Yes, isn't it?" Tobias peered at him. "Julia made considerable changes to her previous will, although her charitable bequests and dispositions remained the same. That was the reason for this afternoon's delay. I wanted to ensure that everything was in order before I spoke to you. Julia had a letter prepared for this occasion, which she instructed me to read aloud. I'll warn you, it's a bit unorthodox."

He picked up the top sheet. "It reads as follows . . ."

Dear boys, and Lauren,

Since you're visiting my lawyer's office, I'll assume that I have departed from this world. I hope you take my death in stride and don't grieve too much. I mean you, Rick. (Rick stiffened in his chair.) I had a great time, and no regrets. I'm leaving a hundred dollar bill with Tobias (the lawyer passed the bill to Warren) for you to go out and have a drink on me when he's done reading this.

Let's get down to the big stuff. As you all know, we had to make some changes to the two companies to ensure our financial survival. I've worked too hard for Westmore Resources and Golden Farm Fertilizer to let things unravel now. So did your father, God rest his soul.

Rick, as Westmore's CEO, I leave you 45% of the company shares. (Kevin gasped, and Lauren's mouth dropped open. Rick stared at Tobias in shock.) With my mentorship and guidance, plus your charisma, I'm confident that you'll take Westmore to new pinnacles of success. You just need more responsibility to help you settle down. I know that you'll do your best for your father and me. Make us proud, son.

Kevin, as the president of Golden Farm Fertilizer, I'm leaving the company to you. Fertilizer might not be as glamorous as oil, but it's a commodity that will always be needed. Your grandfather built that business, and I promised him I'd keep it in the family. Look after it, Kevin, and it will look after you

That leaves 6% of the Westmore Shares, and I'm giving them to Warren. Not that I don't trust you, Rick, but Warren deserves part of the business that his father built. He's a great VP, and I'm sure that the two of you will make a fine team.

Oh, and Rick, I'm leaving you my house. It's the perfect showplace for entertaining clients, plus there's plenty of room to raise a family. It's time to stop acting like a playboy, kiddo.

Well, that sums up the important items. Tobias can tell you about the other details. I love you, boys. See you at the pearly gates.

Mother

Tobias looked up. "Would you like to hear about those bequests and dispositions now?"

Lauren jumped to her feet and dragged a dazed-looking Kevin to his. "This is outrageous! As the eldest son, Kevin should be CEO of Westmore, not president of a ridiculous fertilizer company." She spat out the last words. "We'll contest the will in court."

There was a choking sound nearby. Lauren turned in surprise to stare down at Rick. He was shaking with laughter, one hand covering his face. She stomped a designer-clad foot.

"It's not funny. Stop laughing." But Rick shook his hand weakly, his shoulders still heaving.

"Come on, Kevin." Lauren yanked her speechless husband out of the office.

Rick's laughter sputtered to a stop. "Mother always was such a hoot," he said. He wiped his eyes and looked at Warren, who was contemplating his folded hands on the table.

"I guess you're disappointed with your share of the business?"

Warren peered at his stepbrother, his face a careful blank. "It was Dad's idea to leave everything to Julia with no strings attached. She never made me any promises, and I know you boys always came first with her. I would have been a fool to expect more."

Rick nodded. "If it's any consolation, I couldn't be happier to have you as my senior VP. Hell, I've only been with Westmore for six years, but you've been with us forever. You're one of our top assets. Can we let bygones be bygones and work together as a team?" He held out his hand with an ingratiating smile. Warren stared at it wordlessly. A few seconds passed before he shook hands.

"You're right. I've devoted my life to Westmore. Where else would I go?"

"Where's that hundred dollar bill Mother left?"

Warren fumbled in his pocket and held it out to Rick, who snatched it from his fingers.

"Come on. Let's go have that drink she promised. We'll get big brother and his wife sorted out later." Warren nodded.

Rick turned to Tobias. "You have copies of the will available for us?"

"Yes. You can pick them up from my secretary on the way out."

"Thanks. I think we're going to need them." Rick shook Tobias's hand. "If there are any outstanding legal expenses, send the bill to me." Tobias nodded. "It was good meeting you. Come on, Warren." He put his arm around the larger man and led him away.

While Rick and Warren were sipping fifteen-year-old brandy in a bar across the street from the lawyer's office, Kevin was swilling beer slumped in an easy chair in his bedroom. He had thrown his jacket and tie on the floor, and placed a six-pack next to his feet. Lauren paced back and forth in front of him, ranting about the unfairness of his mother's will.

He had stopped listening five minutes ago, and was brooding over his mangled dream of becoming CEO of Westmore. He was the eldest son. He was entitled. But Mother and Rick had always had a mutual admiration society, going out to lunch together, attending openings at art galleries and theatres, and all that other artsy-fartsy stuff. And what about their love of ridiculously expensive scotch! Plus, they had always had their heads together, laughing at some private joke that they didn't bother to share with him. Well, now the joke was on him. He was royally screwed.

"And another thing. Why did your mother make you take engineering in university instead of business, like your brother? If you had had an MBA like Rick, she would have had no excuse to pass you over. Was she planning on making Rick CEO way back then?" She paused to glance at her glassy-eyed husband. Dropping to her knees, she gave his shoulders a shake.

"Kevin, are you listening to me? Come on, we have to decide what to do about this."

He grabbed her arms and shoved her out of the way. "Lay off, Lauren. I've got one hell of a headache. I need time to think."

She threw up her hands and walked to the bed, flopping down on it.

"The only good thing is, I'll be able to force Oliver to retire as soon as I've got the hang of the business," Kevin said. "I can't stand the old fart. He used to drive me crazy with his pep talks and micro-managing during the summers when Mother forced me to work in the fertilizer plant. Wait until he hears I'm going to replace him." Kevin started to laugh unpleasantly.

Lauren raised her head, frowning. "What about my business, Kev? Will there be enough money for you to continue helping me with the store?"

Kevin's smile was replaced by a scowl. "When was there ever enough money to keep you and your store afloat?" He hauled himself out of his chair and stumbled the short distance to the bed. "When is that business of yours going to pay for itself, eh?" he shouted, towering over her.

Lauren rose up on one elbow. "You know my market is specialized," she said in a soothing tone. "I just need time to find my niche. But business will take off with my new advertising campaign. It will generate all kinds of online orders. You'll see."

Kevin dismissed her with an impatient wave of his hand and collapsed back in his chair. Lauren watched him for a moment before sitting up. Kevin pretended not to notice as she began unfastening her silk dress, button by button. She rolled off the bed and walked toward him, her dress open and her hips swaying. The dress dropped to the floor right in front of him. She was wearing a one-piece, lemon-yellow, leather corset, her breasts overflowing the cups. Leaning forward to give him a better view, she rested one hand on either arm of his chair.

Kevin looked away, muttering, "You can't always use sex to get your way, you know."

She kicked off her stilettos, ignoring his remark. He could smell her jasmine body wash as she pushed her lush black hair over her shoulders. Climbing on top of him, she settled back into his lap

"Let's not fight, baby," she purred. "Together, we make a great team. We both want the same things. Success. Fame. Power." She punctuated each word with a kiss. He tried not to react, but she teased his mouth with her agile tongue until he couldn't help himself. His arms encircled her, crushing her against his chest.

She drew back a bit. "Just make sure that you make a clean break from Westmore. Then we'll figure out a way to use the fertilizer company as a stepping-stone to better things." He nodded and reached for the zipper on her corset.

6

Just over a week had passed since Julia's collapse at the Christmas party. The tragedy was beginning to lose its sadness for Anna. She was taking a stroll around the campus ring road during her lunch break on Friday afternoon. A warm wind had chased away the bitter cold, melting the snow until it was nothing but a damp memory. The sky was blue and the air was sparkling. Anna's mind was occupied with happy plans about the Christmas dinner she was going to prepare for the two special men in her life, Charlie and Ben. In honour of Charlie's English heritage, she was going to roast a goose for the first time. Would her roasting pan be big enough?

Returning refreshed at the end of her break, she sat in her chair to change out of her runners. The light on her phone was flashing. Anna dialled voice mail and slipped on her black pumps as she listened to the message.

"Anna, when you get back from lunch, please come to my office immediately."

Anna frowned as she erased the message. What did Magdalena want now? She'd been more difficult to please this week, presumably because she was worried about Julia's death and its ramifications for Warren. Not that there was anything that Magdalena could do about it.

Anna picked up a pad and pen in case she needed to jot down notes and crossed the hall to Magdalena's office. The door was closed, so she knocked.

"Come in."

Anna opened the door and halted on the threshold, startled to see Detective Soo peering at her from one of the chairs in front of her boss's desk.

"Come in and shut the door," Magdalena said. Anna looked past the detective to her boss. The average person wouldn't have detected the tension in Magdalena's seemingly-composed face, but Anna could see it. She closed the door and walked to the detective with her hand extended.

"Good to see you again, Detective Soo."

The short, compact woman rose to shake hands. Sandra Soo was dressed in a grey pantsuit with a stark white blouse under the jacket, the top button undone. Her close-cropped, black hair was brushed straight back from a bare face. As Anna studied her, she thought that it wasn't that Detective Soo was unfeminine. She wasn't masculine, either. It was as if that part of her personality was incidental to what mattered most to her — being a cop.

"Good to see you, Mrs. Nolan. Rather than ask you back to the Westwinds building for questioning, I decided to visit the two of you here. It's handy that you both work for the university."

Anna nodded and sat down uneasily in the extra chair. "Has something happened?" she asked.

"Yes. We've determined Julia Moreland's cause of death. The final toxicology report just came back from Ottawa this morning. When we didn't get any positive results from the earlier tests, the chief of police asked the lab to do a bunch of tests for the toxins that cause seizures and are native to this area, and we finally got a reaction. Julia Moreland died from ingesting water hemlock."

"What's that?" Anna asked. "Is that the same stuff Socrates was forced to take?"

"No. 'Hemlock' applies to a lot of different plants. Water hemlock is the most poisonous plant growing wild in North America. It's found next to rivers, marshes, and wet ditches. Maybe it grows near Crane, for instance. That's the town you live in, isn't it?"

Anna nodded, staring at Detective Soo in fascinated horror. What did the stuff look like? She had never heard of any poisonous plants growing near the town.

"Probably not. I believe that Crane's water source is subterranean," Magdalena said. Anna glanced at her boss with gratitude. Mounting apprehension was making it difficult for her to think. She was having a severe attack of déjà vu.

"Is that so? But Calgary has two rivers."

"Have you discovered water hemlock growing in Calgary?" Magdalena and Soo contemplated each other, the detective with open curiosity, and Magdalena with studied indifference.

"No," Soo said.

Anna managed to ask, "Do they know how Julia took the poison?"

The detective turned to her. "Not yet, but our forensics team got lucky the night of the party. The kitchen staff managed to isolate the glasses and dishes that Mrs. Moreland used. Now that we know she died from water hemlock poisoning, the lab will know what to look for." She paused to watch for reactions. Anna looked stunned, while Magdalena seemed only politely interested.

"We're taking a closer look at Mrs. Moreland's movements on the night of the party. I already heard from you, Mrs. Nolan, that she met with a man in the Library Lounge just after the dancing began. Any more ideas on who the man was, by the way?"

Anna shook her head. "I didn't recognize his voice, but then I didn't know most of the guests at the party."

"Well, if it comes to you, just let me know. Meanwhile, eyewitnesses told us that Mrs. Moreland was sitting at a table with you two and her stepson before she went out on the dance floor for the last time. She was having seizures twenty minutes later. Do either of you remember the victim eating or drinking anything while she was at your table?"

Anna froze. Julia had asked Warren to fetch her a scotch from the bar. That was the only thing Julia had consumed while she was sitting with them. But if Anna admitted that to the detective, Soo might conclude that Warren had poisoned Julia's drink.

"Yes, Detective," Magdalena said. "Julia asked Warren to get her a Lagavulin from the bar. She drank a little after he delivered it to her. But he was also carrying an orange juice for Anna, so his hands weren't free." Anna quickly nodded her agreement.

"Did anyone else handle it after Warren gave the drink to Mrs. Moreland?"

Magdalena and Anna were silent. Finally, Magdalena said, "As I recall, Warren set the drink on the table next to his stepmother, who picked it up immediately and drank from it. Is that how you remember it, Anna?"

"Yes, that's right."

Soo closed her notebook and stood. "Thanks. That's all I need from you now. I'll be in touch if I have any other questions." She nodded to them and left the office, her boots ringing on the tiled hall.

Dr. Georgiou-Bates stepped into the doorway, ruffling a handful of papers. "Magdalena, do you have a minute? I've got those statistics you wanted on female undergraduate grades."

"Not now, Lou."

The professor looked up in surprise. "What?"

Magdalena sprang from her chair and marched the short distance to her. "Now is a bad time. I'm talking with Anna."

The professor looked over Magdalena's shoulder, seeing Anna for the first time. "But you said you needed the information today."

Magdalena gazed at her coldly. "Later, Lou."

Lou took a step back. "Why don't I just e-mail them to you?"

Magdalena closed the door in the professor's face and whirled to look at Anna. The cold mask of indifference slipped, and Anna saw anger in her eyes.

"What should we do?" her boss demanded.

Anna stared back. "Why did you tell Detective Soo that Warren got the scotch for Julia? If you hadn't said anything, she might have thought that Warren got it for himself, and Julia helped herself to it later. It made him look bad."

Magdalena sank into the chair beside her. "What else could I say? There might have been witnesses who overheard her asking him for it. If I had lied, Detective Soo would have found out anyway. It would only have made matters worse."

Anna stopped to consider. Cops did have a tendency to ask questions for which they already had the answers. "You're probably right."

"But what should I do now? How can I help Warren?"

"What do you mean?" Anna asked warily. "There's nothing you can do."

Magdalena waved a hand impatiently. "But you got involved with both of the Crane murder investigations. You looked for evidence. You followed people."

Anna jumped to her feet. "And that's how I ended up almost getting myself killed. Do yourself and Warren a favour: let the police figure it out."

"Anna, please."

Anna saw annoyance in her boss's face and felt trapped. Magdalena must think that she was holding out on her, that there was something Anna could do to make this right for Warren. Her chest tightened, and her left leg began to tremble.

"Look, please don't ask me what to do," Anna pleaded. "There's nothing you can do to help. Really." She turned and escaped back to the sanctuary of her office.

A young man holding a book was sitting in front of her desk. He stood as she rushed into the room.

"I want to return a book that Dr. Carmichael loaned to me this term, but he's not in his office."

"Here, give it to me. I'll make sure he gets it." Anna's hand was trembling as she reached for the book. The student noticed and looked at her with concern.

"Are you okay, ma'am?"

Get a grip on yourself, Anna thought. She pasted a weak smile on her face. "Just a little muscle fatigue. I've been overdoing it with the weights lately."

The young man relaxed. "Well, take it easy. You don't want to injure yourself."

Anna swallowed nervously. "Thanks for the advice. I'll do that. You have a good holiday, now."

He smiled. "You, too. See you in the New Year."

"I hope so," Anna said fervently.

7

Anna woke with a start. The room was shadowy except for the moonlight gleaming through her curtains. She groaned and rolled onto her side. The digital display on her clock radio said 3:43 a.m. Wendy, her shepherd/labrador cross, padded to the bed and rested her muzzle on the mattress. Anna stroked the dog's sleek head.

"It's okay, girl. Just a bad dream. Go back to sleep."

Wendy sank down on the carpet beside the bed and sighed while Anna rolled onto her back and stared at the ceiling. She had been back in the cemetery with the ghost in the mouldy black shroud chasing her. Just as the ghost had reached out to catch her with its skeletal fingers, Anna had tripped and jolted herself awake.

Damn, she hadn't had that dream for a couple of weeks. Anna rammed her pillow against the headboard and placed her hands on her stomach before trying some deep breathing exercises to relax. It was too late to take one of the sleeping pills her doctor had prescribed. She'd only feel fuzzy in the morning and have trouble functioning all day. Besides, she preferred not to take them anymore unless it was absolutely necessary. She'd just have to get back to sleep on her own.

The mattress bounced, and Anna woke with a gasp. Wendy was standing over her, sniffing her arm.

"Wendy! What are you doing?"

The room was bright. Anna turned to look at the clock. 10:17 a.m. She never slept in that late, even on a Saturday. She threw off the covers and sat up. Wendy bounded off the bed and trotted for the door.

"Sorry, I know it's late. I'll be right there." Anna shoved her feet into slippers and followed the dog down the hall to the living room and into the bungalow's eat-in kitchen. First things first. She unlocked the sliding door to the backyard and tugged it open so that Wendy could go out to do her business. The dog burst past her, and Anna filled the water and food bowls. Wendy was crunching on kibble by the time Anna hurried to the bathroom for a quick shower. She'd have to move it if she were going to catch May and Erna in time for breakfast at The Diner.

Twenty minutes later, Anna was speed-walking the six blocks to downtown Crane. As she turned onto Main Street, she spotted Clive's blue tractor parked right outside the restaurant door. Saturday breakfast-time at The Diner was not as busy now that it was too cold for the motorcycle crowd to make the twenty minute ride from Calgary. At least Clive was still there. Maybe May and Erna were too. Her face pink with exertion, Anna pulled the restaurant door open and hurried inside.

Mary, The Diner's full-time waitress, bustled by with two plates piled high with pancakes, the cords of her white apron tied twice around her skinny waist. "Anna! Thought you were sick this morning," she called over her shoulder as she headed for the tables.

Judy looked up from the counter where she was pouring a refill for Clive. She was dressed in a red plaid shirt, jeans, and cowboy boots with a white Stetson topping her honey-blond hair. Judy helped out at The Diner on Saturdays, but worked as a secretary at the Foothills Premium Real Estate Agency during the week.

"Hey, Anna. What happened to you?" she called.

"What'd you say?" Clive asked.

Judy nodded in Anna's direction, and the hulking man pivoted on his stool to look. "Morning, Anna. Cold enough for you?" he asked.

"Sure is." Anna walked over while pulling her hands from her gloves to clap him on the shoulder. "I had trouble getting out of bed this morning," she said in a clear voice.

"Heard we've got snow on the way. Mother's rheumatism is acting up again."

"Sorry to hear that. Tell your mom I said 'hi,' and that I'm going to make shortbread this weekend. I'll bring some by for the two of you this week."

"Thanks. Mother says your shortbread is the best she's ever had." Clive swung back to his breakfast and raised his mug to his lips. The bell rang on the kitchen pass-through, and Anna glanced up to see Frank, The Diner's owner, laying a plate of bacon, eggs, toast, and hash browns on the counter.

"Hey, Anna, hang on a minute. I need to talk to you," he hollered. Pushing through the swinging door a moment later, he joined Judy behind the counter. Frank was sixtyish with long grey hair pulled into a ponytail and a full beard and moustache. He placed an arm around Judy's waist, and she leaned against him.

"Do you want to buy tickets for the Rotary Club's Christmas Dinner Dance for you and Tremaine? We're raising money to buy a new swing set for the park this year."

"When is it?"

"Next Saturday night, December fifteenth."

Anna shook her head. "Charlie won't be here by then. I'm not expecting him until the twenty-first."

"Too bad. We were wondering if the sergeant is as smooth on the dance floor as he is in an interrogation room." He grinned at Anna, pleased with his joke.

"I don't know. I haven't had the pleasure yet."

"You're joking," Frank said in amazement. "Judy and I go dancing at least once a month. We even dance at home after the dishes are done, don't we, honey?"

"We're just a couple of dancing fools," Judy said with a smile.

"But I'd still like to come," Anna added. "Maybe Erna, May, and I can sit together?"

"Sherman already bought tickets for him and May, and Erna's tagging along with them. You can share a table for sure."

"Are they still here?" Anna asked. She twisted to look around the restaurant.

Judy pointed to a table at the back of the room. "Right beside the Christmas tree."

Anna spotted her friends and nodded. "I'd better hurry over before they leave. Catch you about a ticket on the way out, Frank."

"You want the usual?" Judy asked as Anna turned to join her friends.

"Yes, please."

Threading her way through the tables, Anna paused to greet Mr. Andrews. He was a retired rancher who could be found reading the paper and drinking coffee most mornings at The Diner. He replied with an "hmm," not bothering to raise his head from perusing the Classifieds.

May and Erna waved as Anna approached. May was wearing a green, home-knit sweater with Rudolph, the red-nosed reindeer's face on the front. Rudolph's nose was knit a bright cherry-red.

"That a new sweater?" Anna asked as she sat down.

"Just finished it this week," May said. "Where were you? We were about to give up on you."

"Have another tea and keep me company while I eat," Anna said, ignoring the question. She didn't want to admit to her friends that she had overslept after having had another nightmare.

"Did you have trouble sleeping last night, dear?" Erna asked. Anna shook her head in amazement. You couldn't get anything past those bright, inquisitive eyes of hers. Years of being a high school teacher had honed Erna's perceptiveness, and she hadn't lost any of it since retiring.

"Does it show?"

"Not very much. You're just looking peaked this morning. How was the end of your week? Has anything new happened since Wednesday?" The three friends had met earlier that week at the library's book club.

Their conversation was interrupted by Judy's arrival. She set down Anna's apple juice and a plate with three strips of bacon and two fluffy pancakes. May asked for more hot water, and Anna waited for Judy to refill the teapot before telling her friends about Detective Soo's visit and the results of the toxicology testing. May listened with her chin cupped in her hand while Erna stirred sugar into her tea. When Anna had finished talking, she poured syrup over her pancakes and ate two pieces right away. She was starving, and no one made pancakes like Frank.

"How distressing," Erna said. "Poison is so distasteful."

May nodded. "There's something sneaky about poisoning. Only a rat would kill someone that way."

"I've been researching water hemlock on the internet since I first heard about it," Anna said. "It's also called 'cowbane' because cows have been poisoned by accidentally eating it in fields where they're grazing."

"A girlhood friend of mine had a nephew who died of water hemlock poisoning," Erna said. Anna paused with the fork half-way to her mouth. Trust Erna to have had some personal experience with the poison.

"The boy cut some of the root to make a whistle," Erna said. "The root is the most poisonous part of the plant, plus it's hollow." Erna shook her head. "He was only eight. I went to the funeral. It was so sad." She stared into the distance for a moment before refocusing on Anna. "Anyone who would do that deliberately to someone must be punished."

Anna popped some more food into her mouth and chewed. The pancake didn't taste as good as it had a minute ago.

"Magdalena did ask for my help," she said nonchalantly.

"I'll bet. You've become quite the sleuth," May responded.

"I told her to stay out of it. Let the police do the investigating," Anna added.

May and Erna exchanged a glance. "That was probably wise," Erna said tentatively.

Anna nodded as she cut her bacon. "I mean, what can I do about it? Stick my nose in where it isn't wanted, I guess, and ask questions that would upset people. It's not like I had anything to do with Julia Moreland." The knife grated on her plate, and she picked up the bacon and bit off a chunk.

"Magdalena is my boss, not my friend," she said as she chewed. "It's true that she and I have gotten to know each other better over the past year, but it's not like we're close or anything. She'll just have to get through the investigation on her own." Despite her words, Anna's eyes were troubled as she glanced at her friends.

"What you say is absolutely true," Erna said, patting Anna's hand.

"You've been through a lot this year," May added.

Anna nodded and looked down at her plate.

In a lower voice, so as not to be heard by the couple at the next table, Erna said, "On the other hand, this isn't like you, dear. You've always been so impetuous, charging ahead into danger without weighing the consequences. I've chided you in the past for not using more discipline in your thinking, but I don't like to see you cowed by fear. You mustn't let what's happened change you."

Anna couldn't believe her ears. "Are you saying that I'm a coward?"

"No, of course not," Erna hastened to say.

May blurted, "No way! You've just hit a rough patch, doll."

"You two think I should do something to help Magdalena, don't you? But what can I do?"

Anna's face flushed. This wasn't fair. They couldn't criticize her for being foolhardy one minute and fearful the next. There was nothing wrong with wanting to stay out of trouble for a change.

"We don't want you to do anything. It's what you think you should do that's important," Erna said.

"You're not making any sense," Anna muttered. She picked up her purse and pushed back her chair. "I'm sorry, I have to go. Wendy hasn't had her walk yet, plus my outdoor lights need stringing and I've got baking to do. I'll see you next Saturday."

Avoiding her friends' eyes as she left the table, Anna paid Judy at the cash register and stomped out of the restaurant. If people would just leave her alone and stop picking on her, maybe she could get over the bad memories that still plagued her dreams. Why should she be braver than everyone else? Her friends weren't the ones who had almost died.

Still in a funk when she reached home, Anna collected Wendy and some plastic bags and strode along Wistler Road into the countryside. She always felt better when she was on the move. Exercise helped to clear her head.

Wendy was the perfect companion, running ahead to nose at piles of leaves or chase a squirrel up a tree, leaving Anna to calm down. The fresh air and exercise worked like a tonic. By the time the sun was as high in the sky as it got in December, Anna was unlocking her front door, ready to tackle the outdoor decorating. Wendy darted ahead into the kitchen for a long drink while Anna trotted down the stairs to the basement. After hunting through boxes of Christmas ornaments and gift wrap, she found the outdoor lights. The colourful, solar-powered lights she had purchased on sale two years ago were perfect for the tall blue spruce on her front lawn.

She was standing on her stepladder, weaving the string of lights through the boughs at the top of the tree, when a black BMW skidded into the driveway and parked behind her Honda. Funny. The only person she knew who owned a black BMW was Magdalena.

The car door flew open, and Magdalena jumped out. Anna practically fell off the ladder when she saw her. Her usually chic boss was wearing leggings and a sweat shirt with her hair straggling down her back. Anna scrambled down the ladder as Magdalena dashed across the grass toward her. Magdalena's face was white and taut, and she shuddered in the bitter wind.

"Detective Soo has taken Warren in for questioning," she panted.

8

Magdalena was huddled on the couch under a blanket when Anna returned with two steaming mugs of hot chocolate. Wendy was lying at her guest's feet.

"Here," Anna said, placing the mug into her boss's hands. "Drink this."

Magdalena raised the hot chocolate to her mouth and swallowed automatically, her face withdrawn. She seemed mired in her own thoughts.

Anna sat beside her and took a sip from her own mug. The drink was extra-chocolatey because she had added a dash of chocolate syrup, just the way she liked it. Magdalena looked like she needed the extra sugar, anyway. She leaned forward to place her mug on the coffee table, but Anna said, "No, keep drinking." Magdalena nodded and drank mechanically until her beverage was done.

"Feel any better?" Anna asked.

"A little," Magdalena said in a husky voice.

"Okay, tell me again. What happened?"

Magdalena sat up and pushed back the blanket. "Warren stayed with me last night. It had been a difficult week for him, what with people calling for updates after Monday's press announcement and his stepbrothers and the board of directors worrying him about what to do. Then Detective Soo made everything worse by telling Warren and his brothers about Julia's poisoning at the same time. If she had warned Warren about it first, he could have softened the blow for his stepbrothers. Rick made a scene and left. Warren was afraid that Rick might do something foolish and spent hours trying to find him. He finally did, at a bar. I can only imagine what Warren went through getting Rick home to bed.

"So we slept in late this morning. I was preparing breakfast when Detective Soo arrived with a male constable. I don't remember the constable's name, but he was obviously there as her back-up. She asked if they could come in and talk with Warren, that they had seen his car parked out front. Warren came to the door and invited them inside. While we were sitting in the living room, Detective Soo told us that the toxicology report showed water hemlock in Julia's Lagavulin. The bartender at the Christmas party stated that very few people had requested it that evening, and that Warren was one of them. Detective Soo said that if she could figure out how Warren had poisoned Julia's Lagavulin right before everyone's eyes, she would arrest him for Julia's murder then and there."

"How did Warren react?"

"He was so staggered, he couldn't speak at first. But after he recovered, he asked what possible motive could he have had for killing Julia? Detective Soo said that two witnesses had come forward to report an argument between Warren and Julia that happened a year ago. According to the witnesses, Warren had barged into a restaurant during their dinner with Julia to accuse her of being responsible for his mother's death. They also said that he'd threatened Julia's life. Allegedly, the owner of the restaurant and one of the waiters had to take Warren outside because he was causing such a disturbance."

"Why would Julia have been responsible for Warren's mother's death?"

Magdalena turned to look at Anna. "Did you know that Warren's father left his mother for Julia?"

"Yes. Julia mentioned it to me."

Magdalena nodded. "Supposedly, Warren's mother, Sheila, didn't know about the affair, so it came as quite a shock to her when Robert left. She'd already had some difficulty with post-partum depression after Warren's birth, and had become dependent upon barbiturates. She took the break-up quite hard, and sank even lower into depression and drug and alcohol abuse. Warren staged an intervention when he was an adult to persuade his mother to get professional help, but it didn't work. The argument the witnesses reported occurred on the night Sheila died in a car accident. Her car went off the road in the mountains. The alcohol level in her blood was three times the legal limit."

"I feel so sorry for Warren," Anna said. "I can understand why he'd be angry on the day his mother died. What did he have to say to Detective Soo?"

"He said that, yes, he had accused Julia of being responsible for his mother's death. He had been having a few drinks at a bar across the street when he saw Julia go into the restaurant with her friends. He said that he hadn't threatened Julia's life, however, but had said something like, 'We're still alive, and my mother is dead. She didn't deserve this.' He apologized to Julia the next day, and the incident never came up again.

"Detective Soo replied that the witnesses had quoted Warren as saying, 'Why should you live now that my mother is dead?' Warren just stared at her, as if he couldn't believe what she was saying. She said that since Warren had a motive for wanting Julia dead and his fingerprints had been found on the poisoned glass of Lagavulin, they were taking him into custody as a person of interest. She advised Warren that he could have a lawyer present for the questioning, so he asked me to make the call. He also asked me to contact Kevin and Rick. Then they took him to their cruiser, holding him between them as if he might run away. That was four hours ago. I made the calls, and then I wanted to talk with you. I went to the office and found your home address in the files so that I could come see you in person."

"Have you heard anything from Warren's lawyer?"

Magdalena shook her head. "I phoned the number on Detective Soo's card, but the call went straight to voice mail. I left a message, but she hasn't called back yet. That was two hours ago." Magdalena blinked. "I hope you don't mind my coming."

Anna laid her hand on her boss's shoulder. "No, of course not. I know what it feels like to be crazy with worry over someone you love."

"I wish Sergeant Tremaine were here. He might have some investigative insight to share with us."

"No you don't, because he wouldn't want to hear what I'm about to say."

Anna swallowed hard to push away her fear. She knew how much Magdalena was suffering. She had to help her.

"You don't think Warren is responsible for Julia's death, do you?" she asked.

Magdalena stiffened. "Of course not! He might have blamed her for his mother's death, but he wouldn't have harmed Julia. And certainly not with poison. That's too despicable."

"Then who do you think murdered her?"

Without missing a beat, Magdalena said, "Kevin, or possibly his wife, Lauren."

"Why?" Anna asked, startled.

Magdalena rested her head against the couch. "Kevin didn't like his mother much. I could see it in his face whenever she talked to him. Julia relied on Warren to help run Westmore, and Rick was her favourite — the golden son — but she didn't have much use for Kevin. She told me so herself. I think he realized it and was jealous of Rick. Aside from that, Lauren was like Lady Macbeth in the background, willing to do anything she could to promote Kevin and her business. I honestly don't think she would stop at murder if someone threatened their success. Warren told me how upset Kevin was at the reading of the will when Julia made Rick CEO of Westmore and Kevin the president of her fertilizer company. Obviously, he thought he would become CEO of Westmore when Julia died. Did he poison her to speed up the process?"

Anna paused to think, but shook her head after a moment. "If that's true, I still can't figure out how the poison got into the scotch that Julia drank. Did Warren explain that?"

"He said that it took him a few minutes to get back from the bar because people kept stopping him to talk. He remembers seeing Kevin pass by on the way to the table. It's possible that Kevin introduced the poison into the Lagavulin when Warren was distracted."

Anna snorted. "If Kevin did, he must have balls of steel. And how would he know that the scotch was meant for Julia and not Warren?"

"Warren hates scotch, and Julia was quite fond of Lagavulin. Everyone close to them knew that. Plus, if Kevin were following Julia that night, waiting for an opportunity to use the poison, he'd have overheard her asking Warren to get her the drink."

"Hmm." Anna leaned back against the couch beside Magdalena. Her boss waited patiently as Anna reflected.

"It would be interesting to find out why Kevin couldn't wait any longer to become CEO," Anna said. "Have you heard of any recent changes in his life?"

Magdalena shook her head, her eyes intent on Anna's face.

"I know a good way to find out," Anna said. "Lauren."

"You want me to talk to Lauren about Kevin?"

"Sure. You've got a perfectly good excuse to see her. The police just picked up Warren. Act as if you need her support. Phone her up and invite her to lunch tomorrow so that you can cry on her shoulder."

Magdalena frowned. "Lauren and I aren't very close, so she might be suspicious if I tried to arrange a meeting. Besides, how would I get her to talk about Kevin?"

"That's easy. Wives are always ready to talk about their husbands. Kevin's upset about not becoming CEO. I'm sure Lauren has a thing or two to say about that."

Magdalena nodded. "She did threaten to contest the will in court. Warren told me that."

"Terrific. Then she'll probably be ready to talk her head off."

"I'm not a very good actress, Anna. What if she sees through me? I wouldn't want to put her on her guard. That would be counter-productive." Magdalena hesitated. "I know it may be overstepping the boundaries of our relationship to ask for a favour, but would you come with me?"

Anna stiffened. "What excuse could we give for my coming along?"

"I'm sure Lauren and Kevin must have seen you sitting at the table with Warren and me at the party. She'll assume that we're friends. It's not unnatural that you'd be going out to lunch with me, and that we'd want to talk about Julia's death." Magdalena placed her hand awkwardly on Anna's knee. "Please, Anna? For Warren's sake?"

Anna gazed at her boss's pleading face. In her mind, she heard Erna saying, "I don't like to see you cowed by fear." She wouldn't have been afraid to talk to Lauren a year ago, before the two Crane murder investigations. Had fear altered her? Had she turned her into a coward?

"I'll do it," she said. "Call her now, before I change my mind."

Magdalena sighed. "Thank you, Anna. Thank you very much."

Anna smiled weakly and nodded, but as Magdalena bent to retrieve her cell from her purse, she prayed that her boss wouldn't be able to reach Lauren.

But Lauren answered on the third ring, and Magdalena ended the call after only two minutes. "Lauren said to meet her at the store at eleven tomorrow, and we'll go to lunch afterward."

"The store?"

"Yes. Lauren designs lingerie and sells it from a downtown store. I shopped there once. It's very expensive."

"Great." Anna sighed. Not only would she be hobnobbing with a possible killer, but threatening the limit on her credit card.

"Isn't it?" Magdalena answered.

9

Anna left her car at Magdalena's house the following morning and rode downtown with her. She glanced at Magdalena, so composed and elegant in a cashmere sweater and wool slacks, and realized that her boss didn't look the part of an anxious girlfriend.

"You're going to have to convince Lauren that you're upset about Warren, you know. Have you heard from him, by the way?"

"He called me before I went to bed last night at midnight. The police had released him, and he was back at home."

"That's terrific!" But something in Magdalena's tone made Anna ask, "Was he all right?"

"He said that he was exhausted and didn't want to talk." Magdalena's tone was brisk.

Anna nodded slowly. If she had been close to someone who had been taken into police custody, there would have been a tearful reunion when that person was released. Magdalena did not meet her gaze, however, and her mouth was pressed into a firm line, so Anna didn't ask any more questions. Still, there was something wrong here.

They arrived at the store by eleven and were able to find a parking spot a half-block away amidst the busy shoppers. Anna was curious to see what an upscale lingerie store looked like, but couldn't see inside because black velvet curtains covered the windows. This was definitely the place. "Lauren" was written in silver lights on a purple sign over the door.

"That's weird. Doesn't she want people to know what she's selling?" Anna asked.

Magdalena paused with her hand on the handle. "Lauren doesn't encourage walk-in trade. She feels that they won't appreciate her designs. Most of her customers are referrals from friends, plus she has online ordering." Magdalena opened the door, and they walked inside.

The walls and ceiling were painted a deep violet, making the interior feel dark and dramatic. White lights were focused on black mannequins posed on pedestals, forcing Anna to look up. One outfit in particular caught her eye.

"Oh my," Anna said. The mannequin in front of her was wearing a blood orange ensemble. A leather strap, fastened with a hip ring to a leather thong, crossed diagonally across the torso to cover the right breast. The left breast was bare. The mannequin held a spear.

"I call that 'The Warrior,'" a voice said from behind her. Anna turned and saw Lauren, dressed in a chestnut-coloured leather bodysuit, advancing toward them. Her beautiful, waist-length black hair swung freely behind her.

"Magdalena, what can I say? Kevin is calling everyone he knows to protest Warren's innocence." Lauren laid her hands on Magdalena's shoulders, and the two women air-kissed.

"Thank you, Lauren," Magdalena replied in a quivery voice. "I don't know how I could get through this without the support of my friends."

Anna looked at her in surprise. She had no idea that her boss could be so convincing. Magdalena sniffed and withdrew a tissue from her purse to dab her face.

"I know just what you need," Lauren said. "Shopping therapy. I have something special for you. You'll look so hot, Warren won't be able to keep his hands off you." She put an arm around Magdalena's shoulders and turned to frown at Anna.

"Do I know you?"

"Anna works with me at the university, and she's a good friend," Magdalena said. "She's trying to keep me busy so that I won't worry about Warren."

Lauren studied Anna dubiously. "What size do you wear, dear?"

Anna stole another glance at the "Warrior" mannequin and tried not to shudder. "A ten on top and a twelve on the bottom."

"Hmm. I don't usually carry anything that big. Wait a minute." She snapped her manicured fingers. "I've got this fun little number I created especially for the holidays. It's cut a bit more generously, so you might be able to squeeze into it. Come with me."

Lauren put her other arm around Anna and led the two women toward the back of the store. On the wall facing them were two enlarged photographs of Lauren. She wore nothing but a designer gold watch and a pair of gladiator sandals with some artfully arranged shadows in the first, and crouched naked behind a purse in the second. She looked fabulous.

"Are you a model?" Anna asked.

Lauren paused to study the pictures. "In another life, before I became a designer. Those photographs appeared as full-page ads in all the major North American fashion magazines." She shrugged. "They impress my customers."

She led them through an archway into a short corridor with doors opening on either side. A large, three-way mirror hung on the far wall next to a door.

"Right in here, Magdalena," Lauren said, guiding her into a dressing room. "We'll put Anna next to you."

Anna's stall contained a black upholstered bench, a wall mirror, and an art print of a naked woman in a turban looking serenely over her shoulder. Anna sighed and sat down on the bench to unzip her ankle boots. She was unbuttoning her blouse when she heard Lauren's heels clicking down the tiled hall toward them.

"Here we are," she said from the corridor. Anna heard Magdalena's door open. "I think the black will contrast beautifully with your hair and colouring."

Magdalena murmured her thanks, and the door closed.

Anna's door opened next, and she froze with one arm out of her blouse. "I think you'll find this amusing," Lauren said, eying her impersonally. "Come out and show us when you're dressed."

Anna took the hanger, and Lauren closed the door. She peered down at the outfit. It was a two-piece, red silk outfit with a push-up bra augmented by a swish of fabric and a matching panty. Two white fur pompoms dangled from red cord attached to a rosette between the bra cups.

Lauren had to be kidding. The outfit looked like a teenage boy's Christmas fantasy come true. All she needed was a Santa hat.

"What do you think?" Magdalena called from next door.

"I haven't got it on yet," Anna said. She left on her underpants — there was no way she was going to try on the cheek-baring panties that went with the outfit, even if the crotch did have a protective strip — and quickly donned the bra. She bent forward to adjust her breasts and straightened. The pompoms bounced against her skin, framed between the wispy panels of red silk framing her tummy. She looked in the mirror. Her hair was mussed, her face was pink, and her breasts pointed toward the ceiling.

Now that Anna had reached the age of forty and comfort was more of a priority than sex-appeal, she slept in sleep pants and a tank-top. Sometimes she even wore a flannel nighty on nights when the weather was really cold. Charlie said he liked the short silk slip she wore to bed when he was around, but it still covered a lot more skin than this getup did.

She heard Lauren returning, and the door to her change room opened again. Lauren handed in a pair of feather-covered mules.

"Here, try these on. I think they'll look adorable with your 'Santa's Little Helper' outfit."

Anna dropped them on the floor and slid her feet into them. The heels were two-inch spikes, but at least the shoes fit.

"You're not going to try on the panties?" Anna shook her head, and Lauren rolled her eyes. "Come out and have a look in the big mirror."

"That's okay. I can see how I look in the mirror in here."

"But you can't see the back." Lauren took Anna's hand and dragged her into the hall, towing her to the three-way mirror. Anna concentrated on keeping her balance in the flimsy mules until Lauren stopped her. There was silence. Anna lifted her eyes. Lauren was studying Anna's reflection with her head to one side. The outfit didn't have the same effect with her black cotton briefs, but as she turned and looked over her shoulder, Anna felt that she could have looked worse.

"Actually, the higher waistline works for you," Lauren said, brushing a lock of Anna's hair from her bare shoulder and letting her hand linger there. She caught Anna's eye in the mirror, ogling her with a sexy pout to her lips. Her stare made Anna uncomfortable.

The door to the other dressing room opened, and Magdalena strode out dressed in a black leather outfit that could best be described as a "V" with side straps. She had shaken her hair out of its chignon and left on her high, black leather boots. With her lithe dancer's body, she looked like a queen in her underwear. Or some kind of authority figure.

Anna's mouth dropped open.

"Wait, I've got something that's going to look fabulous with that," Lauren said, rushing past them.

Magdalena sauntered toward Anna with a twinkle in her eye. "We look like we should pose for a poster captioned 'Naughty and Nice.'"

Anna shook her head. "No one's going to take my picture in this outfit."

Lauren rushed back carrying a pair of long, black leather gloves.

"Here, try these on."

Magdalena drew them smoothly up and over her elbows. They fit like a second skin. Magdalena walked toward the mirror, her face a deadpan, as Anna scuttled out of the way.

"All I need is a whip."

Anna burst out laughing. Her boss had always seemed so uptight and ladylike. Anna had never seen this side of her before.

"Whatever floats your boat, honey," Lauren drawled.

A half-hour later, they were back in their own clothes and waiting in a restaurant for their lunch to arrive. Purple shopping bags with "Lauren" emblazoned in silver sat on the floor beside their chairs. Magdalena had bought her queen outfit, but Anna had balked at buying hers when she saw the $400.00 price tag.

"I don't think the Santa's Little Helper outfit is really me," she had told Lauren, "but I'll take the sandals." After all, she didn't want to offend Lauren by not buying anything. "How much are they?"

"$250.00."

"How much?" Anna couldn't hide her shock.

"Those are real ostrich feathers," Lauren said indignantly. She paused by the cash register with the sandals dangling from one hand. "Well?"

"I'll take them," Anna said with resignation. Now they'd better get some worthwhile information out of Lauren to make up for it.

Anna drank her orange juice while Lauren and Magdalena sipped their mimosas. The waiter brought them their food: spinach and mushroom omelettes for Anna and Magdalena, and a caviar and egg white omelette for Lauren.

"It's my treat. Have whatever you like," Magdalena had said when the waiter handed them their menus. Lauren had taken her at her word.

"So, you're married to one of Julia's sons," Anna said, taking a bite of omelette. At least the food was good.

"Kevin. Julia's *elder* son."

Anna smiled. "How did the two of you meet?"

Lauren scooped up some of the caviar from the top of her omelette and licked it off her spoon. "Mmm. So good." Her eyes shone with pleasure. "Rick introduced us."

"Really? I didn't know that," Magdalena said.

Lauren nodded. "We met at a fundraiser for a women's shelter. It was one of Julia's pet projects, but she couldn't make it that night, so Rick was there, representing her. They were auctioning off fashions by local designers, and I was one of the models. Rick hung around afterward to buy me a drink. I guess he'd liked what he'd seen. We went on a date or two after that. He was very charming, but I could see that he wasn't serious about me. When he mentioned that his brother had a thing for Asian women, I told him to give Kevin my number. Kevin and I were married seven months later." Lauren had finished the caviar and was cutting into the egg whites.

"Does it bother Kevin that you dated his brother first?" Anna asked.

"Hardly. There was never anything between Rick and me. The three of us get along great together."

Anna winked at Magdalena, the sign they had pre-arranged. Now was the time for Magdalena to go after Lauren with both barrels.

"I hope that Julia's will didn't do anything to interfere with your friendship. I understand from Warren that you and Kevin were upset about Kevin inheriting the fertilizer company. Didn't your husband think he would succeed Julia as CEO?

Anna had been watching Lauren closely. She saw anger flare in the exotic beauty's eyes for just a moment before she calmly ate another mouthful of egg whites.

"We were for about five minutes until we had some time to think about it," Lauren said. "Golden Farm is a privately-owned company, which means that there are no stockholders and no board of directors. Kevin will have complete control, so he gets to make whatever changes he wants. Rick won't be able to do that at Westmore. Besides, we're honoured that Julia chose Kevin to save the company that her father built. Don't get me wrong. Oliver Sumpter has done a good job of continuing the business as Kevin's grandfather envisioned it, but he hasn't made any improvements, and he's actually lost customers. Kevin is looking forward to bringing the company into the twenty-first century. He'll make Golden Farm western Canada's premier fertilizer supplier."

Lauren glanced at her wristwatch. "Is that the time?" She dabbed at her mouth with her napkin. "We took longer at the store than I thought we would. I'm afraid I have another appointment in twenty-five minutes, so I'll have to run. Thank you so much for lunch, Magdalena." She turned to Anna. "It was a pleasure meeting you. Drop by the store again sometime. I'm sure we'll be able to find an outfit that will reveal your inner woman." Her eyes were full of meaning, and Anna had to work hard not to wrinkle her nose in disgust. Lauren rose from her chair. "Ciao."

When Lauren was safely out of ear shot, Anna leaned across the table toward Magdalena. "Darn! Just when we got her talking about Kevin and the fertilizer company. Was it just me, or did her explanation sound rehearsed?"

Magdalena nodded. "Definitely rehearsed. She and Kevin may be putting the best possible spin on it, but I'm not convinced that they're as happy about inheriting Golden Farm as she says they are."

"I feel kind of sorry for Oliver Sumpter. Have you ever met him?"

"Only once. We spoke for a few minutes at the Christmas party, but Warren likes him very much. You see, Julia insisted that all three boys work at the fertilizer company during their high school summer holidays. The other two didn't take it seriously, but Warren treated it as a learning opportunity. Oliver really took a shine to him. Then, when Robert Moreland died when Warren was only sixteen, and Julia was too busy consoling her own sons to have much time for him, Oliver helped Warren through the grieving process. He and his wife, Beatrix, even took Warren on vacation with them to British Columbia that summer. Warren still respects Oliver's opinion, and uses him as a sounding board for important financial decisions."

"It's nice that Warren had someone he could go to for advice when he was a boy, what with his father gone, his mother with problems of her own, and Julia only interested in her sons. Oliver sounds like a kind man. I'm sorry that Kevin will be forcing him out of a job."

"Yes, that's unfortunate, except that Oliver was talking about wanting to spend more time with his nieces and nephews at the party. Now he can take some well-deserved time off to do just that. I'm sure that Kevin will offer him a generous retirement package, if only because it would look bad if he didn't."

Magdalena caught their server's eye and asked for the bill. "Did you find today's encounter with Lauren useful?" she asked Anna as they waited.

"Sure. We found out a few interesting things. For instance, did you notice that we were the only people in Lauren's store, and that she didn't have any staff? Not to mention that she was able to close up early on a Sunday. Business can't be very good."

"Warren told me that Kevin gave Lauren the seed money to start the business."

"And I bet he's keeping her afloat, which has to be draining their finances. What is his job with Westmore, by the way?"

"Vice President of Production Engineering."

"I bet that as the CEO, and with the income from the stock Julia owned, he was hoping to pull in a lot more money. There might have been other financial perks too. So money and power, as well as jealousy about his mother's relationship with Rick, might have been good reasons for Kevin to want Julia dead."

Magdalena nodded. "Plus, we have only Lauren's word that Kevin isn't jealous about her history with Rick. I don't know how it fits in, but there might be resentment between the brothers."

"Money and sex. They're all part of the puzzle. We'll see how they fit as our investigation continues."

Magdalena smiled at Anna. "Do we have an investigation?"

Anna hesitated, suddenly feeling vulnerable. She had promised herself to stay out of trouble. "Nothing too ambitious. We're just taking a peek at how the members of the family get along with each other."

"Of course, Anna. Whatever makes you comfortable. So, when do you think we should take our next peek?"

"The funeral is on Tuesday, isn't it?"

"Yes. Julia's remains were delivered to Fergusons Funeral Parlour yesterday. Warren told me that while we were having breakfast before the police arrived." Magdalena hesitated, and Anna guessed that she was remembering how Warren had been too tired to talk with her that night.

Hopefully there would be a message from Warren when her boss got home, asking her to call him. What was wrong with him, leaving Magdalena dangling like that?

"Do you know if there'll be any public visitations before the funeral?" Anna asked. "The family would have to attend those too."

"No, I don't believe so. Apparently Julia thought that visitations and open caskets were morbid. So there will only be the church service at 10:00 a.m. on Tuesday."

"I'll go if my boss lets me have the time off work," Anna said with a twinkle in her eye.

"I don't think the dean will object to shutting down the office for part of the day while we attend the service and the reception. Even if it weren't a slow time of year, I suspect that the president of the university will be there, setting an example. Not to mention that Julia is funding the Robert

Moreland Scholarship in perpetuity, so it would be fitting to pay our respects."

"How convenient that it fits in with our plans," Anna replied.

10

The weather was gloomy on the morning of Julia's funeral with below-freezing temperatures and snow that swirled down from a yellow-grey sky. The funeral guests stomped the snow off their boots outside the church and hurried inside to get warm. The first thing they saw was an oil painting of a younger Julia framed on its easel by vases of pink, purple, and yellow orchids. Kevin, Rick, and Warren, wearing black suits, stood at the foot of the aisles to greet the mourners, speaking with them in hushed voices.

Anna and Magdalena waited for a knot of people to move on before approaching Warren. He glanced up and spotted Magdalena before quickly switching his gaze to Anna. Anna held out her hand.

"I'm so sorry," she said. "It's hard to believe that I watched Julia dancing at her Christmas party less than two weeks ago."

Warren patted her hand before releasing it. "Thank you. She'll be missed." Anna nodded, thinking he must have said the same thing forty times already to other people that morning. She stood aside to make room for her boss. Magdalena met Warren's eyes coolly. Neither said anything for a moment.

"You're looking well," he finally said.

"And you, all things considered. I would like to convey our condolences on behalf of the Kinesiology Department. Robert and Julia were generous supporters of our students."

"Yes. I think Dad sometimes regretted going into the oil business instead of kinesiology. He loved sports and was fascinated by how the human body works."

Magdalena nodded and was about to step past him when Warren took her hand.

"Magdalena."

"Yes?"

"Warren, how're you holding up, son?" Oliver Sumpter strode forward to clasp the younger man's shoulder and give it a gentle shake. Warren turned to Oliver, and Magdalena walked away. She preceded Anna up the aisle and ducked into a pew mid-way to the front. Anna sat down beside her stony-faced boss.

When they had met at work on Monday morning, Anna hadn't asked if Magdalena had heard from Warren, thinking that her boss would tell her if she had. Now Anna was bursting to know if there had been any communication between Magdalena and Warren at all.

"Is this the first time the two of you have spoken since Saturday night?" she whispered into Magdalena's ear.

Her boss continued staring straight ahead. "Yes."

"What happened? Why hasn't he called?"

"I have no idea." She turned to Anna, her expression so frosty that Anna didn't dare risk any more questions. Neither spoke again during the service except to recite the prayers with the rest of the congregation.

The church was crowded. Anna calculated that there must be at least two hundred mourners, some of whom she recognized from Julia's Christmas party. Even with this outpouring of support, however, Anna felt bereft and lonely. Somehow it all seemed so impersonal. No one cried, sniffled, or dabbed at tears. The Anglican priest extolled Julia's virtues as a church supporter and upstanding member of the community, but none of the sons got up to pay tribute to her or tell funny stories. Warren, Rick, Kevin, and Lauren sat together in the front pew, Lauren in a black coat and hat with a veil, but somehow they seemed isolated from each other.

The three men filed out of their pew to join the other pallbearers as the organist began the recessional hymn. Together they rolled the casket down the aisle on its silent wheels. Anna watched it pass and said a silent prayer that Julia would find happiness in heaven.

The mourners emptied out of their pews and shuffled to the back of the church. The doors were open, and gusts of frigid air ruffled their hair and caught at their clothes as they waited for the coffin to leave the church. Anna stood beside Magdalena, wondering if her boss was in the mood for conversation.

"Are they going to the cemetery?" Anna asked.

"No. There won't be any ceremony at the grave side. Julia's remains will be interred in the cemetery mausoleum until the spring. There's a reception back at the funeral parlour, however, if you'd like to attend?" The two women had driven to the church in Magdalena's car and would both have to attend the reception if either one of them wanted to go.

Anna studied her boss surreptitiously. Magdalena looked pale and somehow fragile. Her encounter with Warren must have cost her more than she had expected, and now she would be subjected to seeing him again if they went to the reception.

"If you're sure? I'm game if you are," Anna said.

Magdalena nodded. Anna positioned herself at Magdalena's side and accompanied her from the church to the car.

The funeral parlour was tastefully decorated with thick carpet, stained glass windows, and muted lighting. There was even a handy coat check to protect the ladies' valuable furs. Two somber staff members greeted the guests at the entrance and directed them to the correct reception room. Someone must have hurried to bring Julia's portrait from the church because there it was again, stationed just outside the reception room door.

A buffet was set up inside with covered steam trays and bowls of salad and buns. A second table bore plates of squares, cheeses, and fruit, while the third held two large coffee urns, hot water, and an assortment of teas. As the room began to fill with mourners, white-uniformed serving staff removed the lids from the trays. Guests picked up china plates and cutlery and shuffled past the food. There was chicken parmesan, braised short ribs, and seafood paella.

"Wow," Anna said. "This is quite a spread. I've only seen sandwiches and vegetable trays at the funerals I've attended before."

Magdalena half-smiled. "Julia wouldn't be caught dead serving sandwiches to her wealthy friends and business associates."

Anna grinned as the servers heaped food on her plate. She was starving, and the hot entrées both looked and smelled delicious. She helped herself to tea and hovered beside Magdalena.

"Where do you want to sit?"

"How about over there with Oliver and Beatrix Sumpter? I think you should meet them." Magdalena nodded toward a table close to the buffet that was empty except for the couple. It appeared that Oliver didn't have many friends among the oil crowd.

"Okay." The two women made their way to the table and hesitated beside Oliver.

"May we join you?" Magdalena asked.

Oliver smiled and sprang to his feet. "Please do. How nice to see you again, Magdalena."

"You as well, Oliver. This is my friend, Anna Nolan. She's the administrative assistant for the Kinesiology Department at Chinook University."

"I'm delighted to meet you, Anna. This is my wife, Beatrix." Anna and Beatrix smiled at each other before she and Magdalena took their seats. Like her husband, Beatrix had silvery hair, but while he was tall, she was petite and had a rosy complexion and china-blue eyes. With her diminutive stature, she seemed delicate and doll-like.

"Did you know Julia personally, Anna?" Beatrix asked.

"Actually, I met her only a few days before she died. We worked together on choosing a winner for her husband's scholarship, and then she was kind enough to invite me to her Christmas party."

"That's where I know you from," Oliver said. "You seemed familiar." Anna studied him, thinking that he seemed familiar, too, and conversation faltered.

"Do you have children?" Anna asked, casting about for something to say. "Magdalena didn't mention it."

Oliver and Beatrix exchanged a look before Beatrix said, "I'm afraid not. My physical complaints would have made taking care of children difficult." The older woman glanced down, and Anna noticed for the first time that

Beatrix was sitting in a wheel chair beneath the rim of the table. "I have multiple sclerosis and asthma," she added.

"I'm so sorry. I didn't know," Anna said with a flushed face.

Beatrix smiled. "Why should you? Oliver and I came to terms with it before we married. We've had a very full, happy life since then and have loved many children as our own."

"Bea is the Calgary chairwoman for a foundation called 'Nurture the World's Children,'" Oliver added. "She's raised hundreds of thousands of dollars to help clothe, feed, and educate under-privileged African children."

"Well, not single-handedly," Beatrix said. She patted her husband's cheek. "This time of year is particularly busy for me. Every Christmas, each of our chapters sponsors a village. Ours is in Mozambique this year. I've been buying clothing and gifts to send to the children. Friday we'll be packaging everything up because the gifts will be flown out the next day. The funeral is a break for me, but I'll be back shopping again tomorrow."

"Just be careful that you don't overdo it," Oliver said. "Find somebody to help you with the shopping, if you can."

"I'd love to help," Anna said. "My son is in his second year of university, but I used to love shopping for him at Christmas when he was little."

"Oh? What program is he in?"

"Computer Science."

"Very wise," Oliver said. "He'll always be able to find a job working with computers."

"If you were serious about helping," Beatrix said, "I could always use an extra pair of hands."

"Absolutely. I'm done work at four-thirty. I could meet you afterward."

Oliver waved at someone, and Anna looked up. Warren was hesitating a few yards away with a plate of food and a cup of coffee.

"Warren, come join us," Oliver called. The surrounding tables were full, and Oliver gestured at the empty chair beside his. Beatrix smiled welcomingly, and Warren came to the table, sitting down beside the older man.

"The food is excellent," Oliver said. "Fergusons uses a good caterer."

"Yes, we left the menu up to them," Warren said.

"You're looking tired," Beatrix said. "I hope you get a chance to take a few days off soon."

"Good idea," Oliver said. "Maybe you and Magdalena can take a mini-vacation together." All eyes turned to Magdalena, who looked up from her plate at Warren before turning to Oliver.

"That would be nice, except that I have a scholars' symposium in Halifax this weekend." Her foot tapped against Anna's ankle.

"Oh, yes, I forgot to tell you, Magdalena. The symposium coordinator called to confirm your presentation time. It's two o'clock on Friday."

Her boss nodded. "So, unfortunately, Warren will have to vacation on his own." She gazed into his eyes. "Maybe you can finally take that skiing trip to Banff that you're always talking about."

"Maybe I will." Warren turned back to Oliver. "So, did you catch the hockey game the other night? How did the Flames do?" They talked about the game while Beatrix spoke to Anna about the items she still needed to buy for her charity. Magdalena excused herself to get a cup of coffee.

The room was buzzing with conversation as people finished their meals and checked out the dessert table when a high-pitched, hysterical giggle rose above the other voices.

The room quieted and heads craned, searching for the source. When the giggle wasn't repeated, conversation resumed.

"Who was that?" Anna asked Beatrix. Magdalena returned in time to hear her question.

"Rick Moreland," she said quietly. "He's at the table closest to the door." Magdalena glanced at Warren, who nodded and left the table.

"Oh, dear," Beatrix said.

"What's wrong?" Anna asked. Judging by their faces, everyone else at the table seemed to know what was going on.

Beatrix hesitated, and Oliver said, "Julia's death has hit Rick the hardest. He's always been rather high-strung. Sometimes he takes something to calm himself. Looks like he over did it today."

Anna heard another giggle and tried to glance discreetly at Rick. She saw Warren, his head bent, standing next to him. Rick slid a hand behind Warren and patted him on the rear end before bursting into laughter again. Warren grabbed Rick's arm, dragged him to his feet, and towed him from the room. Anna looked around. Everyone was watching.

"What a shame," Beatrix said.

Oliver shook his head. "At his mother's funeral, too. This is going to be difficult to live down."

As if on cue, Jack Upton stood, walked to the middle of the room, and called for everyone's attention. "Now that you've finished your meal and are enjoying a cup of coffee and some dessert, you're going to have to put up with me for a while." That got a laugh. "I'd like to welcome you on behalf of the family and thank you for joining us here today to celebrate Julia's life. She would be delighted to see such a great turnout. No one loved a party more than Julia, right?"

Everyone smiled, and someone called, "You got that right, Jack."

The crowd laughed until Jack held up his hand for silence.

"Yep, if it was Julia's time to go, it was fitting that it was at a party. I know that Julia's watching us from heaven right now, hoping that we're all having a good time. I just want to say that, even though we'll miss her, she has nothing to worry about. Her sons, Warren, Kevin, and Rick, will take good care of Westmore Resources and Golden Farm Fertilizer, as well as all the employees and stockholders who rely on them. With the boys' combined strengths, they'll bring us the success and prosperity that Julia unfailingly delivered. Now, it doesn't seem fitting that I only have coffee to toast her with, but that's the best I've got. So, ladies and gentlemen, if you will join me in a toast, here's to Julia." He raised his cup, and the guests followed suit.

"To Julia," they all said.

Anna glanced at Oliver to see his reaction to the speech. His head was bent, and there was a look of resignation on his face. Beatrix reached for his hand and squeezed it.

Warren returned to the table and reached for the jacket left hanging on the back of his chair. He slipped it on and pulled a cell phone from his pocket.

"How's Rick doing?" Oliver asked.

"He's waiting in the men's room. I'm calling him a cab."

"Good boy. Do you need any help?"

"No, everything's under control. He's calmer now."

Warren made his call as Anna stood up. She hadn't had an opportunity to use the facilities since arriving at work that morning. Warren's mention of the bathroom reminded her that her bladder was full.

"I'm just going to freshen up," she said. "Be back in a minute." She left the reception room and turned right, following the sign's arrow to the bathrooms. She attended to her needs and was just washing her hands when the door opened and Rick stumbled in.

"Well, if it isn't my beautiful dance partner from the Christmas party. How's it going, angel face?" Anna froze as he sauntered toward her, staring at his reflection in the mirror. She turned with dripping hands, and he tried to slide an arm around her waist. Anna sidled away.

"Rick, what are you doing in the ladies' room?"

He giggled. "Ladies' room. Is that where we are?" Pivoting, he ran toward the stalls. "Come out, come out, ladies. Don't be shy." He bent to look under the stall doors and almost fell over. Fortunately, there weren't any women in the cubicles to be embarrassed by him. Anna hurried forward to haul Rick upright.

"Whoops!" He laughed and placed his arms around her, pulling her into a tight embrace. "Dance with me, angel face." Dragged into a drunken two-step, Anna supported Rick so that he wouldn't lose his balance and knock them both down. He backed her up against the sinks.

"You're so light on your feet, I could dance with you all day," he said. Rick leaned forward to kiss her, and Anna struggled to stay upright as his weight sagged against her.

"Rick, are you all right? What are you doing?"

Rick looked over his shoulder, and Anna peered past him to see a handsome young man with a goatee and an ear stud staring at them with a horrified expression.

"Toby! You're not supposed to be in here," Rick said. "It's the ladies' room." He laughed hysterically. "Come and dance with us. Angel face's an excellent dancer. Angel face, this is my boyfriend, Tobias Rapp. Silly name, isn't it?" He giggled again as the other man dragged him off Anna.

"Shut up, Rick," Tobias said. "You're stoned." He looked at Anna. "I'm not really his boyfriend."

"What a terrible thing to say," Rick said. "Don't you love me anymore?" He pouted. "Kiss me with those ruby lips of yours." He leaned toward Tobias, who ducked out of his way.

"Don't be an asshole," Tobias said. Rick tried to put his arms around him, and they struggled.

"Toby's a lawyer. Mother would have approved, wouldn't she, Toby? Lawyers are a good catch. If she had been willing to share, that is. Toby was mother's lawyer."

Tobias looked over his shoulder at Anna while wrestling Rick to the door. "Sorry to disturb you, ma'am. Rick's feeling a bit under the weather with the funeral today. I hope you understand."

"Certainly, certainly."

Tobias smiled and struggled to push a protesting Rick through the door. "Come on, Rick. Warren's looking for you. The cab's here."

"Bye, angel face," Rick shouted. The door closed behind them, and Anna grabbed at the counter. Oh my goodness! Not only was Rick wasted at his own mother's funeral, but he seemed to be having an affair with Julia's lawyer. She stared at her reflection in the mirror. Did the rest of the family know about Rick and Tobias?

The door opened and Magdalena walked into the room. "There you are. I was wondering what happened to you. Rick's causing quite a scene in the lobby."

Anna nodded. "You should have seen the scene he was causing in here. Was Tobias Rapp with him?"

"Who?"

"Tall, good-looking guy with dark hair, goatee, and an ear stud."

"I didn't see anyone matching that description. Warren's trying to drag Rick outside into a cab. Who's Tobias?"

"Julia's lawyer and Rick's lover, if you can believe Rick. Although Tobias denied it."

"Really?" Magdalena leaned against the counter to study Anna. "That's an interesting development. Rick's such a ladies' man. Perhaps his sexual inclination swings both ways."

"Never mind that. If Rick is Tobias's lover, he might have heard the details of Julia's will before she died."

"Which Warren said Julia changed only three weeks before her death. And which gave Rick forty-five percent of the Westmore stocks. That's a very lucrative motive for murder, Anna. Maybe Rick didn't love Julia as much as everyone thought he did."

"Or maybe he loves money more."

"From what Julia said in her letter, she expected that Rick would be Westmore's CEO and that Kevin would be president of Golden Farm by the time she died. Was that because she was ready to retire and thought that Oliver was ready to step down? Was she going to announce that at her press conference?"

"Maybe. Do you think she discussed retirement with Oliver?" Anna asked.

"I don't know, but maybe you could find out. The reason I came looking for you is because the Sumpters are ready to leave, and Beatrix wants to set a time and place for your shopping trip."

Anna picked up her purse from the counter and slung it over her shoulder. "Okay, I'll go arrange that with her. It will give me an opportunity to pick her brains about Oliver and Golden Farm. If Oliver was planning to retire, she'd know."

Magdalena nodded. "I can see why you got caught up in the other investigations, Anna. This sleuthing is quite stimulating."

Anna took hold of Magdalena's shoulder and turned her toward the door. "It's a nasty habit. Take it from me — don't get too involved with this mess. Anything I learn after talking to Beatrix is going straight to Detective Soo. Then we can start minding our own business again."

Her boss nodded, but as Anna followed her from the ladies' room, she worried that it was too late and Magdalena was already hooked. She'd better keep an eye on her.

11

Latona Taylor picked up her cell and punched in some numbers. It was early evening on the day of Julia's funeral, and she had just arrived home. She had managed to speak with Jack Upton before the funeral service began and had the distinct feeling that she was going to be out of a job as soon as she had finished tidying up Julia's affairs. It was imperative that she line up something else right away.

A voice answered on the other end.

"Hi. It's Latona Taylor. I think I've found Julia's thumb drive, the one you asked me to look for before the police went through her office."

"Where was it? I thought you couldn't find it."

"That's the funny part. I was going through my desk after the funeral and found it in an old box with some keys. The only way it could have got in there is if Julia placed it there herself."

"Did you look at what was on the thumb drive?"

"Of course. I didn't know that it was what you were looking for until I opened the file. It's a list of customers, right?"

There was a pause, and the voice said, "Well, what counts is that you found it. Why don't I drop by to pick it up? Are you still at work?"

"No, I'm at home now." She provided the address for her apartment.

"I'll be there in three-quarters of an hour. I'll bring some coffee."

"Fine. Listen, about the job we were discussing earlier. I've been thinking about it, and I feel that the salary should be higher. It has more responsibility than my position with Julia had."

"Why don't we discuss salary when I get there? See you within the hour."

"All right. Goodbye."

Latona ended the call. She didn't want to play hardball with her new employer, but she had to look out for herself. Her past jobs had all been stepping-stones to something better, and she wasn't going to make a misstep now. She was sure she could convince her future employer to see things her way.

Latona smiled as she leaned against the back of her chair. Why had she been so nervous about making the call? Everything was going to work out fine.

Anna was waiting on a bench outside The Great Lakes Department Store at the Trillium Mall the day after the funeral. Weary mothers pushing fretful children in strollers, gangs of students with nowhere better to go, and office workers dashing in to do their shopping on the way home to dinner circled the stores while "White Christmas" played in the background.

There was Beatrix Sumpter now, motoring through the mall in her wheel chair with a service dog walking beside her. The dog was a German shepherd, and he was wearing a harness and saddle bags. They stopped beside Anna.

"Hi, Beatrix. Who's the charmer?"

"His name is Max. Oliver got him for me a year ago when I started losing strength in my hands. He does my carrying when I'm shopping." Max's ears quivered when he heard his name.

"May I pat him?"

"Of course. Relax, Max."

Anna reached out to pat the dog, who licked her chin. Anna laughed. "He's very handsome. I've got a dog, too, a shepherd/labrador mix. Her name is Wendy."

"I hope she's not waiting for you at home right now."

"No, she's fine. I asked my neighbour to let her out and feed her."

Beatrix smiled. "That's good. I'd feel guilty if I were keeping your from her." She indicated the department store. "Shall we get started?"

"Okay. What are we looking for?" Anna fell in step beside Beatrix and Max as the older woman wheeled past the cosmetic counters. Beatrix pulled over next to women's fashions and drew a list from her purse.

"Let's see. We're looking for toys for a three-year-old girl, a six-year-old boy, two ten-year-old boys, and a twelve-year-old girl. I'm glad you're with me, Anna. I'd like to get soccer balls for the boys this year, but they're too difficult to manage when it's just Max and me. The elevator is this way. The toy department and sports equipment are on the second floor."

"That simplifies things. Then all we have to worry about is finding something for the girls."

"Well, and a little something extra for the boys. Let's see what they've got."

After picking up the soccer balls, Beatrix, Anna, and Max passed up and down the toy department aisles, looking at dolls, miniature cars and trucks, board games, books, and craft kits. They chose a doll, a colouring book, and crayons for the youngest girl, and books for the boys, but they didn't see anything for the oldest girl.

"These things are really too juvenile for a twelve-year-old girl, don't you think?" Anna asked.

"You're right. In her society, she's practically an adult."

"In our society, too," Anna said. "How about something pretty? Maybe some things for her hair and a necklace."

"That's a good idea, as long as the necklace isn't too expensive. We'll find those items on the first floor. I'll just pay for these things first." They made their way to the customer service counter, where Beatrix drew the charity's credit card from her wallet. When the transaction was complete, Anna carried the bags containing the soccer balls and the doll while Max carried the books and crayons in his saddle bags. They rode the elevator back down to the first floor, where they found some pretty hair clips before heading to the jewellery department.

"I don't know," Beatrix said as they searched through the racks. "These necklaces seem too mature for a young girl." She pointed at a display on the counter. "What about some earrings?"

"Sure. Let's have a look."

They were met at the counter by a middle-aged sales clerk who looked as if her shoes were pinching by the expression on her face. "Can I help you?" she asked in a dreary voice.

"We're looking for some earrings for a twelve-year-old girl. Maybe a nice pearl stud? Like these," Beatrix said, pointing at the revolving earrings tower on the counter.

The sales clerk took the key hanging by a plastic coil around her wrist to unlock the tower. She removed a couple of cards with pearl studs on gold posts and laid them on the counter in front of Beatrix. Anna bent to look.

"These are pretty," Beatrix said, pointing at the smaller pearls. "How much are they?"

The sales clerk checked the price on the back. "$319.99."

"Hmm. Not quite what we're looking for," Beatrix said. "I suppose the other earrings are even more expensive?"

The sale clerk nodded with an impatient expression. "The pearls are larger."

Beatrix pointed at a display of plain gold chains inside the counter. "Could we have a look at these, please?"

The clerk locked away the earrings before unfastening the case's sliding glass door and taking out the card with the gold chains. "These are all 14K gold. What size were you looking for?"

Beatrix looked at Anna. "Sixteen inch?" Anna nodded.

The clerk removed one of the chains and set it on the counter. "The rose gold rope chain is lovely, and it's on sale for $399.99."

Beatrix held it in her hand, the chain laced between her fingers. "It is lovely, but it's a bit more than I was hoping to spend. Do you have something a little less expensive?"

The clerk removed a finer chain. "This snake chain is also on sale. It's $299.99."

Anna had been studying the necklaces inside the case. "What about the little gold heart?"

The saleswoman turned to see the necklace that Anna had selected. She drew out a pendant with a filigree heart and held it up for them to admire. Inserting her thumb nail into a groove on the heart, she opened it.

"You see, you can put a picture inside. It is pretty, isn't it?" She snapped the heart shut and checked the price tag. "It's $149.99." She held it out to Beatrix, who studied it on the palm of her hand.

"It's perfect for a twelve-year-old, don't you think?" Beatrix asked. Anna smiled and nodded. "I wonder. We're buying holiday gifts for a Calgary charity I chair. The

Nurture the World's Children Foundation? Have you heard of us?" Beatrix removed a card from her wallet and gave it to the sales clerk.

The woman glanced at the card and nodded.

"I wonder if you could do any better on the price? It would be such a lovely gift for one of our girls."

"I don't know. I'll have to check with my supervisor."

"If you wouldn't mind?"

The saleswoman locked the chains inside the case, picked up Beatrix's business card, and walked to the next counter. Anna saw her consulting with another woman, who glanced their way.

"You know, Beatrix, I saw a pretty necklace with amethyst-coloured beads on the display rack over there," Anna said. "It's only $19.99. Maybe that would be more suitable than the locket?"

Beatrix tilted her head back to look up at Anna. "Do you think the gold heart is unsuitable?"

"I don't know what your gift budget is, but I'm a little worried that the gold heart might make some of the other children jealous. Someone might try to take it away from your twelve-year-old."

Beatrix sighed. "You're probably right. I guess I got carried away. I was just picturing our girl's face on Christmas morning when she saw the necklace. But I wouldn't want to cause any trouble for her. Would you mind bringing the beaded necklace over here so that I could have a look at it?"

When the saleswoman returned, Beatrix had the beaded necklace on the counter. "I'm sorry to have troubled you, but we've decided to purchase this instead. It would be more appropriate for our charity, we think."

"As you wish," the woman said with a stony expression. Beatrix handed her the foundation's credit card, and the transaction was completed. Taking the plastic bag from the clerk, Beatrix turned to Max, who had been patiently lying on the floor beside her wheelchair. He stood, and she secured the bag in one of his pouches. He walked beside Beatrix as she and Anna left the department store for the mall.

"Anna, you have been such a big help tonight," Beatrix said. "Would you like to stop by the house for dinner before you go home? Oliver should be there by now. I know he'd love to see you again."

"I wouldn't want to put you to any trouble," Anna said. Secretly she was relieved. She hadn't had an opportunity to bring up Oliver's retirement yet and had been hoping that Beatrix would agree to getting some dinner in the food court so that they could discuss it.

"It's no trouble at all. I put some stew in the crock pot this morning. All we have to do is dish it up."

"That would be lovely. Thank you."

"I'm glad," Beatrix said, taking her cell from her purse. "I'll just let Oliver know that we're coming now."

The Sumpters lived in Signal Hill with a fabulous view of the city. Anna followed Beatrix's specially-adapted Chrysler van to the house and parked on the street while her hostess pulled into the garage. Climbing out and leaning against her Honda, Anna took a moment to enjoy the Santa, sleigh, and reindeer grouped on the Sumpters' snowy front lawn. Jewel-toned lights were tacked along the bungalow's roof and over the porch, giving a festive glow to the scene.

The front door opened, and Oliver appeared. He waved at Anna.

"Anna! Welcome. Come on in." She hurried up the shovelled walk and bounded onto the porch.

"Hi, Oliver."

"Thanks for helping Beatrix with her shopping today. She always enjoys having someone go with her. It's hard to decide what to buy for all those kids on her own." He rested an arm on Anna's shoulder and led her inside, where he hung up her coat while Anna pulled off her boots.

"It was my pleasure. I haven't shopped for children in a long time."

Oliver closed the closet door and smiled at her. "Well, once your son graduates from university and finds a job, he can get busy on making you some grandchildren."

"Just as soon as he finds the right girl."

"Of course. Having the right person sharing your life makes all the difference in the world. I don't know what I would have done without Bea. I'd probably still be planting wheat on my Dad's farm. Come on through to the dining room. I'm just giving Max his supper while Bea gets ready."

"Can I help with anything?"

"No, it's all under control. You just have a seat and take it easy."

He disappeared down the hall while Anna gazed around the formal dining room. Her house only had an eat-in kitchen, so she appreciated the luxury of having a separate dining area. The square table was draped with a white cloth with an ivy-and-berry patterned runner on top. Two white tapers mounted in silver candlesticks glowed in the subdued light from a crystal chandelier. The table was set for three with floral plates, cutlery, glassware, and red cloth napkins.

Oliver returned with an opened bottle of red wine and a pitcher of ice water. "Would you like some wine with your meal?"

"Just a wee bit, please."

Oliver poured her a half-glass and filled the water glasses. "We'll just be another minute."

"Don't hurry on my account," Anna said to his retreating back.

Beatrix zipped into the room in her wheel chair with a basket of rolls and a butter dish in her lap. "Here we are," she said, driving around the table to Anna's side. She proffered the basket. "Roll?"

"Thank you." Anna chose a cheese bun from the collection. "I love these."

"Butter?"

"Why not?"

Beatrix smiled and drove to the place setting without a chair across the table. "Oliver's bringing the stew."

"And here I come," he announced. He entered the room carrying three steaming bowls on a wooden tray. He set a bowl down in front of Anna, and she lowered her head to sniff. Chunks of carrot, potato, celery, and beef floated in the herb-scented gravy.

"Smells wonderful," Anna said.

Oliver served his wife before taking a seat. "Shall we say grace?" he asked.

"Certainly," Anna said, bowing her head. They prayed over the food and began to eat.

"Bea said she was very pleased with today's haul," Oliver said, buttering his roll.

"We did really well, honey. We'll show you what we got after dinner," Beatrix said. "I just set the bags on the kitchen floor for now."

Oliver nodded and tried a forkful of stew. "You've outdone yourself, Bea. This is really good."

"Thanks. It's good to cook for an appreciative audience." Turning to Anna, she asked, "Do you have any plans for Christmas?"

Anna nodded, dipping a chunk of her bun into the gravy. Cheese, butter, and gravy. Heaven. "My boyfriend will be visiting. He's a sergeant with the RCMP, part of a special unit that investigates homicides in western Canada. I haven't seen him since Thanksgiving, so I'm really looking forward to his visit. And my son will be with us on Christmas day, of course."

"How lovely for you," Beatrix said. "Does your boyfriend find his job very difficult?"

"How so?" Anna asked.

"Well, it must be sad to be surrounded by death all the time."

"I should think he finds great satisfaction in bringing criminals to justice," her husband said.

"He finds the work fascinating," Anna said. "Although he's had to develop a thick skin and tries not to get emotionally involved with his cases."

"I should think so," Beatrix said.

"How do you plan to spend the holidays?" Anna asked as she chewed. The stew was really hitting the spot.

"We'll be visiting my sister and her family in Saskatchewan," Beatrix replied. "We don't have any family here in Calgary, although Oliver has family in southern Alberta just north of Lethbridge. But it's my turn this year." She smiled at her husband.

"Normally we take a month's vacation in February to go to the tropics," Oliver added. "The sunshine does Bea good and lifts both our spirits. But we'll have to hold off this year. Kevin starts with Golden Farm after the holidays, and I'll be showing him the operation for four months before he takes over. That was the agreement we reached after the reading of Julia's will."

"Then what will you do?" Anna asked. She was thrilled that the conversation had flowed naturally to Oliver's job with Golden Farm.

"Then I'll be retiring. We'll be free as birds, won't we, honey?"

"That's right," Beatrix said with a strained smile.

"You must be looking forward to it," Anna said.

"Might as well. No point in getting upset," Oliver replied.

There was an uncomfortable pause in the conversation. "I'm sorry. I take it retirement wasn't your idea," Anna added.

Oliver snorted. "Heck, no. I'm only sixty-two. I was planning on working another three years so that we could get the retirement plan with the full medical benefits. With Bea's condition, we were counting on it."

"If you don't mind my asking, did Julia discuss early retirement with you before she died?"

Oliver shook his head. "That's the unfathomable part of all this. I don't know what was going on in her mind. We've always had such a good working relationship. This just came out of left field."

"Do you have any guesses?" Anna didn't want the couple to think that she was prying, but she'd never have another opportunity like this to get the information.

"If you ask me, it was because of the trouble Julia was having with Kevin," Oliver said.

"Oh, Oliver," Beatrix said with a frown.

"Don't 'Oh Oliver' me," he replied tartly, his face flushing. Beatrix put down her fork. "You know as well as I that Kevin got in over his head, buying that expensive house and car for his spoiled wife and trying to stop her business from going down the drain. He was never more than a pencil-pusher at Westmore. There was no way that Julia could have made him the CEO. He doesn't have half the brains or the gumption Warren has. If Julia hadn't had the fertilizer business, I don't know what would have happened to Kevin. Not that Rick's any better with his irresponsible lifestyle."

He wiped some spittle from his mouth and threw the napkin on the table. "I've been with Golden Farm for twenty-six years now and eighteen of them as president, since Robert's death. And now I'm out on my behind."

Beatrix's face was strained as she peered down the table at her husband. "Hopefully Julia's sons will ensure that you get a good retirement package." She glanced at Anna. "Please excuse me." Reversing her wheel chair, she sped away from the table.

"Bea," Oliver called after her, but she continued her retreat down the hall. He turned to Anna with a chagrined expression. "Now I've put my foot in it. I'm sorry to spout off like that. It's been a stressful situation for Bea and me, this forced retirement. I'm afraid I'm still bitter."

"I'm sorry. It was my fault for continuing the discussion."

"Not at all. Please excuse me. I need to apologize to my wife."

As Oliver left the dining room, Anna felt like a rat. Poor Beatrix and Oliver. They were already worried about their future, and now her questions had caused an outburst. She looked down at her bowl of half-eaten stew and pushed it away. She wished there were something she could do for the couple. Maybe if Magdalena worked out her relationship issues with Warren, she could use her influence to get Oliver a really good severance package. But why wasn't Warren looking out for Oliver, if he thought so highly of him? Were Rick and Kevin fighting Warren because they had some sort of grievance against Oliver?

A few minutes later, Bea returned looking calmer. "I'm sorry we had that little spat in front of you, Anna. Even after thirty-eight years of marriage, we still have our disagreements."

"Not at all. What couple doesn't?"

"Oliver's just putting on some coffee, and then we'll have dessert."

Anna jumped to her feet. "Why don't I clear the table?"

"Don't be silly. You're our guest."

"But I want to. You sit and relax while I take these few dishes out."

"It's very kind of you."

"It's nothing."

Anna gathered the dirty dishes onto the tray and took them to the kitchen. It had a wide-open design with lowered counters and cupboards for someone in a wheel chair. Max was chewing a rawhide bone on a dog cushion next to the sliding door while Oliver poured water into a coffee maker. He glanced over his shoulder at her as Anna set the tray down next to the sink.

"Thanks, Anna. That's kind of you."

"It's my pleasure." She saw the shopping bags and Max's saddle bags next to the dog. "How about if I take the Christmas presents to the dining room so that Beatrix can show you what we bought?"

"Good idea." Oliver removed a lemon pie from the refrigerator. "That ought to cheer Bea up."

Anna knelt down on the floor and patted Max's head before opening up the saddle bags. She took out the sacks with the books and crayons, and reached into the other pouch for the hair clips and necklace. There was something lying loose in the bottom, and Anna reached back inside for it. The rose gold rope chain she and Beatrix had admired at the jewellery counter dangled from her fingers.

"Is this slice too big for you?" Oliver asked, standing behind her with a plate. When Anna didn't answer, he peered over her shoulder to see what she was staring at. Anna looked up into his face.

"I don't understand. We were looking at this at the Great Lakes jewellery counter. How did it get into Max's saddle bag?"

Suddenly, Oliver's face looked weary, and his shoulders drooped. He held out his hand for the necklace, and Anna rose to her feet to give it to him. Sighing, he shoved it into his pocket.

"Bea has a problem, Anna. For years now. She gets these blue spells when her physical challenges become too much for her. Sometimes the bouts go on for days, and it's all I can do to get her out of bed to eat her meals. We've tried her on different kinds of medication, but we've never found one that really works without having side effects she can't live with. Sometimes, when life starts to be too much for her, she takes things. Pretty things that make her feel better. Life has been very difficult since we found out about my forced retirement. I should have expected this."

He turned and placed Anna's plate on the counter beside the other slices. Anna took a step closer to him. "But what if she gets caught?"

Oliver gazed at her face. "She has been caught, but the store owners have been sympathetic up until now. I explain about her problem and reimburse them for their loss, and they let her go. I'll be calling the department store manager about the chain after you leave." Suddenly, he threw up his hands. "She's been to counselling. I don't know what else to do."

Anna laid her hand on his shoulder. "I'm sorry. I wish there was something I could do to help."

Oliver looked at her with pleading eyes. "There is something. Please don't tell anyone about this. Bea would be so embarrassed if it got out."

"Of course not. I'm just sorry you have to bear all this trouble on your own."

Oliver picked up two plates of pie and smiled. "She's my girl. I'd never replace her." Anna returned his smile. "Now, if you wouldn't mind taking the other plate, let's have dessert with Bea."

12

Thursday morning at eleven, Detective Sandra Soo was doing something that she hated and that always made her stomach clench — staring down at a dead body. Latona Taylor was sprawled on her bathroom floor. The detective was wearing a white protective suit with booties over her shoes so as not to contaminate the crime scene. The forensics team had already taken pictures and searched the bathroom for evidence and were off scouring the rest of the apartment. One of the staff from the Medical Examiner's Office was on the floor beside the body, preparing to remove it. Bob Schute, a short man with a runner's body and a very expressive face, was scowling.

"What's wrong, Bob?" Soo asked.

"This is the body of a well-nourished, seemingly healthy young woman without any traces of trauma. I hate to see her dead."

"How long would you estimate that she's been gone?"

"My guess would be thirty-six to forty-eight hours. The medical examiner will be able to tell you better when he does the autopsy tomorrow."

Soo nodded. "That fits. The housekeeper at the place Latona worked said that she didn't show up yesterday. She got worried because Latona always phoned in if she wasn't coming. When she didn't show up again today, the housekeeper called Latona's super. He found the body and called 911."

Bob rose to his feet. "Well, I'll be interested to find out what killed her."

"I'll bet you a loonie that it was water hemlock poisoning."

"What?" Bob peered back at the body. "Why would you say that?"

"Because she was Julia Moreland's personal assistant." Soo turned and left the bathroom as Bob whistled. One of the forensics team members approached the detective.

"We found something interesting. A couple of paper cups from a Weber's coffee shop were lying on top of the kitchen garbage. We dusted them for prints and got a nice set on one of them. Funny thing, though. The other cup was clean."

"Send both cups to Ottawa for analysis. Did you find her cell, by the way?"

"No, and there's no land line, either. Weird, eh?"

Soo gritted her teeth. She could imagine Latona's murderer poisoning her and hanging around until the girl was helpless before stealing her phone and leaving her writhing on the floor. Bastard! She couldn't wait to catch the perpetrator on this one.

"I'm leaving," she said. "You guys finish here and secure the apartment. I'm going to Westmore to break the bad news."

Warren was already having a bad day. Jack Upton had turned up without an appointment fifteen minutes earlier, insisting on seeing him. Warren was leaning forward in his office chair while Jack paced in front of the leather sofa.

"It's standard practice, Warren. Whenever there's a change of personnel in an executive position, his department is audited to make sure everything's squeaky clean for the new guy. It was part of Julia's transparency program."

"I know, Jack, but come on. Production Engineering. We're talking about Kevin here."

"I can't help it. The numbers don't add up. What's been pumped out of the ground doesn't match with what's been sold to the distributor. Plus, there are discrepancies between infrastructure spending and the inventory lists. Someone's been skimming. The auditors are trying to track how much and where the money went. It looks bad for Kevin."

Warren rubbed his eyes with one hand. "Can you give me a ball park figure on how much money we're talking about here?"

"Six hundred thousand to a million."

Warren groaned and leaned back in his chair. "How long has it been going on?"

"Over a year."

"Shit. What are we going to do?"

Jack waved his hands. "What kind of a question is that to ask me? I'm the goddamned chairman of the board of directors. I have to report it to the board."

"Can you give us any leeway? Why not wait to tell them until after the auditors track the money? If it wasn't Kevin, it'll make a huge difference. You'll destroy him with this."

"We've got the shareholders' meeting at the beginning of February. We have to have this cleaned up and somebody arrested before we talk to them or stock values will plummet. I can't wait, Warren. I'm sorry."

Warren folded his hands on his desk. "All right, go ahead and tell the board. But make them sit on it until the end of December. You said the auditors should be done by next week. Kevin is leaving Westmore to start with Golden Farm in the New Year. If we have to file charges against him, it would be better to file them against the president of Golden Farm than against Westmore's VP of Production Engineering. It will look better in the papers."

Jack stopped pacing to stare at Warren. "Good point. You've got your father's head on your shoulders, all right. Okay, we'll keep it under wraps until the end of the month."

"Good." Warren stood up and extended his hand. "Thanks for coming to me about this first, Jack."

The older man shook his hand. "Who else was I going to see? That pissant new CEO of ours? Is he even here today?"

"Yeah, but Rick's been keeping a low profile since the funeral."

"Do your best to keep him under control, will you? We don't need a loose cannon like him causing trouble when we've got a potential disaster on our hands. His mother used to keep him on a short leash. Hell, why did Julia have to get herself killed and cause all this trouble?"

Warren's telephone rang. He grabbed the receiver in one ring and growled, "Helen, I told you to hold my calls."

"I'm sorry, but Detective Soo is here. When I told her that you were in an urgent meeting with the chairman of the board, she insisted on seeing you both right away."

Warren stiffened and put his hand over the mouthpiece. "Detective Soo is outside. She wants to talk to both of us."

"Hell," the older man muttered. "What now?"

Warren uncovered the mouthpiece. "Send her in, Helen."

Jack sat down in one of the chairs in front of Warren's desk just as there was a knock and Helen ushered the detective in, closing the door behind them. Soo headed straight for Warren, who rose behind his desk to greet her.

"Thanks for seeing me," the detective said. She glanced down at Jack. "Mr. Upton."

Jack nodded.

"What can I do for you, Detective?" Warren asked. "I thought I made it clear at the Westwinds building last Saturday that I would only answer your questions in future in the presence of my lawyer."

Soo smiled. "I'm not here to ask questions today, Mr. Moreland. I'm here to provide you with information."

"About what?" Warren asked, his voice wary.

"Latona Taylor is dead."

Warren paled and sank slowly into his chair.

Jack slapped the arm of his chair, his face reddening. "Goddammit," he muttered.

"Obviously, her death is connected with Julia Moreland's murder," Soo said, appearing to enjoy their discomfort. "Now, I find myself wondering who might have gained by Ms. Taylor's death?"

Warren shook his head. "I don't know. How did she die?"

"Her super found her in her apartment. There was no obvious cause of death, but my guess is that our poisoner has struck again. We'll be sending a sample for toxicology testing as soon as possible." She glanced from one shocked face to the other. "Latona told me when we arrived with the warrant to search Mrs. Moreland's office that you two beat us to it. Do you want to tell me what you found?"

"Nothing," Warren said.

She looked at Jack, who nodded.

"You didn't remove anything?"

"No," the chairman said. "We didn't find anything that would explain why Julia was murdered. All the company reports and information in her office were the same stuff we all had."

Soo rose to her feet. "I hope that's true, gentlemen, because if you're holding out on me, the poisoner might be searching for that special something too. Maybe he — or she — found what he was looking for in Latona Taylor's apartment. Maybe he didn't. But I'd hate to see anything happen to either one of you because the poisoner thought you held incriminating evidence."

Jack and Warren exchanged a startled glance.

"Give me a call if you want to talk. You've got my card." The two men were silent as the detective stalked out of the room.

13

Anna was in a hurry to see Magdalena when she arrived at her office on Thursday morning, but her boss wasn't there. Checking their shared electronic calendar, Anna saw that Magdalena was in a chairs' meeting until ten. Damn it. She wanted to share what she had discovered about Beatrix and Oliver Sumpter.

She tried to keep herself occupied with some end-of-term clean-up duties, boxing year-old exams and teachers' evaluations for shredding to make room for the current term's records. No one disturbed her for a change. Now that exams were over, the students and part-time faculty had departed for the holidays, while the full-time faculty were shut up in their offices, reporting grades online and preparing for the start of the winter term so that they could go away for the holidays with a clear conscience.

Anna heard the mail cart creaking up the hall and stepped out of the storage room where she was purging the old records. Alice appeared with a Santa hat on her head.

"Ho, ho, ho," she said. "I'm delivering the new 2013 calendars from Document Services. How many copies do you want?"

"I'll take five, in case some of the faculty want one," Anna said. "Step into my office. A couple of the professors gave me candy for Christmas, and I'm trying to get rid of it before I eat it all."

"Yippee!" Alice said, hovering behind Anna as she unlocked her office door. Alice plunked the Kinesiology Department mail in the in-tray and the poster-size calendars onto Anna's desk. "What've you got?"

Anna pointed to the small table next to her desk where a miniature Christmas tree stood, decorated with hand-me-downs from her home collection. The candy was under the tree.

"Chocolate liqueurs, which I don't like, and two chocolate oranges, which I love."

"I'll have a chocolate liqueur." Alice chose a blue, foil-wrapped candy shaped like a bell. She unwrapped it and popped it into her mouth. "How about another one for my coffee break?"

"Be my guest."

Alice rubbed her hands together and picked a second liqueur. She hopped onto the corner of Anna's desk while Anna smacked one of the chocolate oranges on the table, breaking it into sections. Unwrapping the foil, she offered the chocolate orange to Alice, who took two slices. Anna took a slice for herself and bit into it. The orangey milk chocolate melted on her tongue, somehow making life seem less stressful. Anna circled the desk and sat in her chair.

"You're just here for another week, right?" Alice asked.

Anna nodded. "Charlie's coming next Friday on the twenty-first, so that's my last day. I'm taking off Christmas Eve morning."

"Yeah, this place is going to be a graveyard on Christmas Eve, what with the university closing at noon. Everyone other than essential staff takes the morning off."

"I'm not coming back until classes resume on January 7th. Charlie will be staying with me for the full two weeks. I can hardly wait."

Alice smiled. "You two love birds. That's great, Anna. I'm glad for you."

"What are you and Mike and the kids doing for Christmas?"

Alice shrugged. "Same as always. Since Mike's French Canadian, I make a couple of tourtières for Christmas Eve. My daughter is coming from Edmonton with her husband and the kids in time for dinner. Then we all go to Midnight Mass, and they stay overnight. Christmas morning, my son and his family arrive. We have brunch and open presents, and then my mom and dad come, and we open more presents. I make a huge turkey and do the vegetables and the salads for dinner, but my daughter and daughter-in-law are in charge of desserts. Mom and Dad go home, but everyone else stays over Christmas night. The grandkids love camping out on air mattresses in the basement. They never get any sleep."

Anna smiled. "Sounds like fun. I missed all that, being an only child. I guess my son missed out too."

"Well, it's a lot of work, but Mike and I wouldn't have it any other way." Alice hopped down from the desk. "Better be getting back to work. See you, Anna. Thanks for the chocolates."

"You're welcome. See you later."

Magdalena returned from her meeting at 10:10 and stopped by Anna's office to consult with her.

"Magdalena. There you are. I've been waiting for you," Anna said in an excited voice.

"Why? Has something happened?"

"I've got something to tell you. Come in and shut the door."

Magdalena did as she was told, and Anna told her about her shopping expedition with Beatrix Sumpter, Oliver's outburst during dinner, and the discovery of the stolen necklace. Magdalena looked grim as Anna finished her recitation.

"I promised Oliver not to tell anyone about Beatrix's shoplifting, but I'm making you an exception," Anna added. "I thought it was important for us to share everything that might have anything to do with Julia's death. But I feel awful about the Sumpters. Can't Warren help them?"

"I don't know. I still haven't spoken to him, other than at the funeral."

Anna couldn't stand the suspense any longer. "What happened to the two of you? Did you have a fight?"

Magdalena shook her head. "No. He just stopped communicating with me."

"Weird. Has he ever done that before?"

"No. Between his behaviour, Rick's conduct at his mother's funeral, and my suspicion that Kevin and Lauren are responsible for Julia's death, perhaps it's best that I have nothing more to do with him."

Anna's eyes grew large. "I thought you loved him. Can you cut him off just like that?"

Magdalena's face was impassive as she returned Anna's gaze. "If I must. I have to do what's best for me."

They stared at each other for several seconds.

"So, I assume our investigation into Julia's death is over," Magdalena said, breaking the silence.

"Not quite."

Magdalena's eyebrows rose. "You didn't want to get involved in the first place. What do you have in mind?"

"I felt so badly for the Sumpters after I got back from their place last night, I wondered if there wasn't something we could do for them. It occurred to me that if one of the Moreland sons was arrested for Julia's murder, it could be the answer to their prayers. The son who didn't do it would have to be Westmore's CEO, and Oliver could go on being president of the fertilizer company." Anna paused to see if Magdalena followed her reasoning.

"Continue."

"I know you suspect Kevin of being the murderer, but I've been thinking about Rick and the possibility that he knew about Julia's will ahead of time. I think we should check that out."

"What do you propose?"

"I think we should visit Tobias Rapp and see what we can wheedle out of him."

"Hmm. It might work. Do you have a phone number for him?"

"For his law office."

"That will do. Pass me the phone." Moments later, the phone was ringing.

"Koebler and Rapp Legal Solutions. Melanie speaking." Magdalena put the call on speaker phone so that Anna could hear.

"Hello, Melanie. This is Dr. Magdalena Lewis. I'd like to make an appointment to see Mr. Rapp, please."

"Certainly. For what purpose?"

"I'd like some legal advice on drawing up my will."

"Absolutely. I'm sure Mr. Rapp can help you with that. When did you have in mind?"

Magdalena glanced at Anna. "The sooner the better. I was hoping for an appointment today." They heard the sound of computer keys clicking.

"I'm sorry, I'm afraid that I can't fit you in until Monday. Would 10:00 a.m. suit?"

"I'm afraid not. I'll be leaving on holidays tomorrow. I was so hoping to see Mr. Rapp before I go. My father, Jonathan Lewis — that's Jonathan Lewis of Lewis Investments of Toronto — maybe you've heard of him? — has a friend here in Calgary who recommended Mr. Rapp very highly. However, if he is unable to see me today, I suppose I could ask my father's friend for another recommendation."

"Jonathan Lewis, did you say?"

"Yes, that's right."

"Please hold, Dr. Lewis. Let me speak with Mr. Rapp about his calendar."

Generic jazz music played softly out of the speaker. Magdalena winked at Anna, who crossed her fingers.

Melanie was back on the line a minute later. "Mr. Rapp was able to switch some appointments to accommodate you. He can see you 12:30 today, if that will work?"

"That will work beautifully. Please pass my gratitude along to Mr. Rapp. I'll see you then."

"You're welcome, Dr. Lewis. Goodbye."

"We're in," Magdalena said, passing the phone back to Anna.

Koebler and Rapp Legal Solutions was located on the thirty-first floor of a high-rise with a prime real estate address in downtown Calgary. At 12:25, Magdalena and Anna were standing in front of the receptionist's desk, waiting for the young woman to finish a call. She hung up the phone and glanced at them.

"Good afternoon. I'm Dr. Lewis. This is my personal assistant, Anna Nolan."

"Yes, Dr. Lewis. I'm Melanie. We spoke over the phone."

"I'm pleased to make your acquaintance, Melanie. Is Mr. Rapp ready to see us?"

Melanie eyed Anna. "We weren't expecting anyone other than you, Dr. Lewis."

"Oh, I never go anywhere without Anna. She makes records of my meetings for me. Otherwise, I suspect I would leave my own head behind someday." Melanie looked at her doubtfully and Magdalena smiled, trying to look disarmingly imbecilic.

"Well, I suppose it will be all right. Please follow me, ladies." Melanie rose from her desk and led the two women down a hall with floor-to-ceiling windows to a small meeting room with a round table and four chairs.

"Please take a seat. Would you care for tea or coffee?"

"No, thank you. I'd only end up spilling it on my papers." Magdalena held up her briefcase with a smile.

"I understand. Mr. Rapp will join you shortly."

Anna chuckled after Melanie left the room. "I'm not buying the dim-witted routine, and I doubt that she did, either."

"Never mind. It got both of us in here to see him, didn't it?"

Tobias Rapp strode into the meeting room at 12:45. "I'm terribly sorry to keep you waiting, ladies," he said, looking dashing in a grey suit with a burgundy vest. He held out his hand to Magdalena, but hesitated before offering it to Anna.

"We've met before, haven't we? What did you say your name was?"

"I'm Anna Nolan, but we weren't introduced when we first met, Tobias. Or Toby, as Rick was calling you in the ladies' room on the day of Julia Moreland's funeral."

Tobias winced as he sank into his chair. "Now I remember. Rick was upset that day."

"Or very high," Anna said. "His guard was definitely down, whatever he was taking. I remember him referring to you as his 'boyfriend.'"

"What is this about?" Tobias asked, looking from Anna to Magdalena.

"We have no interest in your sexual proclivities," Magdalena said. "But we do want to know more about your relationship with Rick Moreland."

"What is your interest, Dr. Lewis? If you are, in fact, Dr. Lewis, Jonathan Lewis's daughter?"

"I am. I'm also a personal friend of Warren Moreland."

The lawyer's face was blank as he climbed to his feet. "This meeting is over," he said.

"Are the police aware of your relationship with Rick?" Anna asked.

Tobias paused. "For the record, I am not Rick's boyfriend, although our relationship didn't come up when I was responding to the police's questions about Julia's death."

"Whatever your relationship is with Rick, what would interest me more is whether or not he knew the details of Julia's will prior to her death," Magdalena said.

"That would be a violation of my client's privacy, Dr. Lewis."

"Quite."

Tobias shook his head. "As I said before, this meeting is over. But be careful of what you say about this to anyone, ladies. I will file charges against you for slander if I hear any scuttlebutt that I prematurely divulged the terms of Julia Moreland's will to anyone. Goodbye. I'm sure you can find your way out." That parting remark was flung over Tobias's shoulder as he exited the room.

Anna looked at Magdalena admiringly. "You were wonderful, Magdalena. You handled him just right."

"I don't think so. He didn't admit to divulging the details of Julia's will to Rick."

"No, but you riled him. Sometimes it's good to shake things up to see what the fallout is afterward. I'm looking forward to what happens next."

14

It was after ten the same night. Magdalena had spent a couple of hours feeding numbers into a spreadsheet on department spending and performed a half hour of yoga afterward to unwind. She was meditating now, sitting on a mat before the window in the upstairs bedroom she used as an exercise room. She liked to meditate before bed to clear her head. She had turned off the lights so that she could see out over the reservoir, a view she found beautiful at any time of the year. There was a light snow falling, sugaring the spotlit trees in her back yard and the public walkway that separated the shoreline from her property.

The doorbell rang, shattering her peace. Magdalena sighed and rolled fluidly to her feet, something she was still able to do at the age of thirty-nine thanks to years of dance training and yoga. She was dressed in leggings and a cotton tunic with her hair up in a serviceable bun. Trotting down the stairs, she turned on a lamp in the living room before walking to the front door. She flicked on the outside light and peered through the peephole. Rick Moreland stood on her front porch, his arms wrapped around himself and jittering up and down because he wasn't wearing a coat. He must have dashed to her front door from his car.

Magdalena hesitated. She and Rick had always gotten along fine, although she thought he was immature, but he must have come as a result of her interview with the lawyer.

Rick was bound to be upset, even angry, that she and Anna had been intruding in his private life. Still, he didn't look angry as he jiggled in the cold with the snow catching in his blond hair. And Magdalena seriously doubted that Rick was a murderer, no matter what Anna suspected. He was a lightweight, too interested in having a good time to become involved with murder.

Anna had talked about seeing what the fallout might be from their visit to Tobias Rapp, and Magdalena was curious about what Rick might have to say. As a precaution, however, she grabbed her cell from her purse in the living room and slid it into her tunic pocket before opening the door.

"Rick," she said with a nod, wrapping her arms around herself as the cold air seeped past her into the house.

"Sorry to be visiting so late, but I needed to talk with you," Rick said. "I know you saw Toby today because he called me about it afterward. I dropped by Warren's office to explain why Toby and I were keeping our friendship a secret, figuring that Warren would share it with you, but he said you two weren't seeing each other anymore. I was sad to hear it. I always thought you and Warren clicked."

Magdalena blinked. She hadn't expected that Warren would share information about their relationship with Rick, but now she was very interested to hear what Warren had said.

"What did he have to say about us?" she asked aloud.

"Do you mind if I come in?" Rick shivered. "It's so cold out here. I didn't need my coat when I got into the car in the parking garage, but I should have put it on before I came to your door." He looked boyishly charming as he smiled ruefully.

"Come in." Magdalena opened the door wider to allow him inside. Rick kicked off his shoes as she shut the door behind him. "This way."

Magdalena waved toward the living room, allowing him to precede her through the house. Better to stay behind him until she knew what kind of mood he was in. She turned on a second lamp and perched on one of the chairs while he sprawled on the couch.

"What a great view," Rick said, nodding over his shoulder toward the window.

"Yes. You were about to tell me what Warren had to say about our relationship."

Rick grinned. "Don't worry, he was too much of a gentleman to talk about the reason for your split. Although he did seem unhappy that your relationship was over."

"I see." How disappointing. "What did you want me to know about your friendship with Mr. Rapp?"

Rick leaned forward, resting his elbows on his knees. "Well, Toby and I started seeing each other last spring. We were never that serious about each other — not exclusive, or anything — but he made a nice change from all the rich girls and models I'd been dating. Things ran their course, and we broke up in September. All very amiable, you understand. Of course, I didn't tell Mother about us because she wouldn't have been pleased. She'd been after me the past couple of years about settling down and starting a family because it would have looked better to the stockholders. So I didn't tell anyone about us in case it got back to her. I swear our relationship was over long before Mother saw Toby to change her will."

"So you had no idea that she intended you to be the CEO of Westmore or that she was leaving you the majority of her shares?"

Rick sat up and signed a cross on his chest. "Hope to die. Of course, her death came at the worst possible time. It was Mother's intention to train me so that I'd be ready to take over when she got around to retiring. Instead, Westmore's stuck with me as I am. But, have no fear, I'm taking my new position seriously. I've already given up my night life and started burning the midnight oil at the office. Mother trusted me with a huge responsibility, and I'm not going to let the family down." He smiled. "Say, have you got anything to drink? I'd love a nightcap. It's been a long day."

"I was just about to go to bed. It's getting late."

Rick smiled and patted the couch beside him. "C'mon, it's not that late. I've been staring at worksheets all day. Why don't we get to know each other better? Life's been pretty grim since Mother's death. We could both use a diversion."

Magdalena hesitated. Rick seemed to find her attractive. Maybe she could pry some useful information from him.

"All right." She stood up and took the pins out of her hair, running her fingers through it so that it would fall onto her shoulders. Then she sat very close to Rick on the couch. She noticed that his lashes were ridiculously long as they shaded his half-closed eyes. She preferred Warren's rugged good looks.

Rick slid an arm around her shoulders. "I guess it hasn't been easy for you since the break-up. Warren's an idiot, giving up a woman like you."

Magdalena smiled flirtatiously. "What makes you think he had any choice?"

"Oh, you dumped him? Do tell." As Rick leaned in closer, there was a whack on the window that made them both jump. Magdalena whirled to look, but there was nothing there.

"What was that?" Rick asked as he turned to stare at her.

"I don't know."

The doorbell rang, and someone started pounding on the door. Glancing at Rick, who showed no inclination to see who was there, Magdalena strode across the room to check the peephole. Warren was on the door mat, raising his arm to pound on the door again. She opened it abruptly, and he stumbled inside. He glared at Magdalena before pushing past her into the living room.

"Rick! What the hell are you doing here?"

Rick leapt to his feet before Warren could reach him, putting the coffee table between them.

"Warren, I thought you said you were about to go home when I left the office."

"I was," Warren said, leaning toward his stepbrother, "but after what you said, I decided to make sure that Magdalena was all right first."

Hmm, that was interesting. Magdalena studied the two men. They were both tall and well-built, but Warren was older and heavier than Rick. Warren's eyes were dark infernos as Rick took a step backward until his legs pressed up against the couch.

Rick laughed, a starved sound. "What are you talking about? Why wouldn't Magdalena be all right?"

"Are you kidding? You said how mad you were at Magdalena for butting into your private life and practically accusing you and Tobias of collusion, and that you were going to make sure that she never did it again."

"In a manner of speaking," Rick said, holding up his hands. "I'll admit I was angry, but I cooled down on the ride over." He peered past Warren at Magdalena. "I realized how

I sounded to Anna in the ladies' room on the day of Mother's funeral, and how the two of you must have misunderstood about Toby. I just wanted a chance to explain my side."

"Is that what you were doing with your arm around Magdalena just now?" Warren growled. "You looked like you were about to kiss her."

Rick paled. "That's ridiculous. I think I'd better leave."

"That's right. Get the hell out of here."

Magdalena advanced into the living room. "This is my house. Don't you think I should decide who stays and who leaves?" Warren turned to glare at her, and she raised an eyebrow as she stared back.

"Not a problem," Rick said. "You two have stuff to talk about. I'll give you some privacy." He sidled past the couple and hurried to the foyer to put on his shoes. Magdalena swivelled to look just as the door banged shut behind him. She turned back to Warren.

"What's this about? Why the big display of testosterone? I thought you weren't interested in me anymore?"

"I'm not, but that doesn't mean I'm going to stand by while Rick assaults you. Westmore's got enough trouble without you pressing charges against our CEO."

"Assault me? I hardly think so." Magdalena crossed her arms over her chest. "You'll have to do better than that. Why are you really here?"

"What are you talking about?" Warren rubbed his eyes with one hand. "Look, it's been a long day. I don't need another argument. I'm going home." He took a step toward the door, but Magdalena crossed in front of him, blocking his way.

"Not yet. Now that you're here, I want an explanation. Why have you been behaving so badly, Warren?"

They stood inches apart, Warren scowling. Magdalena's expression was frosty, but there was an angry glint to her eyes.

"*I've* been behaving badly? You should be the one doing the explaining," Warren snapped.

"About what? Last time you were here, the police were taking you in for questioning. You asked me to call your lawyer and your brothers, which I did. I'd have done anything to help you that day. Next thing I knew, you weren't returning my calls."

"Done anything to help me? That's not what I heard. According to Detective Soo, you couldn't wait to tell her that I gave Julia the glass of poisoned scotch and that nobody else touched it before she drank from it." Warren edged closer to Magdalena, his dark eyes dangerous. "You were afraid that you might be implicated in a murder investigation, so you threw me to the wolves." He grabbed her arms.

"Take your hands off me," she warned in a charged voice. Warren ignored her.

"I thought you were different. I thought you were strong. I loved you, but the first hint of trouble, you betrayed me. You're weak and self-serving, just like Dad and Mom were. They were never there when I needed them. Julia never pretended to love me, but at least I was important to her."

"I'm telling you one last time, Warren," Magdalena said in a barely-constrained voice. "Take your hands off me."

"Or what?" he jeered

She bashed his ears with both of her hands. Warren staggered backward, holding his head and moaning.

"I warned you!" She jabbed her finger into his chest, her face white with anger. "Of course I told Detective Soo that you gave Julia the Lagavulin. Did you want me to lie and let her think that you had something to hide? She had witnesses, Warren. She'd have found me out, and then where would you have been?"

Warren grabbed her arms, and she strained against him. "Do you think you're the only person who's ever been betrayed?" Magdalena shouted. "That you've got a monopoly on being disappointed by the people you love?"

They struggled, and she shrieked, "Let go of me!" She kicked him, but Warren held on.

"Stop it!" he roared.

He wrapped his arms around her, trapping her arms at her sides. She struggled furiously to break free and they rocked back and forth, grunting with effort.

Suddenly, Magdalena stopped. She raised her eyes to his, panting, her hair hanging in her face. "This is ridiculous. We're behaving like animals." He dropped his arms and she half-turned, but when he moved to walk away from her, she grabbed his shirt.

"I never meant to betray you, Warren. I didn't know what else to say to Detective Soo." She gazed deep into his eyes so that he could read the truth in them.

Warren stared back before covering her hand with his. "I'm sorry. I should have trusted you."

"I've done everything I could think of to help you since they took you in for questioning. Anna and me both."

Warren shook his head. "You shouldn't try to help. What if you got hurt? I couldn't bear to lose you. I found that out tonight, when I saw Rick with you on the couch. It made me crazy."

Magdalena raised her hand to stroke his face. "I love you."

Pulling her into his arms, Warren kissed the top of her head. "We'll get through this somehow. We can't let it break us apart." They kissed over and over, their hunger intensifying, until he picked her up and carried her to the couch.

Magdalena turned on her side and reached for Warren in the darkness. The bottom sheet was still warm from where he had been lying.

"Warren?" She peered around the shadowy room, but he wasn't there. The bedroom door was closed. Worrying that something had happened, she slid out from under the covers and padded to the door. Opening it onto the darkened hall, she noticed light spilling out from under the bathroom door. She could hear Warren's voice.

"Don't worry. Everything will be fine. I promise."

She rapped on the door and peeked inside.

"Warren? What's happening?"

He was leaning against the counter, talking on his cell.

"I've got to go now. Bye." Warren ended the call and frowned. "I'm sorry, I didn't mean to wake you."

"Who were you talking to?"

"Oliver. Beatrix was having trouble breathing, so he took her to Emergency. He was calling to let me know."

"I didn't hear your phone ring."

"No, I had it switched to vibrate."

"Oh. I woke up and you weren't there." Magdalena gathered her long hair in her hands and draped it down her back. "I hope that Beatrix will be all right."

Warren sighed. "It's not the first scare Oliver's had with her. I think I should go to the hospital. It's hard for him to wait alone, and he's got no family close by."

"Of course. Whatever you think."

Warren nodded and walked past Magdalena into the hall. She followed him to the bedroom, where he bent to pick up his clothes from the floor. The window was cracked open, and she shivered.

"You're cold. You should go back to bed," he said.

She hurried to crawl under the covers. Warren followed her and drew the duvet up to her chin as she gazed up at him.

"Please tell Oliver that I hope everything turns out well for Beatrix."

Warren kissed her forehead. "I will. Listen, why don't I stop by your office on my way to work in the morning to let you know how she is? Maybe we can grab a cup of coffee together."

Magdalena smiled. "I'd like that."

"Okay, sweetheart." He kissed her lips. "Get some sleep. I'll see you later."

"Bye, Warren." He left the room, and Magdalena listened to his footsteps thudding down the stairs before closing her eyes.

15

The next morning was beautiful with the rosy glow of sunrise as Anna pulled into the parking lot at Chinook University. She was in a happy mood, anticipating Charlie's arrival in a week from today. She climbed out of the car with her purse and a tin of thumbprint cookies she'd made to share with the department. Brr, it was cold. Her boots crunched in the fresh snow as she rushed across the lot to the sidewalk leading to the main building.

After waiting for one of the maintenance staff to finished shovelling out the entrance, Anna rushed inside and stamped her boots on the rubber-backed carpet between the double doors. She walked down the main hall, past the Registrar's Office and the Bookstore, to the door opening onto her department hallway. She was early, a good fifteen minutes before the building was supposed to open, and she had to swipe her employee card through the security device on the wall to gain access. The light on the reader switched from red to green, and she gripped the handle to swing the door open. The air in the corridor was stale; the ventilation system hadn't kicked in yet.

Anna whistled a Christmas carol as she walked past the faculty offices. As she approached her own office, she spied something on the floor outside her door. It was a box of chocolates tied with a pretty red ribbon.

"Isn't that nice. I wonder who they're from?" she asked aloud as she bent to pick it up. Anna froze. A small envelope was tucked inside the ribbon. Her first and last names were spelled out in colourful letters cut from a newspaper or magazine. The envelope looked just like the one Julia had received.

Anna didn't want to touch the box. She unlocked her office door, reached inside to flip on the lights, and kicked the box into the room. Searching her pockets for her leather gloves, she pulled them on over trembling fingers. Then she picked up the candy, staring at the envelope as though it might bite her.

She had to open it, had to know what the message inside said. It was the only way to find out how much danger she was in. She pulled a tissue from the box on her desk and spread it over a clear space on the wood. Setting the chocolates on the tissue, she grabbed the letter opener from her desk organizer, slid the envelope from under the ribbon, and slit it open. Twitching out a folded slip of paper from within, she flipped it open. The message was written in the same cut-out letters.

"Life is full of nasty surprises. Mind your own business, or die." Anna dropped the note and screamed.

Someone came running down the corridor. Anna whirled, clutching at her throat. Magdalena burst into the room, still dressed in her boots and coat.

"Anna! Anna, what's wrong?"

Anna grabbed her boss's arm, her eyes wild with fear.

"Magdalena, he sent me a note! The murderer sent me a note!"

"What?"

Anna waved at the box of chocolates and the message on her desk. "There!"

Magdalena stepped around her to reach for the paper.

"Don't pick it up with your bare skin! It might be poisoned."

Grim-faced, Magdalena pulled on her gloves and picked up the sheet of paper. She read the note and frowned. Anna crept closer, peering over her shoulder.

"That's just how Julia's message looked," she whispered. Magdalena flipped the page over, turned back to the message, and glanced at Anna.

"Come with me to my office. I've got Detective Soo's card in my desk. We'll call her immediately."

Anna nodded and stuck to Magdalena as she unlocked her office door and went inside. Anna paused to switch on the overhead light while Magdalena hurried to her desk, opened the drawer, and retrieved the card. She sank into her chair and jabbed the buttons on her phone. Once it was ringing, she put the call on speaker phone.

"Detective Soo here."

"Detective, it's Dr. Lewis. Anna and I are at the university. She just found a box of chocolates with a threatening note at her office door." Magdalena read the message out loud, glancing at Anna, who trembled in a chair in front of her desk. "She's half-scared to death."

"I'll be right over. Try to find a clean plastic bag to put the note in, and make sure no one touches those chocolates!"

"Right. See you shortly."

Anna smacked her forehead and jumped out of the chair. "I should have locked my office door before we left." She hurried back across the hall, only to discover Dr. Brian Carmichael standing in front of her desk with his back to her.

"Brian!" she shrieked.

He jumped and turned to stare at her with a chocolate in his fingers.

"What?"

Anna raced over to slap the chocolate from his hand.

"Ow! Hey," Brian complained.

She grabbed the front of his sweat shirt. "Did you eat any?"

"What? No."

"Let me see. Open your mouth."

He stared at Anna as if she were crazy. She thumped his chest with her hand.

"Open your damn mouth!"

He did as he was told and Anna grabbed his ear, forcing his head down to where she could see inside. There was nothing in his mouth. His breath smelled of garlic, not chocolate.

"Thank heaven," Anna muttered. She heard the sound of the ocean roaring in her ears. Brian grabbed her shoulders as she teetered.

"Anna, what the hell is wrong with you?"

She opened her eyes. "The chocolates may be poisoned. I was just coming back to lock them in my office." They peered together at the open box, an enticing assortment of milk, white, and dark chocolate nestled in a black tray. One of them was even wrapped in gold foil.

Anna grasped Brian's arm. "Come on. Let's get out of here."

He nodded, and with his arm around her waist for support, led her to the hall. Anna fumbled for her keys inside her purse and turned to lock the door.

Magdalena met them in the corridor. "Is everything all right? I heard shouting."

"What's going on?" Brian asked.

Magdalena ignored him to ask, "Are you feeling all right, Anna? You look shaky."

Anna couldn't respond. The rushing sound was back and there were spots in front of her eyes.

"Brian, help me get her into my office," Magdalena said.

They took Anna's arms and supported her across the hall to a chair in front of Magdalena's desk. Quickly, her boss removed Anna's coat.

"Bend over. Put your head between your knees." Magdalena glanced at Brian. "Get some wet paper towels from the bathroom." Brian opened his mouth to speak, and Magdalena said, "Now, Brian!"

As he hurried from the room, Detective Soo passed him in the doorway. She took in the scene with one glance.

"She didn't eat one of the chocolates, did she?"

"No, she's just feeling faint."

"Good. At least she's not going to die. Where're the note and the chocolates?"

Magdalena went to her desk drawer. The paper and the envelope were inside in a resealable plastic bag. She held it out to Soo.

"We wore our gloves to read the message. The chocolates are across the hall, locked in Anna's office."

"I need to see them."

Magdalena returned to Anna, who was bent double in the chair, and knelt beside her.

"Anna, are you still with us? I need the keys to your office."

Anna held up her hand, the keys still clenched in her fingers. Magdalena gently extricated them and patted Anna's shoulder. "We'll be back as soon as we can."

"And when we do, I need to ask you some questions," Soo said. Magdalena frowned at the detective.

They heard the mail cart rumbling down the hall toward them.

"Excellent timing," Magdalena said. She pushed past the detective to stick her head out the door. "Alice, can you come here, please?"

"Sure." Alice walked to the office doorway, nodded at Detective Soo, and spotted Anna in the chair. Her smile vanished. "What happened?"

"Anna's had a scare and now she's feeling faint. This is Detective Soo, who's investigating the deaths of Julia Moreland and Latona Taylor. I have to show her something in Anna's office. Could you stay with Anna, please?"

Alice's mouth dropped open. "Of course." She squeezed past Magdalena and crouched beside her stricken friend as Soo and Magdalena left the room. Anna turned her face toward Alice.

"Did she say 'the death of Latona Taylor?'"

"I think so. Who's she?"

Anna groaned. "Julia's personal assistant."

"Gee." Alice rubbed Anna's back. "Sounds like you're right in the thick of things again."

Anna began to sob as Warren stepped into the office.

"Where's Magdalena?" he asked.

16

An hour later, Anna was feeling much better. Alice had brought her a cola from the vending machine, and the extra sugar was helping her to feel stronger. They were all crowded into the chair's office — Warren, Magdalena, Detective Soo, and herself — while the forensics team the detective had summoned worked across the hall. Soo was calling Campus Security, asking them to ready the footage from the previous night's surveillance cameras.

"Does a cleaning team come through here at night?" the detective asked with her hand over the mouthpiece.

"Not on Thursday nights," Magdalena said.

Soo nodded. "What time did the two of you leave last night?"

Anna and Magdalena glanced at each other.

"I left right at four-thirty," Anna said.

"I left about a quarter after five," Magdalena added.

"I presume you would have noticed a box of chocolates on the floor outside Anna's door?"

"Certainly," Magdalena replied.

Detective Soo removed her hand from the mouthpiece. "Make that the footage outside the Kinesiology corridor from 5:00 p.m. Thursday night to 8:15 this morning. I'll be over to have a look at it when I'm finished here." Soo hung up the phone. "Too bad you don't have security cameras in these side corridors, too."

"Both our corridor doors open into the main hall," Magdalena said. "If someone entered our department through either door, the cameras should have caught it. You realize that if someone came in after hours, he or she would have required an employee card to get in."

The detective nodded. "We already checked the lock. It hasn't been tampered with."

"You mean that whoever left the chocolates and the note at my door was a university employee?" Anna asked in a tight voice.

"Maybe," the detective said. "We'll have to see what's on that tape."

Anna stared at Magdalena. The only person she knew who was both a university employee and connected with Julia and Latona Taylor's deaths was her boss.

Magdalena caught Anna's expression and frowned.

"Don't be ridiculous."

Anna looked away furtively.

"Anna, listen to me," Magdalena said. "I know that you have a vivid imagination, but you have to stop suspecting everyone as being the killer. Would I have invited your help in investigating Julia's death if I had been the murderer?"

"Well . . ."

"What are you two talking about?" Soo demanded. She glowered at the two women as Magdalena provided a summary of their investigative efforts, omitting only Beatrix's shoplifting. Warren, who was perched on the edge of the desk, crossed his arms over his chest and listened with a stony face.

"Just when were you going to tell me about the relationship between Rick Moreland and Tobias Rapp?" Soo asked, her pen pausing over her notepad.

"I left a voice message for you yesterday afternoon, Detective, but you didn't return my call," Magdalena replied.

"I've been busy," Soo snapped. "I've had some investigation work of my own, remember? I can't believe you two." She took a deep breath and sighed. "Listen, as long as you're all here, I've got some news for you. We arrested Kevin Moreland last night."

Warren jumped to his feet. "What? Why didn't you call me?"

"We tried, but you didn't answer your home phone, and your cell appeared to be turned off. Where were you last night?"

Warren glanced at Magdalena. The detective watched their silent exchange.

"I was with Magdalena for part of the night until I left to visit a friend who was taken to Emergency. I had to turn my phone off inside the hospital."

"That's right, Detective," Magdalena said.

Anna smiled. With all the upset about the chocolates and the anonymous note, it hadn't occurred to her to wonder what Warren was doing in her boss's office. At least the two of them were back together again.

"Why arrest Kevin?" Warren asked.

"We've been investigating him since your stepmother's death," Soo said. "For one thing, his finances are a mess. He's got two mortgages on his house, a personal loan, plus he and his wife's credit cards are maxed out. He's been pouring every nickel he's got into his wife's business, which isn't doing so good. Your stepbrother seemed to have the most to gain from his mother's death, given his assumption that he was going to become the CEO of Westmore Resources and inherit her company shares. Then, while we were investigating the crime scene at Latona Taylor's apartment yesterday, we found two disposable coffee cups in her kitchen garbage, one with Kevin's fingerprints on it. We've rushed samples from the victim and the coffee cups for toxicology testing, and I'm betting they'll find water hemlock in both. We'll have those chocolates checked out, too," she said, nodding at Anna.

Warren's face looked grim. "I knew about Kevin's financial problems, but I never imagined him capable of committing a crime, much less killing someone. But there's something you should know, Detective, something I just found out about yesterday."

"What's that?"

He explained about the Westmore audit and the money that had been skimmed from the Production Engineering Department. "Jack Upton and I agreed that we weren't going to move on this until the auditors traced the money back to the embezzler. There's absolutely no proof that Kevin took it. It may only be a coincidence that the money is missing from his area. But in light of his arrest, I thought you should know."

Soo made notes on her pad. "Thank you, Mr. Moreland. You've done the right thing. I'll get someone from our Economic Crime Unit to contact Jack Upton so that we can interface with your auditors. The sooner we find out if Kevin Moreland is responsible for the embezzlement, the better." She stood up and stretched. "We searched his house and took his computer when we arrested him, so maybe we'll get lucky. It's going to be harder to convict your stepbrother of Mrs. Moreland's death, but if Latona Taylor died of water hemlock poisoning, that'll make the case stronger. Meanwhile, stay in touch in case we have more questions."

She was leaving when Anna said, "Detective Soo?"

The detective turned, her hand on the door knob. "Yes, Mrs. Nolan?"

"There's just one thing that doesn't make sense to me."

"What's that?"

"If Kevin was arrested last night, then who left the chocolates and the anonymous note at my office door?"

Soo paused to think. "I assume that Kevin did prior to his arrest. I'll check the surveillance footage to see if we recognize him."

"When was he arrested?

"Shortly before midnight. He was in bed when we caught up with him, but that doesn't mean he didn't have time to leave his surprise for you first."

"But if he didn't? What then?"

The detective leaned against the wall. "Look, Mrs. Nolan, I know you had a nasty shock this morning, but stop worrying. I'll check the tape right away. If there's any problem, I'll let you know. Until then, try to relax. Kevin Moreland's safely behind bars. He's not going to be bothering anyone anymore. Okay?"

Anna nodded, but her face looked doubtful.

"All right," Soo said. "I have to check in with the forensics team. They'll give you back your office as soon as possible. I'll be in touch. Goodbye."

Anna watched her leave and turned to look at Warren and Magdalena. He was holding her hand as he stood beside her.

"I'm sorry, but I have to leave. The office is probably turning into a nuthouse with the news of Kevin's arrest. Somehow, we've got to hold Westmore together."

"I know. Call me when you can. Let me know how you're doing."

Warren bent to kiss her. "At least we're all right. I don't know how I'd get through this without you."

Magdalena smiled, and they gazed into each other's eyes.

Warren straightened and said, "See you." He walked past Anna and added, "Take care of yourself."

"Thanks. You, too," she replied.

He left the office, and Anna glanced at Magdalena and did a double-take. Her boss's face was serious as she studied her.

"Perhaps you should go home and rest," she said. "You've been through a lot this morning. I have to visit the dean to explain what the police are doing here." Magdalena rose and walked around her desk to Anna, who peered up at her from her chair.

"If you don't mind, I think I'm going to stay. I don't feel like being alone right now. I can spend some time cleaning out the faculty mailboxes, and if the police haven't finished with my office by then, I can take an early lunch. Besides, I'd like to be here when Detective Soo looks at the surveillance footage. Just in case."

"All right. Whatever makes you feel comfortable. But you really can stop worrying now. The police have arrested the right man."

"You always thought that it was Kevin."

Magdalena nodded. "Although I don't take any pleasure in being proved right. Poor Warren. What a blow this is for him. He's done so much for Westmore and for Julia and her family. They don't deserve him."

"No, they really don't. Well, good luck with the dean. I'll see you later."

Anna had been in the photocopy/mailroom for half an hour when a policeman came to tell her that the forensics team was leaving. She was back at her desk when the phone rang. The caller ID indicated someone from Security. Her stomach clenched. Was something wrong after all?

"Good morning, Anna Nolan speaking."

"Hi, Anna. This is Dave from Security."

"Hi, Dave."

"I've got Detective Soo here with me. She wants you to see something from last night's security camera footage. What's that?" Anna heard muffled talking. "Detective Soo would like Dr. Lewis to come, too."

Oh, no. This can't be good. "Sure, Dave, but I'll have to see if she's back yet. Dr. Lewis left to meet with the dean half an hour ago. We'll be there in a few minutes if she is, or I'll have to come alone."

"Okay, I'll pass that on. See you soon."

"Bye." Anna quickly locked her office door and hurried across the hall. Magdalena's door was open, and she was working on the computer.

"I just got a call from Security. Detective Soo wants us both to see something from last night's surveillance footage."

Magdalena's eyebrows rose. "Very well."

They strode to Security next to the building's main entrance. One of the security guards ushered them into a back room not much bigger than a closet where Detective Soo and Dave were concentrating on a computer screen. They looked up when Anna and Magdalena squeezed in.

"I'm glad you're both here," Soo said, rising. "I'd like you to see this." She turned to Dave. "Play the footage beginning at 2:12 a.m., please." Soo stood in the doorway looking over their shoulders as Anna took the empty chair and Magdalena stood beside her.

They watched black-and-white footage of a man wearing a parka and jeans coming toward them through the parking lot entrance and passing under the camera. The parka's hood was pulled up and his head was lowered, leaving the man's face in shadow. He had something tucked under his arm and was wearing a backpack.

"What's he got?" Anna asked.

"Just keep watching," Soo said.

The man was picked up by a second camera as he proceeded down the main hall and paused outside the door to the Kinesiology corridor. He tried the handle, but the door didn't budge. Taking the item from under his arm, he flipped it open.

"It's a laptop," Magdalena said.

Glancing over his shoulder first, the man sat down on the floor and began typing into the computer balanced on his lap.

"What's he doing?" Anna wondered aloud. She noted the time in the screen's upper right corner before watching the man typing some more. Two minutes passed before he rose to his feet, the laptop in one hand, and took hold of the door handle again. This time it opened, and the man disappeared inside the corridor.

"Wait for it," Soo said. The man was gone for only a minute when he came back through the door, trotted down the hall away from the camera, and left through the same entrance.

"Thanks, Dave. That's enough," the detective said.

Anna and Magdalena turned to peer at her. "How'd he do that?" Anna asked. "How did he use his computer to get inside?"

"He hacked into the system," Dave said. "We used to have to physically authorize the employee cards to get them to work, but that all changed a year ago with our system upgrade. Now we can authorize cards long distance through the computer. We can even open the door without an employee card. It saves everyone a lot of hassle."

"But it allowed our hacker to break into the corridor and leave Anna his surprise. I assume he had the note and the box of chocolates in his backpack," Soo said.

Magdalena turned to Dave. "How good does a hacker have to be to break into the system?"

"Pretty good. We paid a lot of money for the program."

"Hmm," Magdalena said with a frown.

"So he broke into the department after 2:00 a.m.," Anna said to the detective. "After Kevin Moreland was arrested."

"That's right." Soo was blank-faced as she stared at Anna. "You didn't recognize our hacker, I suppose?"

Anna shook her head. "The camera was always looking down at him. Besides, his face was covered by his hood."

"Magdalena?"

"Sorry, I didn't recognize him either. Although it could have been Kevin. The size was about right, given that his coat was bulky, and he moved like a young man."

"Except that Kevin Moreland couldn't have delivered those chocolates," Soo said. "Thank you, Dave. Ladies, I have to get back to the station now." She left the room as Anna and Magdalena exchanged a glance.

"Hey, Detective," Anna called, running after her. Magdalena followed, and they caught up with Soo in the hall. "What are you going to do now? Release Kevin?"

"Of course not. Just because he didn't deliver those chocolates doesn't mean he didn't poison Latona Taylor and Julia Moreland. Although it will be interesting to see if there's water hemlock in your candy." She gazed at Anna. "We could have a copycat on our hands."

"Or an accomplice," Anna said.

"Right. Stay on your guard, ladies. Both of you. And don't try any more private investigating. If you had kept your noses out of this, Mrs. Nolan wouldn't have received her gift this morning." She nodded and walked away. Anna and Magdalena stared after her for a moment before falling into step headed back to the department.

"She's not very comforting," Magdalena murmured.

"I sure don't feel comforted. Copycat or an accomplice? Maybe they just arrested the wrong man."

"The only thing to do, Anna, is give the writer of that note what he wants, as Detective Soo suggested. From now on, we'll refrain from further investigation."

"What if that isn't good enough?" Anna asked with a shudder. Magdalena glanced at her. Anna's eyes looked haunted. "What if he thinks we already know too much and decides to do something about it?"

"Which is why you're going to make yourself scarce today by going home to Crane. You'll notice that the chocolates were delivered here, not to your home. Maybe he doesn't know where you live."

"It wouldn't take him long to find out. He could look up the address on the internet."

"No, it wouldn't. But you live in a small town amongst friends. Everybody knows everybody else, right? If someone you know from the city suddenly turned up, he'd stick out like a sore thumb." They reached the door to the department corridor, and Magdalena held it open for Anna.

"That's true," Anna said slowly as she passed through. "But that's not true for you."

"Me? I'm not worried."

"But I am. We pooled our information. Whatever the murderer thinks I know, you know. What if the murderer realizes that?"

"Except that you were the only one to overhear the argument between Julia and the mystery man on the night of the party. Maybe he's afraid you can identify him."

"If I could, I'd have done it by now." They paused in the hallway between their two offices.

"You talked alone with Julia in the ladies' room. Are you sure she didn't say something that might have a bearing on all of this?"

Anna shook her head. "Only that she was having some sort of problem that she wished her husband could help her with. And that she was still young enough to have fun. I don't see how that could help."

"Neither do I. What was she going to announce at that press conference?"

"And what did Latona Taylor know that got her killed?" Anna stared at Magdalena. "Come home with me this weekend."

"What? What good would that do?"

Anna grasped her boss's arm. "I can look after you there. Otherwise, I'll worry about you all weekend."

Magdalena patted Anna's hand and slid her arm from its grasp. She turned to unlock her door. "I'm a big girl. I can take care of myself."

Anna followed her into the office. "All right, then come home to Crane to look after me. I'm scared witless. We'll be safer together than apart. You're right — if anyone from Calgary comes looking for us there, we'll notice. You don't know who to trust here in the city. Even Warren."

"I beg your pardon?" Magdalena said, frowning as she slipped into her chair.

"What time was it when he left you last night?"

Magdalena shrugged. "I have no idea."

"How can you not know? Didn't you look at the clock?"

"I don't have a clock in my bedroom. I don't like artificial light when I'm sleeping. Besides, I don't need one. I always wake up at six-thirty on weekdays."

"Really? You're kidding. You really are a robot, aren't you?"

Magdalena shook her head at Anna before waking up her computer.

"What I'm saying is, Warren went out last night. He might have been the man in the parka who dropped off the chocolates. Is he really good with computers?"

Magdalena kept her eyes on the screen, ignoring Anna as she typed.

"Okay, scratch that. Warren is a saint. We don't have to worry about him at all. But come home with me, anyway. Humour me. You'll enjoy it. My son's coming home for dinner. You can get to know him better. We'll have breakfast with May and Erna at The Diner tomorrow. They've always wanted to meet you. We'll take Wendy for walks and you can help me with my Christmas baking."

Magdalena continued ignoring Anna.

"Oh, I almost forgot. I'm going to the Rotary Club Christmas Dinner Dance tomorrow night. It'll be great fun. You can dance with all the bachelors. Okay, Clive and Mr. Andrews aren't the greatest dancers, but I'm pretty sure neither one of them will be wearing work boots when they step on your toes."

Still no response.

"All right, you're forcing me to do this. You owe me, Magdalena. You came to me for help when Detective Soo took Warren in for questioning. If it weren't for you, I wouldn't be mixed up with this case, and my life wouldn't be in danger now." She folded her arms over her chest and tried to look formidable as Magdalena stopped typing to rest her hands in her lap.

"What a despicable thing to say."

Anna nodded. "I know, but I'm desperate."

There was silence as Magdalena thought and Anna squirmed, waiting for her response.

Finally, Magdalena sighed. "What does one wear to a Rotary Club Christmas dinner dance?"

17

When Ben came into the kitchen that night, a garbage bag jammed with dirty laundry over his shoulder, he was surprised to see Magdalena setting the table. Ben was twenty and tall, with broad shoulders, slim hips, and his mother's brown hair and eyes. He was wearing his hair longer so that it brushed the edge of his collar.

Wendy rose from under the table to greet him, and he patted her head absent-mindedly while staring at Magdalena.

"Dr. Lewis. I didn't expect to see you here."

"Hello, Ben. Your mother is in the basement fetching vegetables from the freezer." They turned as Anna pounded up the stairs and bustled into the kitchen.

"Hi, honey."

Anna hugged Ben with one arm, the other hand holding a bag of frozen peas. "I see you two have already bumped into each other."

"Yeah." Ben gave his mother a puzzled frown.

"Why don't you start your laundry, and then we'll eat. We got home from work early today, so I had time to make pork chops and fried rice. I'm just about to add the peas."

But Ben deposited his laundry on the floor and sat down at the table. "Why don't you tell me what's going on instead? No offence, Dr. Lewis, but since when do you bring your boss home for dinner, Mom?" Magdalena nodded as she laid the cutlery on the table.

"Ben! Don't be rude," Anna said. She used a scissors to snip open the peas and poured them into a glass bowl. "Did you notice the Christmas lights outside on the tree?"

"Yeah. They looked nice. So . . ."

"Excuse me. I'll just go wash up," Magdalena said, leaving them alone in the kitchen.

Anna opened the microwave door and set the peas inside. She punched in the defrost time and turned to meet her son's eyes.

"It's a bit complicated."

"I've got all night."

Anna sighed, hit the microwave's start button, and joined him at the table. "Remember me telling you about Julia Moreland dying two weeks ago? After her Christmas party?"

"Yeah."

"Well, what I didn't tell you was that she was poisoned. Thursday morning, the police found Julia's personal assistant, Latona Taylor, dead in her apartment. They think she may have been poisoned, too. This morning, when I went into work, I found a box of chocolates with an anonymous note attached to it. I felt a little nervous about that, so I invited Magdalena to spend the weekend with me. I didn't want to be alone."

Ben had started scowling as soon as he heard the word, "poisoned."

"What did the note say?"

Anna looked away. "It said, 'Life is full of nasty surprises. Mind your own business, or die.'"

Ben moaned, "Not this again," and buried his head in his hands. A moment later, he glanced up at Anna. "Mom, you promised never to get involved with another murder investigation. How could you let this happen again?"

Anna patted Wendy, whose solid presence was comforting against her knee. "Magdalena needed help, so we've talked to a few people. That's all. Nothing dangerous. Just a little conversation."

"What about your nerves? How are you feeling after finding the note this morning? Did you tell the police about it?"

"We called Detective Soo, the chief investigator in the Julia Moreland case, directly after Anna discovered it," Magdalena said, appearing in the kitchen doorway. "The detective sent the chocolates away for chemical testing."

The microwave timer "dinged," and Magdalena took the peas out of the microwave and stirred them into the fried rice resting on the stove. She returned to the table with an opened bottle of white wine.

"Detective Soo arrested Kevin Moreland, Julia's elder son, for the crimes. I think that she's arrested the correct person, but your mother isn't as certain." She poured wine into Anna's glass and into her own. "Do you care for wine, Ben?"

"Yes, please," Ben said, staring at Anna's boss.

"The only difficulty is that the person who hacked into the university's security system to leave the note and the chocolates for your mother was not Kevin Moreland, so it was either a copycat or an accomplice who threatened Anna. It's unlikely that this person would follow her here to Crane, but your mother was concerned that I might be threatened next. She invited me to stay with her this weekend for my own protection and not because she was afraid."

Magdalena set the bottle on the table. "Personally, I doubt that I'm in any danger, but your mother's had a difficult day, and I didn't want to upset her. So, Ben, I think your best course of action would be not to over-exaggerate the seriousness of the situation and allow us all to enjoy a pleasant meal before you go home. How does that sound?"

Ben looked at his mother and frowned. "I think I'll go start my laundry now." He jumped to his feet, hoisted the bag over his shoulder, and clumped down the stairs to the basement.

"Thank you," Anna said to Magdalena. "I don't think I could have stood a scene with Ben just now. Although I can't blame him. He's been through a rough year with me."

"Nonsense. He's young. He can endure it."

They did not raise the topic of murder, poisoned chocolates, or threatening notes during dinner, but after returning from taking Wendy for a walk, Ben cornered Magdalena in the living room. Anna was putting on the kettle.

"Should I be worried?" he asked. Magdalena noted the anxiety in his eyes and touched his shoulder.

"No. Your mother is surrounded by friends here, and we'll be cautious next week when she's at work. I can't promise you that this will all be over soon, but Sergeant Tremaine will be arriving next Friday, and she'll be safe here with him, plus having a two-week break from the case. I honestly don't see how your mother could be in any real danger."

Ben nodded. "Okay, but promise that you'll keep me posted. If I have to, I'll cut work next week to stay here with Mom."

Magdalena smiled. "I'll keep you informed, Ben."

"Thanks." He raised his voice to call, "Bye, Mom."

Anna hurried into the living room. "You're leaving already? Don't you want tea?"

"Nah. The guys are meeting up for a darts tournament at the pub. I thought I'd drop by for an hour before I go home." He kissed Anna's cheek. "I'll see you next Friday, if you're sure you want me to come for dinner the first night Tremaine's here."

"Sure. We've got the orgy planned for after you leave."

Ben rolled his eyes and picked up his clean laundry. "Nice seeing you, Dr. Lewis. You have a nice weekend."

She looked up from the magazine she was paging through on the couch.

"You, too. Good night."

After closing the front door behind him, Anna said, "That went pretty well. Tea?"

"Yes, please."

Anna woke up screaming. Flailing her arms and kicking, she fought to release herself from the bedclothes. Wendy stood beside the bed and barked. Magdalena rushed in, flicking on the overhead light as she passed, and grabbed Anna's shoulder.

"Hush," she said. "It's all right. You're perfectly safe."

Anna stared at her, a sob bursting from her lips. "I'm s-so sorry. I had a nightmare."

Magdalena sat on the edge of the bed. "I used to have stress nightmares years ago when I was studying for my comprehensive exams."

"Did you?" Anna wiped her eyes, trying to get a grip on her emotions.

Her boss nodded. "I did. I dreamt that I couldn't find the examination room, and when I did, no one was there. I screamed the house down on more than one occasion. My two roommates took to sleeping together in the back bedroom to get away from me. They wore ear plugs, too."

Anna hiccupped. "That's not nice. You couldn't help it."

"I can hardly blame them. They were studying for their own comprehensives as well. I used to wake up refreshed in the morning, while they were both basket cases. Fortunately, they passed, or I would have been beholden to pay their fees for the extra term it took them to rewrite their exams."

"Can you write your comprehensive exams more than once?"

"Of course. But my point is, stress can do funny things to the subconscious. I'm sorry that Julia's death is costing you sleep."

Anna sighed and rolled over to pull a couple of tissues from her bedside table. She noticed Wendy staring at her from beside the bed and scratched behind the dog's ears.

"I'm sorry to have woken you, too, girl." Anna blew her nose and glanced up at Magdalena, who was examining her.

"Don't Julia and Latona's deaths frighten you?"

"No."

"Why not?"

"Because I know two things. Your problem is that you're looking at this situation from a victim's point of view."

Anna tossed the crumpled tissues into the waste basket beside her bed and sat up. Magdalena had touched a sore point. Being called a victim was too close to being called a coward.

"Well, I sure wish you'd share those two things with me," she grumbled.

Magdalena folded her arms over her chest. "Number one, I know that I'm more intelligent than the killer."

"How could you possibly know that? You don't even know who the killer is."

"Nevertheless, I know that I'm more intelligent than he or she." Anna gazed into her boss's eyes and realized that Magdalena completely believed what she was saying.

"And number two?"

"Number two is that I would kill the murderer without hesitation to protect myself or someone I cared about."

Anna rolled her eyes. "How can you say that? You don't know how you'll react until there's a gun pointed at your head."

"I know because I know myself. I would not hesitate to kill if the situation demanded it. Any person who threatens another's life deserves death. And I am more intelligent than any murderer. I would not fail. Therefore, I have nothing to fear."

Anna shook her head and asked, "How did you get to be like that?"

Magdalena shrugged. "It's what I was raised to believe."

"Were you raised by a bunch of gangsters?"

"No. Bankers."

"Well, gee, remind me never to break into their banks."

Magdalena rose from the bed. "That would be inadvisable. I'm going back to bed now. See you in the morning, Anna." She turned off the overhead light and left the room.

"That's the darnedest thing I've ever heard," Anna muttered. "You think you know a person." Still, as she snuggled under the covers in a contemplative mood, she felt safer. If only she could have just a quarter of Magdalena's confidence, she'd never have nightmares again.

When Anna woke again later that morning, the room was already bright. Glancing at the floor beside her bed, she saw that Wendy was gone. She looked at the clock. It was nine-thirty. She'd overslept.

Springing out of bed, Anna trotted to the kitchen. Magdalena was reading the newspaper with a mug of coffee in her hand while Wendy was gnawing a rawhide bone under the table. Her boss was dressed and made up with her hair in a chignon. She glanced up at Anna.

"Good morning. I thought you needed the extra rest, so I took Wendy for a half-hour walk and fed her her breakfast." The dog's tail thumped on the floor.

"Thanks, that was kind of you. Have you had anything to eat?"

"No, because you said we were going to The Diner for breakfast. I've been looking forward to it, in fact."

"Great. Just give me ten minutes, and I'll be ready."

"Don't rush."

Anna took a quick shower, slapped on some moisturizer, pulled her hair into a ponytail, and dressed in corduroys and a warm pullover. She grabbed her purse and headed for the front door, where Magdalena was zipping up her boots. Her boss was wearing a green-and-blue print wrap-around dress with dark tights.

"What's it like outside?" Anna asked. "Do you want to walk, or take my car?"

"It's nippy, but there's no wind, and it's not snowing. I'd prefer to walk. Don't you, normally?"

"Sure, but I thought you might get cold. You're not dressed very warmly."

"I'll be fine. I want the full Saturday-morning-breakfast experience."

Anna grinned as Magdalena slipped into a tweed coat and eased a chocolate-brown beret over her hair.

"What?"

"Nothing. No two experiences are alike, though. I hope you enjoy yourself." Anna pulled on her cozy parka and bent to lace up her waterproof walking boots. Wendy lay on the floor, watching them from a short distance away.

"She seems to understand that she's not going with us," Magdalena said.

"She's used to my Saturday morning routine." Anna pulled a toque over her head and grabbed her mittens. Magdalena had just finished looping a woollen scarf in shades of brown and cream around her neck.

"Ready?"

Anna opened the door, and a gust of wind blew wet snow into her face. "Looks like the wind and the snow are back. Let's go."

They stepped onto the porch, climbed down the stairs to the driveway, and walked out into the road. There were no sidewalks on this part of Wistler Road. It was a six-block walk to Main Street, and they leant into the wind and crunched through ankle-deep snow most of the way. When they reached the downtown, Anna pointed out her friend's store, "May's Groceries and More," next to The Diner.

"May has an apartment over top of the store," Anna said as they paused outside the restaurant. "And that's Clive's tractor." It was parked in the choicest spot right outside the door.

"Just as you described it," Magdalena said. Her cheeks were flushed with cold.

"How do you do it?" Anna pointed at Magdalena's face.

"Do what?"

"You look perfect, with your face all pink and white, while my face is red and my nose is dripping." She pulled a tissue from her pocket and blew.

"Oh, Anna." Magdalena took her arm and pulled her up the walk to The Diner.

Once inside, her boss paused to study the glass display case containing one of Elvis Presley's Las Vegas costumes. It was positioned in pride of place next to the door. She looked questioningly at Anna.

"Didn't I tell you? Frank is a big Elvis fan." Anna pointed at the old-fashioned juke box next to the chrome counter. "He's got at least eight of Elvis's singles on that thing. Come on, I'll take you to meet Frank." She towed Magdalena to the counter, where Clive was eating his breakfast.

"Hey, Clive, I want you to meet my boss," Anna said, shouting into his ear.

"Huh?" Clive took a look at Magdalena and rose hastily to his feet, his napkin still tucked under his chin.

"Clive, this is Dr. Magdalena Lewis. Magdalena, this is my good friend, Clive Wampole."

"Pleased to meet you, Dr. Lewis." Clive's rough hand engulfed Magdalena's as he pumped it up and down.

"Please call me Magdalena. And don't let me interrupt your breakfast." Magdalena stared down at his plate. "Good heavens, what is that you're eating?" Clive's sausages, eggs, and hash browns were swimming in a red-brown fluid.

"Oh, Clive likes his hot sauce," Anna said.

The big man grinned. "Can't be too hot for me." He sat down again as Mary bustled up to the counter with a stack of dirty plates and cutlery in her arms. She paused, tilting her head at Magdalena.

"Hey, Anna! Who's your friend?"

"Morning, Mary. This is my boss, Dr. Lewis."

Judy sauntered out the swinging door from the kitchen just in time to hear the introduction.

"Your boss? She doesn't look old enough to be anybody's boss. Pleased to meet you, Dr. Lewis." She shook Magdalena's hand as Mary bumped the kitchen door open with her hip and disappeared inside.

"Thank you very much . . ."

"Judy. I'm Frank's girlfriend. Hey, Frank," she called, "come on out and meet Anna's boss."

Frank appeared a moment later, pushing Mary ahead of him through the door. He wiped his hands on his apron before offering one to Magdalena. She smiled as she shook it.

"Magdalena Lewis," she said. "Please call me Magdalena. Anna's told me what a great cook you are."

Anna smiled. "Keeps me coming back for breakfast every Saturday. *And* for dinner, when I'm too lazy to cook."

"Anna didn't mention how beautiful you are," Frank said. Judy elbowed him in the stomach.

"Oof!"

"You old flirt," Judy said with a smile.

Frank rubbed his stomach. "Hey, ladies, I've got a batch of the special in the oven, if you're interested."

"Interested?!" Anna turned to Magdalena. "You're in for a real treat."

"What's the special?"

"It's a kind of soufflé with eggs, cream, Swiss cheese, mushrooms, spinach, and ham. I serve it with baking powder biscuits," Frank said proudly.

"Frank's cooking brings the crowds in from Calgary whenever the weather's good," Judy said.

"Sounds wonderful," Magdalena replied. "I'd love to try it."

"Coffee?" Judy asked.

"Yes, please."

Judy turned to Anna. "Apple juice?"

"You bet."

Judy nodded and pushed Frank back into the kitchen.

"Catch you later, ladies," he called over his shoulder.

Anna turned to scan the dining area and spotted her friends at their table. Taking Magdalena's elbow, she pointed and said, "Erna and May are over there." Her friends waved. "They like to sit at the back so they can see what everyone else is doing. This way."

They weaved past the other diners, a family of four with a squalling baby and a toddler intent on emptying the salt shaker onto the table top, a mature couple placidly chewing their food without speaking to each other, a middle-aged man showing the latest pictures of his "darling" dogs to his boyfriend, and Mr. Andrews. He was sipping his coffee while working the crossword puzzle from the Saturday paper. Anna paused beside him.

"Morning, Mr. Andrews."

"Hmm."

"I'd like to introduce you to my boss, Dr. Lewis."

The retired rancher glanced up, glanced back at the puzzle, and did a double-take. Hopping to his feet, he winced and rubbed his right hip before extending his hand to Magdalena. He was smiling so broadly that Anna noticed a gold molar she had never seen before.

"That's Tom Andrews, ma'am," he said. "I'm real pleased to know you."

Magdalena smiled and gave him her hand. "Please call me Magdalena."

"I'd be happy to." He raised her hand to his mouth and kissed it. Anna almost toppled over with shock. Mr. Andrews just didn't do things like that.

"You know, it's a funny thing," Mr. Andrews added. "You're the spittin' image of a little girl I used to date back in high school. She had the same pretty green eyes as you, and the same blond hair. The colour of moonlight shining on a pond. Yessir, you sure do bring back happy memories to a fellow." He winked. "I'm still a bachelor, you know."

"That was Posy Miller, wasn't it, Tom?" Erna was standing right behind him, peeking over his shoulder. He glanced back at her and nodded.

"I haven't thought of her in years. What do you suppose happened to her?" Erna asked.

"She's had six kids and buried two husbands, last I heard. She's also self-published a knitting-pattern book."

"Did she really? Good for her. We all need something to occupy our golden years." Erna smiled at Magdalena. "But you're monopolizing Anna's guest, Tom, and here comes Judy with their breakfasts."

Mr. Andrews started. "Am I? Sorry about that, ladies. I'd better get back to my crossword puzzle so you gals can eat." He released Magdalena's hand and bowed. Anna couldn't take her eyes off him. It was like an old dog had suddenly learned new tricks.

"It was a pleasure meeting you, Tom," her boss said.

Mr. Andrews nodded and waited for the women to be seated at their table before resuming his place. Laying two steaming plates of the special before Anna and Magdalena, Judy returned with their beverages. Magdalena broke the band bundling her cutlery inside her paper napkin and picked up a fork.

"This certainly looks and smells delicious," she said.

Anna was peering at the retired rancher. "I've never seen Mr. Andrews pay much attention to anyone before, much less kiss a woman's hand and pay her compliments."

"You should have known him back in high school, dear," Erna said. "He had the soul of a poet then."

"You're kidding."

Erna shook her head. "I imagine that inheriting his father's ranch at the age of seventeen and running it for the next fifty-six years didn't give him much of a chance to develop it, but talents don't die completely." Smiling at Magdalena, Erna added, "We haven't been introduced yet. I'm Erna Dombrosky and this is my good friend, May Weston."

May nodded at Magdalena with a smile on her square, ruddy face. "Pleased to meet you, Magdalena."

Anna was still staring at Mr. Andrews and missed the exchange. She was trying to imagine him as a seventeen-year-old boy with a talent for writing poems to a pretty girl named Posy. Erna cleared her throat audibly, and Anna started.

"Huh? Sorry, I was wool-gathering." She removed her cutlery from her napkin and began eating. Erna and May were still eating their own breakfasts; May, apple pancakes and sausage, and Erna, maple-flavoured oatmeal topped with granola.

"We're so happy to finally meet you," Erna said to Magdalena. "Anna has told us so much about you. What brings you to Crane? I hope that nothing else has happened since Julia Moreland's death?"

"Any news about the poison?" May asked, propping her elbows on the table. Magdalena looked from them to Anna.

"I've been filling them in each week," Anna said. "I hope you don't mind."

"Not when your friends were so helpful with the other investigations," Magdalena said. "Go ahead."

"Let's see," Anna said, staring into space. "Detective Soo took Warren in for questioning last Saturday because they found poison in the glass of Lagavulin that Warren gave to Julia. But they let him go the same day."

Erna "tsked" and gazed sympathetically at Magdalena. Anna had already told them that Warren was Magdalena's boyfriend.

"At brunch with Lauren Moreland last Sunday, she said that Kevin was pleased to be president of Golden Farm Fertilizer, but Magdalena and I don't believe her."

May nodded.

"Rick Moreland was drunk or stoned at his mother's funeral last Tuesday, and told me that Julia's lawyer, Tobias Rapp, was his boyfriend. But when Magdalena and I visited Tobias's office on Thursday, he swore that he hadn't disclosed Julia's will prematurely to Rick. We don't know what to think about that.

"I went Christmas shopping with Beatrix Sumpter and had dinner with her and Oliver on Wednesday. He's the president of the fertilizer company, remember? According to Oliver, Julia didn't tell him that she planned for Kevin to be president of the company. Plus, I found out that Beatrix shoplifts."

"I thought you said that she's disabled?" May asked.

"She is. She has multiple sclerosis and asthma."

"Poor thing," Erna said.

"Latona Taylor, Julia's personal assistant, was found dead in her apartment on Thursday."

"No!" Erna and May said together.

"The police are testing to see if it was water hemlock poisoning again. Someone sent me a threatening note with a box of chocolates at work on Friday. The police are checking the chocolates for poison. The university surveillance footage showed someone hacking into the security system outside our department corridor around two o'clock that morning, but the police had already arrested Kevin by then because his fingerprints were found on a disposable coffee cup found in the trash in Latona's apartment. So we don't know how Kevin could have delivered the note and the chocolates to my office when he had just been arrested, but Magdalena still thinks Kevin poisoned both Julia and Latona." She turned to her boss. "Have I forgotten anything?"

"Someone's been embezzling money from Kevin's department at Westmore." Magdalena gestured at her plate with her fork. "The special is truly delicious."

"Right." Anna turned to May and Erna. "That's it."

There was a moment of silence before Anna's friends began squawking.

"Thanks for meeting me today, Mr. Moreland," Detective Soo said as she stepped from the elevator outside Westmore's executive offices. Warren nodded and indicated that she should precede him.

"I'm happy to. Anything I can do to help." He followed her through the deserted halls and past his secretary's empty desk to enter his office. He shut the door behind them, just in case.

"Have a seat." Soo took one of the chairs in front of his desk while he sat behind it.

"Are you normally at work on a Saturday?" the detective asked.

"That depends on how busy we are. I can get a lot done when there aren't any interruptions."

"Then I'll try to be brief."

"No, no, I didn't mean . . ."

Soo waved her hand. "Don't worry about it. I'm busy, too. Do you have a recent picture of Kevin? I tried to download one from the Westmore site, but I could only find pictures of you and Mrs. Moreland."

Warren stared at her. "I'm not sure. Maybe. Why?"

The detective leaned back in her chair. "Just dotting the i's and crossing the t's."

"Oh? Is there anything wrong?"

"No. Your auditors were very helpful. They were able to show our Economic Crime Unit the trail the embezzled money took through Westmore, but that was as far as they could go. Our guys pursued it through a couple of dummy bank accounts until it showed up in a personal account belonging to Kevin. They also discovered some transactions he had made from his home computer. Kevin wasn't particularly careful in covering his tracks. Between that and his prints on the coffee cup found at Latona Taylor's apartment, it looks pretty bad for him. It won't be long before we get the toxicology reports back. If they show water hemlock in the contents of Ms. Taylor's stomach and the coffee cups, we'll be able to begin building a case that he poisoned your stepmother, too."

"I'm sorry to hear that," Warren said. "Kevin and I were never close, but I find it hard to believe that he's a murderer and an embezzler."

"Why is that?"

"I don't know. He's always been so reliable. Kept his head down, worked hard, and did everything Julia told him to do."

Soo nodded. "Sometimes the quiet ones are the ones you have to watch out for."

"What does Kevin have to say about all this?"

"He denies it all. He says he must have been set up. So that's why I'm being so careful. When our guys were tracking the transactions on Kevin's bank account, they found a cash withdrawal for eight thousand dollars made a couple of months back. Do you know what that means?"

Warren shook his head.

"For that much money, your brother would have been forced to have seen a teller. No ATM machine carries that much money, plus there are limits on how much money you can withdraw. I've got the branch location, and they're open until two today. So I'm going to check it out myself."

"That's why you want Kevin's picture?"

"Right. I figure anyone who withdraws that kind of cash is going to be remembered. So, can you give me a picture?"

Warren pushed back his chair and stood up. "There's a picture of him in the annual report. Let me get it for you."

Anna and her breakfast companions were still sorting out the murder investigation details long after they had finished eating. The dishes had been cleared, and they were sipping tea.

"I think I finally have it straight," Erna said, "but you really should have called us during the week." She peered over her cup at Anna, still looking like a disapproving school teacher.

"Sorry. It all happened so quickly."

"That's all right, dear. I understand how engrossing these cases can be."

"I'm interested to hear what you think," Magdalena said. "Anna said you're always insightful."

Erna smiled at the compliment before responding. "Obviously, the police have arrested the wrong man."

Magdalena raised her eyebrows. "Why do you think that? Because Kevin was arrested before the man on the university surveillance footage arrived with the chocolates?"

"Not necessarily. He could have had an accomplice," Erna said. Magdalena nodded. "But embezzling money from a big corporation like Westmore and successfully hiding it for a year requires a superior understanding of accounting practices and computer systems. Would you say that Kevin Moreland possesses that?"

"No, his background is in engineering," Magdalena replied. "But an accomplice may have had that knowledge."

"Terribly risky, to give someone that much power over you, wouldn't you say?"

Magdalena's face was impassive as she gazed wordlessly back at Erna.

"And Kevin had overtaxed his personal finances, too," Erna said. "Two mortgages, a loan, and credit cards over their limits, I believe Anna said. If he were embezzling money from Westmore, why would he allow his situation to become so desperate?"

"Perhaps to hide his criminal activities?"

"I wouldn't think so. That's going too far. Better not to draw attention to himself by living quietly within his means. And Kevin would have to be incredibly stupid to embezzle from his own department, not to mention leaving the coffee cup with his finger prints in Latona Taylor's apartment."

Magdalena shrugged. "If it wasn't Kevin, then who do you think is responsible?"

"I honestly don't know. I assume that Julia discovered the embezzlement and was about to denounce the person responsible to the press. When she wasn't deterred by the threatening notes, the embezzler was forced to kill her. Latona Taylor knew something to implicate the murderer, so she had to be silenced too. How tragic that both women were killed so shortly before the embezzling was discovered. It's as if their murders were for nothing."

"It's stupid that Julia was killed for money, period," May said. "When you think of all the dough she must have had, why didn't Kevin just ask her for help?"

"I don't know," Magdalena replied. "Perhaps he did, and Julia wouldn't give it to him. Warren didn't mention it."

May glanced at Anna. "What do you think, doll?"

Anna checked her watch. "I don't know, but it's getting onto noon. Frank's going to want us to leave before the lunch crowd arrives. Isn't it time we cleared out?"

"Wow, is it that late?" May asked. "My son was expecting me back at the store five minutes ago. My daughter-in-law wants to go Christmas shopping this afternoon. I've got to run." She jumped to her feet.

"It's been fascinating," Erna said, rising with the other women. "Thank you for sharing your thoughts with us."

"Yeah, I can't wait to hear how it turns out," May said, wrapping her jacket around her shoulders. "What are you two doing this afternoon?"

"Baking," Anna said.

Detective Soo was shown into a small office at the bank. It was totally depersonalized except for a framed photograph of a smiling man and a woman holding a baby in her arms. Soo picked up the only reading material and began paging through a report on mutual fund investments. Just when she was about to shoot herself from boredom when a young blonde wearing a pink blouse over a black skirt walked into the room. She shut the door and turned to look at the detective. Soo patted the chair beside her, and the blonde perched next to her.

"I'm Detective Sandra Soo of the Calgary Police." Soo showed the young woman her ID. "You're . . ."

"Kellie Lester."

"You're a bank teller, right?"

The young woman nodded.

"How long have you worked at this branch?"

Kellie paused to think. "About eleven months. I started right after Christmas last year."

"Excellent. Now, Kellie, the police want to identify a man who withdrew a lot of money from a personal account last October 17th. Eight thousand dollars, as a matter of fact. Your manager said you remember helping him?"

"That's right. It was such a large sum, I couldn't forget. Besides, he was so good looking, and friendly, too. We joked around a lot during the transaction. He was very nice."

"Glad to hear it." Soo pulled the Westmore annual report from her lap and opened it to a spot marked by a yellow sticky note. She folded the page back and held it up for the teller to see. It was a colour photograph of Kevin Moreland wearing a suit and tie.

"Can you tell me if this was the man you helped?"

Kellie stared at the photo with a slight frown. "I think so. He looks kind of different there, though. Kind of stiff. He was dressed more casually when he came to the bank. In jeans and a nice cashmere sweater. I remember because he said the sweater was blue to match his eyes."

"I see." Soo flipped through a few more pages and held up the report again. "How about this photo?"

The young woman smiled. "That's right. That's a better picture of him. Maybe it's because he wasn't smiling in the other picture?"

Soo nodded. "That's probably it. Now, if you could just give me your contact information, I'll let you get back to work."

In The Diner, Erna asked, "Do you do much baking, Magdalena?"

Magdalena managed to snort gracefully. "Never."

"I didn't think so. Well, I'm looking forward to seeing you and Anna at the dinner dance tonight. The Rotary Club always decorates the community centre so nicely."

"Plus the food is good because Frank does the catering," May said, still lingering. "Hey, Judy, what's Frank giving us for dinner tonight?"

Judy looked up from stacking clean mugs next to the coffee machines. "Roast beef."

"Good. He always makes roasted potatoes with beef instead of mashed," May said. "Much nicer. Come on, Erna. I'll run you home before I go back to work. There's too much snow for you to walk."

The four women spent the next few minutes paying their bills before waving goodbye on the sidewalk. May and Erna turned to the grocery-store parking lot while Anna and Magdalena retraced their steps home. During their walk, Anna noticed that Magdalena was being unusually quiet.

"I hope you weren't offended by anything Erna said at breakfast," Anna said when they were only a block from the house. "She's used to calling a spade a spade."

"What?" Magdalena glanced up from the road. "No, I wasn't offended. I prefer people to be direct."

"That's good, because they don't come any more direct than Erna and May. I just wondered when you didn't say anything after we left."

"I've been reconsidering. Erna made some good points about Kevin."

"Really?" Anna was impressed that Erna's reasoning had affected her boss. Usually it took a ton of arguing to change Magdalena's mind.

"Yes. Erna is looking at the case from an outsider's point of view. I, on the other hand, have allowed myself to get caught up in the emotions of the crimes. Just because

Kevin disliked Julia more than Rick and Warren did doesn't mean that he killed her."

"That's true."

"It certainly gives one something to think about."

Anna let them into the house, where Wendy greeted them with much rear-end wiggling and tail wagging. "Yes, I love you, too," Anna said, getting down on one knee to hug her pet. Magdalena watched them from the door.

"So, are we really going to bake?"

"Don't you think it would be good to try it just this once?" Anna asked with a smile.

Magdalena shrugged. "I'll try almost anything once."

Anna bustled ahead into the kitchen. Opening the cupboard door, she removed milk-chocolate chips, graham wafer crumbs, sugar, shredded coconut, and a tin of sweetened condensed milk.

"Okay, we're going to make 'Hello Dolly' squares. They're one of my favourites. Do you like chocolate?"

"It's pleasant."

Anna rolled her eyes. "Ohmigod." She cut off the corner of the chocolate chips' bag and held it out to Magdalena. "Give me your hand."

Magdalena held out her hand obediently, and Anna poured a small pile into it. Magdalena stared down at the chocolate.

"Eat them," Anna said.

"Isn't that wasteful?"

"Oh for heaven's sake, eat them!"

Magdalena threw the chips back into her mouth as if she were downing a shot and chewed.

"Well?"

"Very nice."

Anna smiled. "Good. I used to make my squares with semi-sweet chocolate, but when they came out with milk-chocolate chips, they worked even better."

She opened the fridge and took out a tub of margarine. Nudging the door closed with her hip, she measured a half cup into a bowl and set it to melting in the microwave. While that was happening, Anna pulled out a baking tin and set it on the table next to Magdalena. Ripping a sheet of waxed paper from its roll, she handed it to her boss with the margarine tub.

"Here, you grease the pan."

"How much should I use?"

Anna scooped out a chunk with the waxed paper. "That much."

Magdalena greased the pan while Anna retrieved the melted margarine and began mixing it with the graham wafer crumbs and sugar.

"So, while we're baking, why don't we do something else you've never done before?"

Magdalena raised her eyes inquiringly.

"Girl talk."

"That's fine, although I have done that before. What do you want to talk about?"

"Men, of course. Tell me what attracted you to Warren?"

Magdalena leaned back in her chair and watched Anna press the crumb mixture into the pan.

"Warren and I were introduced by a mutual friend at a symphony concert. Warren was very attractive, of course, and was able to talk quite competently about classical music during the intermission, so I agreed to going out for a drink with him afterward."

Anna nodded while scattering chocolate chips and coconut over the crust.

"I researched him on the internet the next day and discovered that he had held a series of responsible positions with Westmore, the country's second-largest oil company. He was also blameless of any criminal or scandalous activities, or at least none drawing the attention of the press."

"Go on," Anna said, pausing from dribbling the condensed milk over the other ingredients to stare at her. "You fascinate me."

"He was a supporter of the arts, sat on the committees of two international charities, and even volunteered occasionally at a soup kitchen. On subsequent appointments when we had dinner together, or, on one occasion, attended the Edmonton Ballet, he voiced sympathy for feminist issues and disparaged the provincial government's practice of inadequately funding education. That led me believe that our belief systems might be compatible."

Anna popped the pan into the oven and shut the door. "This bakes for thirty minutes. Then what happened?"

"I determined that Warren was more than acceptable as a companion. As a matter of fact, he had excellent potential as a life partner. I'm thirty-nine, Anna. It was not in my plan to marry any sooner because I had to finish my doctorate degree and concentrate on my career first, plus I have no interest in having children. But I believe that allying myself with a mate supportive of my goals and interests will be beneficial to my emotional and physical wellbeing, to the point of prolonging my life."

Anna stared at her from across the table. "Really?"

Magdalena nodded. "Studies have shown that married men live longer. Although there are differences in the emotional requirements of men and women, and I've never seen a study on the life-prolonging effect of marriage on females, I presume that it still holds true for women."

Anna clutched her boss's arm. "But how does Warren make you feel, Magdalena? Do the two of you laugh together, for instance?"

"Sometimes. Fortunately he is not amused by slapstick humour or crude jokes. I couldn't abide a man who would laugh at someone breaking wind or doing himself an injury." She closed her eyes and shuddered.

"And how are you in bed together?" Anna asked in a lower voice.

She saw a glint in her boss's eyes.

"That is *more* than satisfactory," Magdalena said. "You were speaking to Alice about my ballet career the other day. I've seen my share of men at the top of their careers wearing nothing more than a dance belt and a leotard. Warren fares well by comparison."

Anna grinned and nodded. "Good on you, boss."

"And what about you and Sergeant Tremaine? I remember that your relationship was more antagonistic than sympathetic in the beginning. Have you remedied that?"

"Mostly. I lead more with my heart than Charlie does. He also plays everything by the book when it comes to work, which drives me crazy sometimes. But we agree on the important things, such as honesty and loyalty. He's an old-fashioned guy at heart, which I like."

"Wasn't there another young man here in town who fancied you? An RCMP constable?

Anna nodded, fingering some graham crumbs on the table top. "Steve Walker. Yes, he's still around. We're good friends, though. More like a brother and sister, really. Not to mention he's involved with Tiernay Rae now."

"I remember you telling me about her. She's the young witch who runs a holistic store, isn't she?"

"Yes, plus she's a massage therapist. She seemed to be quite a handful for Steve at first. I thought the two of them were going to burn each other out, judging by the way they couldn't keep their hands off each other, but they're still together. Of course, it's only been a couple of months."

"Will I see them tonight at the party?"

"You should."

"Good. I'll let you know if you've made the right choice."

Anna rolled her eyes and got up to wipe the table.

18

Anna and Magdalena were late arriving at the community centre that night. Anna had taken one look at Magdalena when her boss emerged from the bedroom and shaken her head.

"I won't do?" Magdalena asked. She peered down at her sleeveless black dress with silver beading that glittered as she moved.

"No, you look beautiful, but Mr. Andrews is going to be awfully disappointed if you don't wear your hair down."

"But your hair is up."

Anna had taken special pains with her hair that evening, styling it into a soft updo with tendrils that curled around her face. She was wearing a strapless red dress with a fitted top and flared skirt, teaming it with a lacy black shrug and black heels.

"But I always wear my hair down, so having it up is special for me. Besides, I don't have hair 'the colour of moonlight shining on a pond.'"

Magdalena smiled. "All right. I'll wear it down for Mr. Andrews' sake."

They arrived at the event in Magdalena's black BMW, but had to jump across a snowbank in their heels to reach the shovelled sidewalk leading to the centre's door. Anna was glad that the hall looked as homey and inviting as it did once they were inside. It made her feel proud in front of her boss, who she knew was more accustomed to big-ticket events than small-town gatherings.

The hall was wood-panelled with tables of six arranged before a glowing Christmas tree with prettily-wrapped boxes beneath. The tree must have been freshly cut because Anna could still smell its delicious pine scent. Each table was covered in white linen and lit by three red candles placed beneath a hurricane lamp. The candlelight glittered softly on the tables' place settings and water glasses and was echoed by the artificial candles decorated with ivy and berries on the windowsills.

"We're sitting at table number eight," Anna said, leading Magdalena across the floor as she nodded to friends along the way. Anna had lived in Crane for four years now, and while she had lived in cities with more attractions — like Toronto and Montreal — the little town was the only place that felt like home anymore.

Sherman Mason stood when Anna and Magdalena arrived at their table. The cemetery custodian had put on a few necessary pounds in the past month and a half since he had started eating May's cooking, so the navy suit he wore didn't bag quite as much as it had at his wife's funeral the previous winter. May, who sat next to him, had visited Amy Bright, the town's beautician, and her short hair curled attractively around her face. She was wearing a long, blue-and-black print dress with a matching black jacket that she had worn to her son's wedding many years before. Erna was sitting on May's other side, her white hair dressed in its usual bun, but she was wearing delicate pearl drop earrings and a strand of pearls that she had inherited from her mother over a grey lacy dress.

"Sherman, I don't think you've had a chance to meet Dr. Lewis yet," Anna said.

"How do you do, Dr. Lewis?"

"Very well, thank you. Please do call me Magdalena."

Sherman nodded, and the two women sat down beside Erna. There was an open bottle of red wine on the table, and Erna had a glass of it beside her plate. She passed the bottle to Anna, who poured some for her boss and herself before offering it to May.

"No, thank you," May said. "Sherman and I don't care for any." She winked at Anna, who knew that May wasn't imbibing in support of Sherman, who was an alcoholic.

Dinner was delicious. Anna had expected as much from Frank and his hired staff. He sat at a table with Judy, eyeing the wait staff as they served the salad. The main course was roast beef and roasted potatoes, as had been promised, with a dab of horse radish mayonnaise and green and yellow beans. Dessert was a thick slice of homemade chocolate yule log. Even Magdalena seemed to enjoy it, finishing half of her dessert before lowering her fork.

When the dishes had been cleared and people were relaxing with cups of coffee or tea, Rotary Club President Eddy Mason, who was also the staff sergeant at the Crane RCMP station, strolled into the middle of the floor holding a microphone. He was a short, rotund man who played Santa Claus for the kids at the Rotary Christmas party.

"How're you all doing this evening? Having a good time?"

People smiled and nodded.

"That's great. It was a good meal, wasn't it?"

More smiling and nodding.

"You bet. Let's have a round of applause for fellow-Rotarian Frank Crow, who not only made us a delicious meal, but donated his services tonight. You did good, Frank. Stand up and take a bow."

Smiling, Frank stood while the guests applauded and hooted.

"We'd also like to thank the decorating committee, who did such a terrific job making the centre look nice," Eddy added, "and the ticket sellers, who raised $712.00 toward a new swing-set for the park. Let's give all those hard-working folks a big round of applause." He nodded his approval as people applauded enthusiastically.

"That's right. Now we have some door prizes to hand out. Your ticket stubs were all mixed together before the party started, and I had the honour of pulling out the three winning numbers. You all look at your tickets now as the numbers are called out. First prize is a manicure at The Bright House of Beauty. Hey, Amy, why don't you come over here to announce the winning number?"

Amy, a curvaceous woman about Anna's age, was wearing a short, strapless green dress with a plunging neckline. When she stood up, there were whistles mixed with the applause. More than one frowning woman turned to shush her husband.

Eddie handed her the winning ticket stub and the microphone. In her stilettos, Amy stood a half-head taller than the staff sergeant.

"The winning number," she said in her breathless, husky voice, "is 1282."

"I won!" Betty Hiller shouted. Anna's plump next-door neighbour was sitting with her husband, Jeff, at a table directly across the floor. Amy smiled and waved at Betty before sashaying back to her seat.

"Now, the next prize is for an hour-long massage with Tiernay Rae at The Healing Hands store. I don't mind telling you that I would love to win this prize. Guys, wouldn't you love to win this one, too?"

More whistling and foot-stomping.

"Uh-huh, but I can't, because I pulled the winning ticket stub. Here it is, ladies and gentlemen. Tiernay, why don't you help me by calling out the number?"

Anna looked at the table beside hers. Tiernay was sitting there with Steve's arm draped around her shoulders, her smooth cap of flaming-red hair hard to ignore. She rose, a graceful goddess in a high-waisted white dress with long, fluttering sleeves and flat sandals. As she strode across the floor, her shapely leg flashed in a thigh-high slit. She stared imperiously at Eddy, who handed her the winning stub.

"1194," she read in a clear voice.

There was silence as the guests glanced at each other.

"Everyone, check your tickets, please. That's 1194," Eddy roared.

"Hey, Clive, that's you," a man shouted. "You won!"

The farmer, who was seated at the table with his mother, blushed a beet-red. There was laughter mixed with the cheering and applause this time. Tiernay studied Clive with an appraising look before crossing the floor to squat down and talk with him.

"And now for the third and last prize," Eddy announced. "This lovely floral decoration, donated by May Weston of May's Groceries and More." Eddy was holding the arrangement in his arms, a red-and-green sleigh stuffed with red roses and ivy. "You all had a chance to check it out when you entered the hall this evening. May, will you announce the winning number for us, please?"

May jumped up from her chair with a big smile and trotted toward Eddy. She waved at the audience, most of whom she had known for the twenty-eight years since she and her now-deceased husband, who had died unexpectedly of a heart attack six years before, had opened the store. Eddy handed her the winning ticket stub with a bow.

"The number is . . . 1232. That's 1232." May looked inquiringly at the audience.

"I believe that's me," Magdalena called out. Anna looked at her boss with delight. How nice that she had won the prize.

Magdalena walked across the floor to May and Eddy amidst enthusiastic applause. Many heads bent as people whispered to each other. No doubt they were wondering who this elegant woman was with her sparkling dress and silky hair swinging half-way down her back.

Eddy handed her the flowers while May grinned. "Thank you very much," Magdalena said into the mike before heading back to the table with the flowers in her arms.

"Congratulations," Anna said. "Now you have something to remember us by." Magdalena nodded and looked pleased.

The guests pushed the tables back against the walls and spent the next couple of hours dancing to music provided by a DJ. Sherman obliged all four women at his table by asking them to dance, a sheen of perspiration on his leonine face by the time he got to Magdalena. She had not lacked for other partners, either, including two dances with Mr. Andrews, who two-stepped her around the hall, and Steve, who gyrated with her to a popular number. Anna had done pretty well for herself as well, dancing with Sherman, Frank, Clive, and John Fox Child, the corporal who had headed up the Halloween murder investigation. John had just escorted her back to her table, and Anna was thinking that she was just about ready to go, when a hand touched her shoulder. She looked up into Steve's darkly handsome face.

"Care to dance?" the young constable inquired.

Anna smiled. "Sure."

She was glad that Steve had asked her to dance. She hadn't seen much of him over the past two months since he and Tiernay had become a couple. Tiernay's jealousy of their friendship had been the problem, but if he had felt comfortable enough to ask her to dance tonight, perhaps the young woman had gotten over it.

Steve escorted Anna to the floor, his hand resting lightly on her back. A new song began playing, Etta James's sultry "At Last." As Steve pulled her into his arms, Anna couldn't help wondering if Tiernay was watching. She relaxed, however, when she spied the young woman swaying with John on the dance floor.

"You look beautiful tonight, Anna," Steve said.

"Thanks. You look handsome, too." She meant it. Steve was wearing a black shirt with black dress pants and a slim green tie. The fitted clothes showcased his tall, muscular frame.

He'd had a birthday in November and now he was twenty-nine. Eleven years her junior. The age disparity had been a problem, and had also been a problem when she fell for Charlie, who was nine years younger than she. Anna was glad that Charlie had convinced her of its unimportance, however, and glad that Steve had found someone else to love. She only hoped that Tiernay was worthy of him.

"Been staying out of trouble, Steve?" she asked.

He grinned lazily down at her. "Haven't broken any laws yet." The smile evaporated. "But what's this I've been hearing about you being mixed up with Julia Moreland's murder? What's that about?"

Anna shrugged. "It's nothing, really. They've arrested one of her sons, and now the Calgary police are just putting all the pieces together."

"I'm glad. I never seem to get tired of worrying about you."

Anna patted Steve's cheek. "I know. You're a good friend."

He rested his head against hers, and they didn't talk for the remainder of the song. Anna noticed that he hadn't mentioned Charlie even though the two men had worked together last spring. Steve must have heard that Charlie would be arriving for the holidays. Well, she'd better not bring Charlie up, too.

The song ended, and Steve escorted her back to the table. "Have a good Christmas, Anna," he said, raising her hand to his lips and kissing it. When he turned to go, Magdalena raised her eyebrows, but Anna shrugged. Reclaiming her seat, she even yawned.

"You ready to go home yet?" Anna asked.

Magdalena nodded.

"Me, too." But it took half an hour of goodbyes, Magdalena with her prize in her arms, before they finally reached the centre's door and escaped.

Sunday morning, Anna tiptoed out of bed at eight thirty to take Wendy for a walk, letting Magdalena sleep in. Returning to the bungalow, however, she smelt bacon frying and hurried to the kitchen to check it out. Magdalena, wearing a cream-coloured silk robe, stood at the stove cooking bacon and eggs. She smiled and suggested that Anna had better get busy making toast. The two women enjoyed a leisurely breakfast and were still able to make ten-thirty Mass. Anna had been surprised when her boss had volunteered to come with her.

"It will be nice to see some of the people I met last night," Magdalena said on the walk to church. "And I find religious services peaceful. They give me time to think."

Returning home, Anna asked her boss if she had given any more thought to Julia's murder investigation, and Magdalena nodded.

"The more I think about it, the more it seems true that Kevin didn't embezzle the money. Still, I wish that we could provide Detective Soo with proof of his and Lauren's innocence. We wouldn't want the real killer to get away with the crimes."

"Hmm." Anna turned the key in the lock. "Maybe there is something we could do."

"What do you have in mind?" Magdalena asked as the two women removed their coats and boots.

"Well, Kevin was arrested over two days ago. That's enough time for things to cool down, don't you think? What do you suppose Lauren is doing right now?"

"I have no idea. Discussing her husband's defence with his lawyer?"

"She was kind enough to talk to us when you were upset about Warren. What do you say we return the favour? Let's give her a call and see how she's doing with Kevin's arrest."

"Good idea." Magdalena pulled her cell phone from her purse and punched in Lauren's number. "I'll put the call on speaker phone," she added. Anna nodded and counted the rings. The call was answered on the fourth.

"Yes? What is it?" Lauren's tone was impatient.

"Lauren, it's me, Magdalena. How are you? I was so sorry to hear of Kevin's arrest."

"Magdalena, thank goodness it's you. I've been going crazy with all the phone calls from the press." Lauren sounded as if she were about to cry, and Anna and Magdalena exchanged an incredulous glance. Lauren's abrupt change of emotion was suspicious.

"I thought as much. This ordeal must be almost as hard on you as it is on poor Kevin."

"More so, because Kevin isn't being peppered with phone calls in prison."

That's true, Anna thought. *Just questions from the police and his lawyer, lucky guy.*

"I truly feel for you, dear," Magdalena said. "Is there anything I can do to help?"

"What? No!" In a calmer voice, Lauren added, "I'm afraid not, although it's sweet of you to ask. I'll just have to be strong until Kevin can prove his innocence and be set free."

"You poor thing. Are you sure I can't take you out for dinner? It will take your mind off things."

"No, that's impossible. I can't leave the house. I'd be swarmed by reporters. Some of them are out front right now."

"The vultures. What if I dropped by to sit with you instead? I could bring some take-out. I wouldn't mind braving the reporters."

"You're a darling, Magdalena, but I'll have to say no. I was just about to lie down. I got no sleep at all Thursday night when the police took Kevin. They had a search warrant and they tore the place apart. It was terrible watching them violate our privacy. I hardly slept last night, thinking about it."

"Of course not. I understand perfectly. Well, you've got my number if you need anything. I'd be happy to help, Lauren. Anytime at all."

"Thank you, you're so kind, but I really must go now, darling."

"Take good care of yourself. Goodbye."

Magdalena ended the call and looked at Anna. "What do you think?"

"It sounded about what I expected from Lauren. She was more concerned about herself than she was about Kevin. Still, she did seem in a big hurry to get rid of you.

You'd think she'd have enjoyed wallowing in your sympathy." Anna paused to think. "I wonder."

"What do you wonder?"

"Well, there are two things we could do this afternoon. I could teach you how to make fudge, or we could drive into Calgary to see if there really are reporters swarming Lauren's house. You were calling her cell phone. We can't even be sure that she was at home."

Magdalena nodded. "To tell you the truth, I don't really want to make fudge."

"You're kidding? Don't you want to impress Warren with your domestic skills? You know that the way to a man's heart is through his stomach."

Magdalena stared at her impassively.

Anna smiled. "I was just yanking your chain. All right, let's visit Lauren."

19

Anna and Magdalena parked on the street outside Lauren and Kevin's home. The weather had turned nasty with sleet. The house was a spacious two-storey, featuring a stone façade and a turret, and was situated across the street from a park. A squirrel skittered across the road in front of them. On the miserable Sunday afternoon, it was the only thing moving.

"A decided lack of reporters," Magdalena said, shutting off the engine.

Anna nodded. "Let's see if she's at home."

They slid across a sidewalk slick with ice to the front door. Magdalena rang the doorbell while Anna climbed into the bushes to cup her hands and peer through the picture window. She shook her head as she stepped back up onto the porch.

"She's not in the living room or in the kitchen."

Magdalena nodded and pressed the doorbell again. Anna left to clamber down the porch stairs and peer up at the second floor windows. Maybe Lauren was peeking at them from a bedroom, but there was no sign of her. Magdalena joined Anna on the walkway.

"She doesn't seem to be home."

"No," Anna said. "How about we check out the store, as long as we're here? She may have decided to do some work this afternoon rather than take a nap."

"Yes, we should give her the benefit of the doubt." They slid back to the car and drove downtown through the sloppy streets. The stores surrounding Lauren's were closed, the few pedestrians on the sidewalk hurrying purposely through the cold. Magdalena was able to park directly in front of the store. The two women climbed out of the car and jogged to the door.

"Brr, I think it's getting colder," Anna said. The sleet had stopped, but a snowflake caught on her eyelash. "Oh, good," she said in a sarcastic tone, blinking it away.

The black curtains were still drawn across the store windows. Anna raised her hand to rap on the door, but Magdalena caught her arm.

"What?" Anna asked, glancing over her shoulder.

"Rather than informing Lauren of our presence, should she be inside, let's have a look around the back. If she lied to us about being at home, I'd like to know what she's doing here at the store."

Anna hesitated, the familiar fear making her stomach tighten again. It was one thing for the two of them to brazen it out with Lauren at the store door, but spying on her around back? Anna wasn't sure that she was up for it.

"Just a look," Magdalena urged. "She may not even be here."

Anna nodded. It was silly to be afraid of nothing.

The women followed the sidewalk around to the lane-way behind the stores. It was dusky with buildings surrounding them on all sides. In fact, as Anna crept down the lane-way behind Magdalena, it felt as if the buildings were closing in on them.

They counted the stores to determine which one was Lauren's. When they found the right back door, they discovered a van parked next to it with a light on over the stoop. Magdalena and Anna exchanged a look before

Magdalena bent low and scuttled up to the driver's door. Straightening, she peered inside. After a moment, she turned and gave Anna a "thumbs-up" signal. Then Magdalena circled the front of the van and disappeared along its side. What was she up to now? Anna held her breath. There was a "click," and the rear passenger door slid slowly open, Anna wincing at every squeak. The van swayed gently as Magdalena climbed inside.

Was her boss crazy? Craning her head in every direction to make sure that no one was watching, Anna hurried around the vehicle. Magdalena was kneeling inside with her back to Anna.

"What are you doing?" Anna whispered. Magdalena turned, holding a purple box with white tissue paper draped over the sides. In the van's interior light, Anna glimpsed something yellow

"There are half a dozen boxes in here," Magdalena murmured. "It looks as though Lauren is preparing to make some deliveries."

Anna leaned forward to grasp her boss's arm. "Nothing wrong with that. Leave it. Let's get out of here before she comes back." Magdalena nodded, refolded the tissue, and slipped the lid back on top. Then she crawled backwards out of the van, climbed back down to the pavement, and eased the door shut. Anna sighed and turned to go.

"Wait a minute," Magdalena whispered, taking Anna's arm. Anna flinched. "I'm just going to have a peek inside the back door."

"No way!" Anna's voice was shrill. "She's bound to see you."

"I'll be very careful." Anna heard something jingle, and Magdalena pressed her keys into Anna's hand. "I won't be more than a minute or two. You go back to the car and start the engine. Stay warm."

"Magdalena!" Anna mouthed after her, but her boss was already scurrying to the back door. Anna grimaced. Part of her wanted to stay, but the other part, a much bigger part, wanted to get the hell out of there. She watched Magdalena reach for the door knob. Anna made up her mind. If the door was unlocked, she would go wait in the car. There was no way she'd be able to watch Magdalena open the door. This was so stupid, spying on a woman who was just trying to get caught up on her orders.

The knob turned, and Magdalena eased the door open. That was it for Anna. Running on her tiptoes all the way down the lane-way, she rounded the corner and slid onto the sidewalk. She half-expected someone to say, 'Aha! Caught you,' but there was no one there. Sighing in relief, Anna hurried to the car, unlocked the driver's door, and dived behind the wheel. She locked the doors behind her and turned the key in the ignition. They'd only been gone seven or eight minutes, so it wasn't long before comforting warm air began to blow out of the heater. Anna turned the fan up high and leaned back against the seat, letting the heat melt away her tension. Fear was exhausting.

Anna lay against the seat for several minutes, her head nestled against the headrest and her eyes closed. After that, however, a niggling doubt began to chip at her sense of wellbeing. Where was Magdalena? She should be back by now. Anna opened her eyes and glanced at the time on the dashboard. At least it had stopped snowing, but the mid-afternoon light was waning under an overcast sky. She'd give her boss five more minutes. Maybe Lauren had come out with more packages, and Magdalena was hiding in someone else's doorway, waiting for Lauren to finish packing the van.

Anna frowned. On the other hand, maybe Lauren had caught Magdalena, and her boss was spinning some excuse for being in the building. Maybe they were arguing right this minute. Anna twisted in her seat so that she could keep an eye on both the store door and the lane-way. But five minutes passed without any sign of her boss.

Anna glanced at her purse on the car floor. Her cell was inside. Maybe she should try calling Magdalena? Then she wouldn't have to leave sanctuary of the car. But she gave up the idea immediately. If Magdalena were still in hiding, the ring would give her away.

She was two minutes past her five-minute deadline. Anna stared out the car window, trying to decide what to do. A third minute passed. Damn, it was inevitable. She had to get out of the car and go back to the lane-way.

Wrenching the key in the ignition, she turned off the engine and shoved the key ring into her coat pocket. Anna locked the car behind her and muttered at Magdalena's stupidity as she strode down the sidewalk, trying not to think about what she was about to do. She slackened her pace on reaching the lane-way, however, to sneak past the other stores. There was no sign of Magdalena as she approached Lauren's. Anna hugged the wall to edge past the van, peering inside, but there was no one there.

Willing her boss to emerge as she tiptoed closer, Anna reached the door, but it remained stubbornly closed. If it were still unlocked, she was going to have to slip inside to look for Magdalena.

Trying to calm her thudding heart, Anna emerged from the shadows into the yellow light pooling around the door. Quickly she removed her right glove and stashed it in her pocket. The keys jingled as she brushed against them, making her wince. Her left leg began to tremble uncontrollably. Anna reached for the door knob, her fingers gripping the cold metal, and eased it to the right. There was no resistance, and she rotated it slowly until the mechanism made a small "click."

Holding her breath, Anna inched the door open. She could glimpse a portion of grey wall inside. Without warning, someone grabbed her from behind. All of the air burst from her lungs with a "whoosh." One arm crushed her waist, while a hand was clamped over her mouth.

"Hey, angel face," a voice whispered into her ear.

20

Anna was hoisted through the door, kicking and thrashing, the hand over her mouth muffling her screams. A hard shove made her trip, and she crashed to the floor. Scrabbling to her feet, she thrust her back against the wall. Rick was grinning at her wolfishly. He closed the door, blocking the exit.

"Lauren," he shouted. "Come here. We have another visitor."

There was a bang, a loud curse, and Anna heard footsteps running toward them. Lauren appeared at the end of the hall with a gun in her hand. It was ugly and black and pointed straight at her. Anna cringed against the wall.

"I told you she wouldn't be far behind," Lauren muttered. Her hair was pulled back into a thick braid and there was a smudge of something dark on her cheek. Anna stared at it, afraid of what the smudge might be.

"Don't worry," Rick said quickly. "Magdalena's taken care of. She won't interrupt us again. Now that Anna's here, maybe she can help."

"What did you do to Magdalena?" Anna whimpered.

"Shut up," Lauren said. She edged closer, studying Rick's eyes. The pupils were dilated. "Did you do some coke while you were in the car just now?"

"Just a couple of lines. It was getting too tense in here. You could use some."

"You idiot! You need to stay sharp. And you know I never touch the stuff. You don't shit where you eat."

"Nice, very nice." Rick shook his head. "Don't worry about me. I'm fine. Now, shall we get back to packing?"

Lauren grabbed Anna by the arm. "Maybe that's a good idea. Come on, you."

She pushed Anna up the short hall. There were two doors on the end, one closed and the other opening into a lit workroom. The room was a shambles. A small mound of sealed, purple boxes, the same size as the box Magdalena had examined, was dumped on the floor to the left of the door. Flattened boxes, still waiting to be assembled, were propped against a worktable in the middle of the room. Styrofoam chips were scattered on the floor beneath it, and sheets of tissue paper were strewn across the top next to a cardboard box. Wooden shelves were attached to the back wall with a confusing jumble of multi-coloured leather, shoes, jewellery, gloves, and other accessories.

Lauren shoved the gun at Rick. "Keep an eye on her," she said.

Rick nodded and pointed the gun at Anna. She flinched, and he snorted with laughter.

"Go stand by the shelves and bring me what I tell you," Lauren told Anna. Anna stumbled to the shelves while Lauren stood by the worktable. Rick leaned against the doorway with his arms folded over his chest, the gun in one hand.

As Lauren assembled a box, she said, "Bring me one of the orange bustiers."

Anna turned to scan the shelves. There was a pile of orange leather on the bottom. She squatted to grab the top item. A sales tag fluttered from it as she hurried to the table, holding the clothing before her. Lauren was smoothing some sheets of tissue with her hands when she glanced up at

Anna, her face filling with irritation. She snatched the item from Anna's hand.

"Not a mini-corset, dummy. Don't you know anything about lingerie? A bustier. It's longer." She threw the mini-corset into Anna's face, and it fell onto the floor.

"And be careful with the merchandise. That stuff's expensive."

Anna nodded and scurried back to the shelves. She stowed the mini-corset on the bottom and searched through the rest for an orange bustier.

"Hurry up! We've got to get all this stuff packaged before we can get out of here."

Anna saw something orange on the top shelf and reached for it on tiptoe. It was an orange corset.

"That's right," Lauren called. "Now bring it over here."

Anna rushed back to the table and handed it to Lauren. Lauren had lined the box with tissue paper and scattered a half dozen small plastic bags on top. Anna stared at the bags. They contained a white powder.

"What's that?" she croaked, pointing at them.

"What do you think?" Lauren asked. She laid the bustier on top of the bags and folded the tissue over top. Placing a lid on top, Lauren used oval, silver stickers to seal the sides. Anna took a closer look at a medium-sized cardboard box on the tabletop. It was almost filled with bags of white powder. She stared back at Lauren, her eyes widening.

"I think Anna's beginning to get the picture," Rick said with a chuckle. Lauren glanced up at her.

"How much coke is that?" Anna asked, pointing at the box.

"Four hundred thousand dollars' worth," Rick said.

"Keep your big mouth shut," Lauren snapped, glaring at him. She dropped the sealed box on the floor with the others.

Rick frowned and turned to Anna, as if looking for support. "We've been saving up to make one final, big score. We just didn't expect to have to make it so soon, so now we're in a hurry. One of our customer's coming to pick up her order tonight. We'll be delivering the rest."

Putting two-and-two together, Anna gasped. "You're the embezzler, not Kevin."

Rick touched his nose with his finger. "Got it in one."

Lauren smiled and slung an arm over Rick's shoulder. "How else do you think we paid for this? Certainly not from the money Kevin's been nickeling and diming me."

"And while my salary from Westmore has increased substantially, now that I'm CEO, it would never have been as profitable as this. Although Mother could have warned me that she was going to leave me all those lovely shares. Now I'll never be able to use them."

"Don't worry, Ricky," Lauren said. She kissed his cheek. "With the money we're making on this sale, we'll be able to start all over again. With my talent and your disarmingly boyish face" — she squeezed his cheeks — "we'll always come out on top." He crushed her body against his and they kissed, his hand massaging her buttocks while she ground her hips against him.

Anna stared at them feeling sick to her stomach. What a thoroughly loathsome couple they were. Together they had killed Julia and Latona and framed Kevin. Her boss must have interrupted them earlier in their packing. As she thought about Magdalena, a tear dripped down her cheek. Where was she?

Magdalena woke up in complete darkness. Her head ached, and she felt cold and dizzy. She tried to move, but realized that her hands were bound behind her back and that her mouth was gagged. Her face was resting on something soft and textured. Gingerly, so as not to jostle her head too much, she stuck out a foot and touched the side of her enclosure only inches away. Reaching with the other foot, she banged into something. It made a sloshing sound. Some kind of fluid, then.

A car horn blared not far away. Of course. She was imprisoned in the trunk of a car. A blaze of panic flamed inside of her, but she quashed it immediately. Fear would destroy her. Discipline and reason were her tools. They would carry her through this, somehow.

She paused to remember what had brought her to this impasse. Opening the back door to Lauren's store, she had heard whistling inside. Surprised, she had snuck down the hall to a storeroom, where she discovered Rick cutting open a cardboard box with a knife. Reaching inside, he drew out a small plastic bag filled with a white powder. Cocaine, no doubt.

In her astonishment, she must have become less vigilant, because someone had stolen up from behind and struck her. It had probably been Lauren, returning from the lane-way. Since she wasn't being held prisoner inside the van, one of them must have had a car parked somewhere close-by. They had bound her and imprisoned her in its trunk. Either they were going to leave her to succumb to the cold — the temperature would be dropping several degrees below freezing tonight — or they would be back to dispatch her. It didn't make any difference. She would have to free herself before either scenario could occur.

Magdalena spared a thought for Anna. Would she have called for help when Magdalena failed to appear? Probably not. Anna wouldn't know of her danger. It was more than possible that Anna had knocked on the store's front door, demanding to speak with Lauren, and Lauren had lured her inside. She couldn't count on Anna's help to secure her release.

Magdalena wiggled, using her hands to feel the inside of the trunk. There was a device inside her own vehicle which, when pulled, would enable one-half of the back seat to be lowered. There it was! She grasped the knob and pulled. She heard a "click." Taking a minute to rotate her position, Magdalena kicked at the back of the trunk. It took only two attempts before the seat gave way and wan light illuminated her enclosure. She blinked and wiggled feet-first through the opening until she was able to sit up inside the car. Now she had only to find something to help loosen the cord binding her wrists.

Lauren and Anna had made a lot of progress with the inventory on the shelves, the mound of boxes on the floor tripling since they had begun. Rick carried the boxes to the lane-way door, sticking the gun in the back of his belt first to free his hands. Now that the gun was no longer so convenient, should she try to escape? Anna decided against it. Even if she could get past Lauren, she would be a sitting duck if Rick took a shot at her in the hall.

There was a banging noise, and the two women stopped to listen. Rick stuck his head around the storeroom door.

"Someone's knocking up front," he said.

"Damn that Shania. I told her not to use the front door," Lauren muttered. She looked at Rick. "I'll take care of this. You stay here with Anna. If she tries anything, shoot her." She glared at Anna and shut the storeroom door behind her. Rick sat down on a stool next to the door to wait. A half-minute passed, and Anna heard voices coming from the store. The conversation moved down the hall past the storeroom and continued to the back door.

Anna glanced at Rick. He was playing a game on his cell.

Rick was the weak link in this operation. His playboy lifestyle and cocaine addiction were the result of self-indulgence. Lauren was the type of woman who would never let a man out of her clutches once she had caught him, and she and Rick had had a relationship before her marriage to Kevin. Maybe the embezzling had been all her idea.

Anna stole another glance at Rick as she tidied up the table. She figured that he would shoot her if it was in his best interests to do so, but she didn't think that he would enjoy it. He was selfish and immoral, but not cruel or sadistic. He had murdered with poison so as not to dirty his hands. Come to think of it, maybe Lauren had done the poisoning. Murder was more her style than his.

With only Rick guarding her, now might be her only chance to escape. She had to think of a way out of this, not only for herself but for Magdalena. If she were still alive. The thought filled her with dread, and she tried to thrust it to the back of her mind. No time for weakness now.

Anna cleared her throat.

"Yes," Rick said impatiently, not bothering to lift his eyes from his game.

"I was just thinking about the first time we met. At the Christmas party when you asked me to dance. Was that your idea or your mother's?"

"How nostalgic of you. Even if Mother hadn't suggested it, I would have asked you to dance. You looked so pitiful sitting there on your own. You're an attractive woman, Anna, but you don't know how to take advantage of your looks. You could use a lesson or two from Lauren."

"That's true." Anna took a couple of steps toward Rick. "I've never been good at parties. I don't know how to talk to strangers."

"It's not difficult. You just need to relax." Rick ended the game and looked up. Slightly unfocused blue eyes met hers across the table.

"You're good at making people feel comfortable. Were you born that way or is it the coke speaking?"

He smiled. "Oh, cocaine's a great conversation starter. You never tried it?"

"Just a little pot when I was away from home for the first time. I'm not very adventurous, you know."

Rick shrugged. "That's too bad. I guess you'll never have the chance to find out."

Anna winced. She didn't want Rick thinking about her imminent demise. He noted her expression and hopped down from the stool.

"I snagged a few packages out of the box. Why shouldn't I? We got this stash from my supplier, so I deserve a finder's fee. Lauren's going to be busy for a while. Why don't you give it a try? You look pretty tense. It may help you to relax."

"Do you think so?"

"Sure. I don't worry about anything when I've got a good buzz going. As a matter of fact, I'm beginning to feel kind of tense myself. What do you say we have a little party, just the two of us, while everything's nice and quiet?"

"Really? Here?"

Rick shoved the tissue paper out of the way, sending several sheets flying.

"Okay," Anna said. The sides of her mouth twitched into a nervous smile.

She watched as Rick removed a pouch from his pants pocket and dropped it on the table. Reaching back inside, he drew out a credit card and flicked it beside the cocaine. He opened the pouch and poured out some of its contents, expertly dividing the white pile into six lines with his credit card. Anna walked the rest of the way around the table to stand beside him. The gun was only a few inches away in the back of his belt.

"How do you sniff it?" she asked.

"Watch." He pulled a handful of bills from his pocket and removed a twenty. Smoothing it on the table first, he rolled it into a tight cone.

"You just sniff it up using this." Bending, he quickly inhaled four lines of powder, two into each nostril. A moment passed before a beatific smile lit up his face.

"Ahh, that's better." His eyes closed, and Anna reached for the gun. The door sailed open, and Lauren marched into the room. Anna clenched her empty hands behind her back. She had been a moment too late.

As she took in the table top, Lauren's face contorted with anger. She strode up to Rick and slapped his face. His eyes opened, and he stared at her, the smile fading.

"What did you do that for?"

Lauren grabbed the gun from his belt and pointed it at Anna. "Don't think I don't know who's behind this. I've got a good mind to . . ."

Something clattered in another part of the building. Lauren cocked her head to listen.

"Did you hear that?" she asked Rick.

"Sure. I can hear everything. Absolutely everything." Rick's eye twitched.

"Oh, you're useless." Lauren shoved him aside and grabbed Anna's arm, twisting it behind her. Anna grimaced with pain.

"I know I locked the back door after Shania left. That noise was coming from the store. Let's go find out what it was."

She thrust Anna ahead of her with Rick following right behind. Moving quietly down the hall, they passed into the area with the change rooms. A dim light had been left on, and the hall was deserted. The threesome crept past the cubicles, their heads darting from side-to-side, before rounding the corner into the store. The room was dark except for the soft glow coming from the corridor behind them.

"Who's there?" Lauren called. Her words echoed slightly in the silence. With the deep purple on the walls and ceiling, Anna felt like she was in a cavern.

"You go first," Lauren said, shoving the gun muzzle into Anna's back. "The light switch is on the wall next to the front door. Head in that direction."

Anna raised her hands and stepped into the room. She threaded her way around the first mannequin's pedestal, her eyes straining to see in the darkness.

Please don't let this be one of Lauren's customers trying to cut a better deal, she prayed to herself. Rick giggled crazily, obviously enjoying himself.

The muzzle pressing into her back was even more insistent. Anna felt in front of her with her foot, edging forward one step at a time. If only those blackout curtains weren't drawn, she'd be able to see something. Passing the second pedestal, Anna felt something swoop in the blackness above her, making her hair stand on end.

Anna shrieked and ducked, covering her head with her arms. Lauren was knocked to the floor and the gun exploded. Anna dove for safety. There were people on the floor behind her, rolling and punching. Someone screamed with rage. Anna quickly crawled away, feeling her way with her hands. If only she could make it to the door before Lauren or Rick caught her.

The door burst open and the lights flashed on. "Freeze!" someone shouted.

Anna found herself pressed up against a wall and clambered to her feet. Detective Soo was crouched in the doorway, her gun pointing into the room. Relief flooded Anna's body, making her knees so wobbly that she almost collapsed. Looking across the room, she saw Magdalena straddling Lauren. Both of Magdalena's hands were wrapped in her adversary's hair with Lauren's head only inches from the tiles. Rick was on his back behind them. Sirens howled in the distance.

"Where's the gun?" Soo shouted. "I heard gunfire."

Magdalena released Lauren, whose head thudded to the floor. Lauren moaned.

Good. Anna grabbed the window ledge in front of her. At least Magdalena hadn't killed her.

"I kicked it across the floor," Magdalena called. "Somewhere toward you, I should think, Detective."

Soo rose from her crouch to step into the room. With her arms still extended in their firing position, she searched the floor with her foot. Something clattered across the tiles.

"Found it." Soo bent and straightened again, two guns in her hands now. Brilliant red and blue light flashed across the walls. Anna heard car doors slam. Six more officers, with their guns pointing and wearing body armour, rushed into the room.

Rick lurched into a sitting position. "Hey guys, what's happening?"

21

The police rounded them all up and took them back to the Westwinds building for questioning. Anna was given a blanket and tea syrupy with sugar to calm her chattering teeth. She was left alone in an interrogation room for half an hour until the detective who had been questioning her returned with her statement. After she had signed it, Anna was allowed to sit with Magdalena and was eating a chocolate bar when Soo popped into their room.

"I know you have a lot of questions, but I don't have time to answer them," the detective said. "How about I drop by the university later this week to bring you up to speed?"

Magdalena nodded slowly. "If that's the best you can do."

"It is," the harried detective replied. "I'll call you."

Then a police officer drove Anna and her boss back to Magdalena's house. Magdalena was given the opportunity of being dropped off at Emergency to have her head injury checked out, but she declined. The officer tried to insist, but Magdalena was adamant.

"I'll be fine, Constable. It's a mere headache. Two pain tablets with a cup of tea, and I'll be as good as new."

The officer shrugged. "It's your decision, ma'am."

When they reached the house, Warren was waiting in his car with the engine running. Magdalena had called him from the Westwinds building to inform him of her and

Anna's ordeal. He jumped out of his car as soon as the cruiser reached the curb and ran over to help Magdalena from the vehicle. They were wrapped in each other's arms, Warren kissing Magdalena's forehead, by the time Anna climbed out onto the street.

"Thanks for the lift," Anna said, patting the side of the cruiser. The officer nodded and waited for Anna to step onto the sidewalk before pulling away.

Anna glanced around the block. Most of Magdalena's neighbours had decorated their homes with tasteful red-and-white lights, and every house had a wreath on the door. It all looked so ordinary and safe. She breathed in several lungfuls of cold air. It was blessedly quiet after the fracas at Lauren's store and the persistent questions at the Westwinds building. She turned to look at Warren and Magdalena. They were still kissing. It was hard to believe that Magdalena had been bashing Lauren's head on the floor only a few hours before.

The couple broke apart, and Magdalena turned to Anna. She held out an arm. Bemused, Anna wondered if her boss wanted to hug her. Instead, she rested a hand on Anna's shoulder.

"Come inside with us. I'll get you a drink, or heat up some soup. You look dead on your feet." Magdalena lifted her wrist to glance at her watch. "It's after eight."

"That late? No thanks. I've got to get home to Wendy."

"Has she been alone all this time?"

"No. I called a neighbour to go over and feed her, but Wendy's been on her own most of the day. Besides, Charlie usually calls on Sunday nights unless he's tied up with something. But thanks for the invitation."

Magdalena nodded. "Give my regards to Sergeant Tremaine." She glanced back at Warren, who put an arm around her waist. He looked as if he were afraid to let her out of his sight.

Anna hesitated. "Look, Magdalena, I just want to say thanks. If it weren't for you, I can't imagine what Lauren and Rick might have done to me by now."

Her boss shook her head. "Don't think about it, Anna. Nothing insurmountable happened to either one of us today. It's over. Case closed."

Anna nodded and turned toward her car. "I'll see you tomorrow."

"Yes. Don't forget, you've got to call Scheduling tomorrow morning to change the room location for KIN 3020 for next term."

With her face hidden, Anna rolled her eyes. How could Magdalena compartmentalize her emotions like this?

"I'll remember to call first thing in the morning," Anna said, pivoting to face her.

"Good. See you tomorrow."

Anna walked to her car parked behind Warren's. It had been sitting at the curb during the day's sleet and snowfall, but someone had cleaned it off. She must have Warren to thank for that. Climbing inside, Anna started the engine. It hesitated before roaring into life. Good old car. She flicked on her lights, waved at Magdalena and Warren, and pulled away.

Back at home, Anna was in the bathroom towelling her hair dry when the phone rang. She dashed to her bedroom and settled on the edge of the bed to answer.

"Hello?"

"It's me, love. How are you? I just got in from work and heated a ready meal."

"Oh? What're you having?" Anna asked nervously, stalling for time. She knew she couldn't hide the day's events from him, but she really needed to hear his voice.

"Some kind of beef and pasta thing. It's actually not bad. But never mind that. How was your week? Did anything new happen in the Julia Moreland case?"

Anna took a deep breath and said, "Funny you should ask." Lying down on the bed, with Wendy settling on the floor beside her, Anna told him what had happened. She heard one or two sharply indrawn breaths, but Charlie was a good listener and didn't interrupt. When Anna had finished, she could hear him mumble. Sometimes he literally had to count to ten during their conversations.

"So, you're all right?" he finally said.

"Just fine. Not a scratch on me," she said in an overly-hearty voice.

"At least we can be thankful for that."

"There's one good thing about all this. Kevin Moreland is being released. The detective who brought me my statement told me so. Apparently, Kevin's even threatening to file charges against the police for false arrest."

Tremaine sighed. "It happens. Your average citizen will call 911 whenever the wind blows the wrong way, but he doesn't take kindly to mistakes. How long was Kevin in jail?"

"Just three days. You'd think he'd be grateful. He had no idea that Rick and his wife had betrayed him until the police informed him."

"Poor bastard. By the way, I don't suppose there's any point in telling you that you could have avoided all this danger by keeping your nose out of a police investigation?"

"You can't blame me this time, Charlie. It was Magdalena's idea to spy on Lauren's store. I was just in the wrong place . . ."

". . . at the wrong time. I know. I know. I'm glad they found the right culprits and it's all over. You lie low, love, and if anybody else asks for your help this week, just say no. I'll see you Friday afternoon at the airport."

"I wish you could come home sooner, Charlie," Anna said in a wistful voice. She was remembering Magdalena and Warren kissing on the sidewalk.

"So do I, darling, but my superiors want everything tied up with a shiny red bow before I leave. There's nothing worse than having the guilty party get off because of sloppy police work."

"I know. I'll see you Friday. Maybe I'll show up at the airport wearing a big red bow." Her voice dropped to a whisper. "Then you can take me home and unwrap me."

"I can't wait to get you all to myself," he said in a husky voice. "Just thinking about it is making me want to take a cold shower."

"Not me. I've just had a nice hot bath, and now I'm stretched out on my bed naked."

"Ouch! You're not helping."

Anna laughed.

"I'd better go," Tremaine said. "I've got an early start in the morning. Love you, darling."

"Love you, too. Bye, Charlie."

It was late Thursday afternoon before Detective Soo made good on her promise to update Magdalena and Anna on the investigation. They had invited Warren to the meeting so that he could hear all of the details directly from the detective. The four of them were crowded into Magdalena's office, Soo looking pleased as she relaxed back in her chair.

"Start at the beginning, Detective," Magdalena said. "Let us know what brought you to Lauren's store in the first place last Sunday."

"Well, as Mr. Moreland here knows from when I dropped by his office on Saturday, I was sure that Kevin Moreland was our guy, but I wanted to confirm it," Soo said. Warren nodded. "I asked him for a picture of Kevin. We had a record of an eight thousand dollar cash withdrawal from Kevin's account in October, and I wanted a visual ID from the bank teller who had waited on him. So Mr. Moreland gave me a copy of this year's annual report. It had pictures of all the executives in it, including the VP's." Magdalena and Anna nodded.

"I figured no one who had helped a guy with such a large withdrawal could forget him, and I was right. The teller did remember him. But when I showed her Kevin's picture, she hemmed and hawed, not really sure if that was the guy she had helped. Then I had a brainwave. I showed her a picture of Rick Moreland, and she recognized him right away. She thought it was just another picture of the same guy, in fact. They look enough alike that I could understand her confusion. That was my first suspicion that Rick, not Kevin, might be our guy.

"I dug around a bit and discovered that Rick had minored in computer science during his undergraduate degree. That fit. Any guy who was able to hide his embezzling from the chief financial officer, plus hack into the security system at the university, had to be pretty clever with computers. Plus, he was the chief operations officer at Westmore, which meant, according to the annual report, that he was responsible for coordinating manufacturing as well as being responsible for corporate financial review. It was the perfect position for enabling our embezzler to hide the money so deep that it didn't set off any alarms.

"Then I got to thinking about the account transactions we'd discovered on Kevin's home computer. If he hadn't moved the embezzled money in and out of his account, then the only other person who could have done it was Lauren. She could have provided Rick with the identification to open an account in Kevin's name as well.

"I already knew that Rick and Lauren had dated before Rick introduced her to Kevin. What if the two of them had always planned to con Kevin? What if they had even continued seeing each other after Kevin had married her? I showed a picture of Lauren to Rick's concierge and the woman who cleaned for him, and they identified her as someone who sometimes visited Rick at his condo.

"So I started following Rick on Sunday morning, and I got lucky right away. He took me to the address of a person the police already suspected for drug peddling and money laundering. Rick stayed inside for half an hour before coming back out with a cardboard box. That was interesting, and then he drove downtown to Lauren's store, pulling into the lane-way behind it. I couldn't follow him there without being spotted, so I parked down the block from the front of the store. I saw you two ladies pull up a couple of hours later," Soo said, looking at Anna and Magdalena. "Then both of you went into the lane-way, but only Anna came back. You waited in the car about half an hour, Anna, before returning to the lane-way, but you didn't come out again. I knew the two of you were friendly with Lauren, so that got me worried. I hated to think that you were tied up with Rick and Lauren somehow."

Anna and Magdalena exchanged a glance. It was strange to think that their lives were being threatened while Detective Soo was out front wondering if they were criminals. Anna shook her head. How ironic was that?

"A woman I didn't recognize arrived in a van and knocked on the front door. Lauren let her in, which confirmed that she was actually in the store. Five minutes later, Lauren and the woman came out the back and drove the van into the lane-way. Something was definitely up, but I didn't know what. I left my car after the van left for a closer look. I was on the sidewalk when I heard a scream and a shot. I called for back-up and went in. You know the rest."

"Yes," Magdalena said. "I escaped from Rick's trunk, which was parked next to a dumpster in the lane-way, and snuck back inside when Lauren was with her customer. The door to the storeroom was closed, but I heard you and Rick talking, Anna, so I knew that he had you. I hid in a change room while Lauren was conducting her business, where I developed the idea of taking the place of one of the mannequins in the store. I reasoned that no one would notice me in the dark if I remained still, so the warrior mannequin and I exchanged places. Remember her, Anna?"

Anna nodded.

"Circumstances quickly grew desperate when I heard Lauren shouting and threatening you. The mannequin came with a spear, which was little more than a prop, but made quite a noise when I dropped it on the tiles. The noise lured the three of you into the store. I waited for Lauren to pass on her way to the light switch, and then I attacked."

"Did you know she had a gun?" Anna asked.

"The possibility had crossed my mind, but I chose to ignore it." Warren sighed, and Magdalena shrugged. "Fortunately, Rick was incapacitated in the ensuing struggle, and Detective Soo arrived in the nick of time."

"I don't know about that," Soo said. "You were doing pretty well on your own." Magdalena accepted the compliment with a nod.

"What happens now, Detective?" Warren asked. "And what about the deaths of my stepmother and Latona Taylor? Is there anything to tie Rick and Lauren to them?"

"The test results came back on Ms. Taylor at the beginning of the week. We know that she died from ingesting water hemlock, and that the poison had been in the coffee cup marked with Kevin's fingerprints. Lauren could have got a disposable cup with Kevin's fingerprints, no problem. Either Lauren, or Rick, or both, could have taken the poisoned coffee to Ms. Taylor. It would help if we could find the equipment they used to distill the poison or could tie them to an area where the plant grows, but we're still working on that."

"Neither one of them has confessed to the murders?" Anna asked.

Soo shook her head. "Don't worry, we'll get them. It's just a matter of time." She rose to her feet. "I'm sorry that you had to go through such an unpleasant experience, ladies, but it sure helped us put those two away. We're grateful."

"Thank you for explaining all this to us, Detective," Magdalena said. Warren began rising, but Soo waved him back down.

"Don't bother, Mr. Moreland. I'll show myself out. Have a good Christmas, everyone. You certainly deserve it."

"You, too," they murmured.

After she had left, Warren said, "Life has certainly been interesting at Westmore since Kevin was released. Kevin says that it's illegal for Rick to profit from Julia's death, so he wants the Westmore shares she left him, plus he wants to be CEO."

"What's going to happen to Oliver and the presidency of Golden Farm Fertilizer?" Anna asked.

"Kevin says he's willing to let Oliver stay on as president for now, but I don't know how that's going to work out. Kevin still owns the company, and he's got a lot of changes in mind. As a matter of fact, I'm headed over to

Oliver's after I leave here to talk with him about them. While I'm there, I'll check in on Beatrix."

"Why? Is something wrong with her?" Anna asked.

Warren looked at her in surprise. "Didn't you hear? She just got out of the hospital on Tuesday. Oliver took her to Emergency last Thursday night because she was having trouble breathing. It's her asthma again. They played with her medications while she was in the hospital. Her breathing's improved, but it's still not great."

Anna shook her head. "Poor lady. I heard you say that you visited someone in Emergency, but I didn't realize that it was Beatrix. I wish that I had known. I would have visited her."

Warren glanced at his watch. "It's almost five. Do you want to come with me?"

Anna hesitated. She normally went straight home at the end of the day to look after Wendy. If she visited the Sumpters first, she'd have to call Betty to feed Wendy and let her out. Anna had done that a lot lately, and she didn't want to impose again. On the other hand, Charlie was coming home tomorrow. If she didn't visit Beatrix now, when would she find the time?

"Sure, I'll come." Anna hopped to her feet. "Just give me a minute to make a call first. I'll follow you in my car."

"All right."

It hadn't snowed since the weekend, so Calgary's main thoroughfares were bare, and they made good time. Anna glanced at the dashboard just as she drew up behind Warren's car. Five-thirty. She'd stay for a half hour, tops, and be on her way. Hopping out of the car, she followed Warren to the porch and rang the Sumpters' doorbell. The curtains were drawn over the front windows, but there were lights on inside.

Oliver opened the door. He was slightly out of breath, as if he had just run from somewhere. He smiled.

"Warren! Good to see you, son. And Anna. What an unexpected pleasure. Are you here to see Beatrix?"

"Yes, if that's all right? How's she doing? I'm sorry, I would have visited her in the hospital if I'd known that she was there."

"Of course you can visit. Bea will be thrilled to see you. Come inside, the two of you, before you freeze. The temperature's starting to drop. Let me take your coats. Bea had a bad spell for a few days there, Anna, but she's doing better now. She's resting in her bedroom at the moment."

Anna looked up from the front mat where she was removing her boots.

"I won't be disturbing her, will I?"

"Not at all. She had a nap, and I just took her a cup of tea. Can I get you one, too?"

"No, thanks. I know that you and Warren have business to discuss, so why don't I find my own way to Beatrix?"

"If you don't mind? She's down the hall on the left, just past the living room."

"Great. I'll stick my head into the office to say goodbye before I leave."

"We'll be right in here," Oliver said, nodding at the room to the right of the door. "See you then."

Anna walked down the hall. The door just past the living room was half-closed, so she tapped on it gently before tiptoeing inside.

"Beatrix?"

The only light came from a bedside lamp. Beatrix looked up from reading a book. She was dressed and lying on top of the bed with a green throw over her legs. A gilded cup and saucer with pink roses sat in easy reach on a nightstand. Anna noticed a wheeled oxygen tank leaning against the bed, the mask resting on Beatrix's knee.

"Anna? I didn't expect to see you here today. How kind of you to come." Beatrix's voice was weak and she looked tired, but her smile was warm and welcoming.

"How are you feeling today?"

"Much better, thanks. Sometimes I have these little spells when the weather gets cold and damp. That's why we head south for part of the winter. Poor Oliver, he's had to give Max all his walks since I've been under the weather."

Anna heard a tail thumping on the floor and walked to the other side of the bed. The German shepherd's head was raised from where he was stretched out on the floor.

"I didn't see him there. Hi, Max," Anna said, closing the distance to the dog and patting his shoulder. He rolled over to let her scratch his stomach. "Good boy."

"He likes to keep me company when I'm not up and about. How are you, Anna? All ready for Christmas?" Beatrix patted the bed, and Anna roosted beside her.

"Just about. Tomorrow is my last day at work, and then I don't go back until January 7th. One of the perks of working for a university is that they close over the holidays. How about you and Oliver?"

"We're still planning on visiting my sister in Saskatchewan, if I'm well enough. So I haven't done any baking this year. Just picked up a few gifts for Oliver and the family."

"I went all out this year, since my boyfriend is coming. Fruitcake, cookies, squares. I'll probably put on ten pounds."

Beatrix laughed. "Well, you just have a good time and don't worry about it. Christmas was made for self-indulgences."

"Yes, it's good to have a time of year when we don't worry about the calories. I've heard some good news about Oliver not having to retire, by the way. Congratulations."

"Yes, we are happy about that. Now we don't have to worry about health benefits and Oliver's pension plan. Oliver's feeling so much more relaxed lately."

"I'm pleased for you both," Anna said, rising. "Well, I don't want to tire you out. I just wanted to say 'Merry Christmas,' and that I'm glad things have worked out for you and Oliver." She took Beatrix's hand where it lay on the covers and gave it a gentle squeeze. Beatrix smiled at her.

"You have a merry Christmas with that sergeant of yours and your son. Enjoy the holidays."

"I certainly will."

"Bye, Anna."

Anna smiled as she walked back up the hall. Maybe it might not be smooth sailing for Oliver with the plans Kevin had for Golden Farm, but it was a finite period of time before his retirement to achieve a desired result. She was glad that the Sumpters' future was now secure.

She heard Warren's voice as she walked to the office and paused in the doorway. Oliver looked up from behind his desk and stood.

"Anna! Warren was just telling me about your adventures with Magdalena since last we saw you. Come in and take a seat."

"Just for a minute. I really have to get going." Anna sat down on a small sofa next to Warren. "My dog is waiting for me at home."

"Certainly, certainly. But I can't get over what you and Magdalena have been through. Held captive by Lauren and Rick! You must have been terrified."

"I was pretty scared, I have to admit. Magdalena's the one with the cool head."

"Anyone would have been frightened under those circumstances. And you also received an anonymous note with chocolates you thought might be poisoned. It must have been terrible, reading that threatening message with those black-and-white, cut-out letters."

"Coloured letters this time. Yes, that was scary. Warren saw me that day."

"I thought you were going to faint. You were as white as a ghost, Anna," Warren said.

"Who wouldn't have been? Thank goodness it's all over now, and they've got the right culprits in jail," Oliver said. "Poor Kevin, to be falsely imprisoned."

"Well, it's not quite all worked out yet. Detective Soo said they're still looking for evidence to connect Rick and Lauren to Julia and Latona's murders," Anna said.

"I'm sure something will turn up," Warren replied.

Anna frowned. "I hope so. Neither one of them has confessed to the murders. That worries me. What if it wasn't one of them?"

"Of course it was one of them," Oliver said. His eyes shifted to Warren and back again. "Who else had as much to gain?"

"No, I'm sure it was them," Warren said.

"That's right," Oliver replied. He rose to his feet. "Thank you for coming today, Anna. I appreciate you looking in on Beatrix."

"It was my pleasure," Anna said, also rising. "And congratulations on still being president of Golden Farm."

"Yes, I have a lot to be thankful for this Christmas," Oliver said, smiling brightly.

Anna turned to Warren, who stood up. "In case I don't see you again, have a wonderful Christmas," she said. "I know this must be incredibly difficult for you, with first one stepbrother being arrested, and then the other. Not to mention what it must be doing to Westmore."

"Thank you, Anna. I'll do my best. I'm lucky I've got Magdalena."

Anna smiled. "She's lucky too. Goodbye."

Anna retrieved her coat from the front hall closet as Warren and Oliver resumed their conversation in low voices. After lacing up her boots, she looked into the office from the front door. Oliver and Warren were leaning toward each other as they talked, their faces grave. They were probably discussing Kevin's plans for the company. It wasn't going to be much fun for Oliver.

As if sensing that she was thinking of him, Oliver looked up and smiled. Anna waved and stepped out the door. Maybe Warren was giving him some good advice on how to handle his stepbrother.

Climbing into her car, Anna sighed. What an exhausting family the Morelands were with all their jealousies, schemes, and now murder. And Magdalena was considering marrying one of them. Warren seemed like a good man, but Anna believed that she would think twice before making him her husband. Warren must have been damaged by his father's desertion and his mother's descent into depression, alcoholism, and drug addiction. After that, he had spent years working for Julia, the woman he blamed for his mother's death. Anna shivered and turned on the heater. Still, Magdalena was a complex woman herself, and very strong. If anyone could handle Warren, she could.

Anna looked over her shoulder and pulled away from the curb to begin the drive home. She had better things to think about. Charlie was coming home tomorrow, and Christmas, her favourite time of year, was less than a week away! She switched on the radio and hummed along to some Christmas music.

The drive west on Highway 22X was pleasant. It was a clear night with moonlight casting a silvery glow on the snow-crested fields she passed. Some of the ranch houses were lit up with strings of multi-coloured lights, and a giant, inflated Santa waved to her from a front lawn. Anna smiled, thinking of her own spruce tree. The solar lights turned on automatically at dusk, making her house as pretty as a Christmas card. It would be the first thing Charlie would see when she brought him home from the airport tomorrow night.

Turning south onto Highway 22, Anna saw the flashing lights of a roadblock and a detour sign up ahead. She'd have to drive the back way into Crane, the range road leading into Wistler. It would probably be fine. The school bus used that road, so they kept it plowed. She slowed to turn left onto the narrow road and turned on her brights.

There weren't any other cars as she drove past the white fields. It was past six-thirty, and rush hour traffic was over. Most of the people who lived along here were ranchers, farmers, or retired folk, so they'd be inside eating their dinners.

No, someone was behind her. She caught the headlights in her rear view mirror. He had on his brights. They disappeared as she rounded a bend, but reappeared behind her. Anna frowned as the car drew nearer and the driver still didn't dim his lights. Some people were so inconsiderate. He was also driving way too fast for the twisting, two-lane road, careening around the last curve. Well, she wasn't going to speed up just because of him. He could either slow down or pass her.

But he did neither, racing closer and closer without turning on his indicator to show that he was going to pass. Anna gripped the steering wheel nervously with both hands. Was he crazy? As his headlights filled her rear window,

Anna was sure he was going to hit her. She rammed the steering wheel to the right and slammed on the brakes. The car slid on the soft shoulder and rolled. Anna screamed, tumbling upside down. An airbag exploded from the door.

The car lurched to a stop. Anna's heart thudded in her chest as she dangled upside down from the shoulder harness and seat belt, gasping for air. The belt was digging into her stomach and crushing her right breast. Her knee ached — had she banged it into something? — and so did her cheek. She had a memory of her purse hitting her in the face as the car rolled. She touched her cheek and felt something wet. Blood. Anna groaned. She looked out through the windshield. The car was tilted nose-down into the ditch. The headlights were still on, shining dazzlingly into the white snow. She began to sob hot tears into her hands.

Over the noise of her crying, Anna heard a car door slam. She froze. Somebody had seen her. Somebody was coming to help. She wiped her face with her hands and craned to look up through the window. The airbag had deflated without her noticing. She saw a dark figure in a long coat climbing carefully into the ditch.

"Help!" she shouted. "I'm in here. Help!"

Her rescuer struggled through the snow to reach the car. A gloved hand reached for the door handle and pulled. Nothing happened. Anna's fingers flew to the button release and unlocked the doors. The hand yanked the door open, and the interior light flipped on.

"Thank God," Anna cried. "Someone tried to run me off the road." A face bent to look at her. Oliver's.

Anna's eyes opened wide. "Oliver, what are you doing here? How did you find me so fast?"

"It's all right, Anna," he said, kneeling down in the snow. He took off his gloves.

"I have to get out of this seat belt." Anna turned to find the release. She pushed the button, but the clasp didn't separate from the holder.

"Help me, Oliver," she said, turning back to the door. He was holding a hypodermic needle in his hand. It was empty. Anna stared at it with horror.

"What are you doing with that?"

Oliver reached for her shoulder, and she beat at him with her left hand.

"Don't worry, Anna, it's not poison. There'll be no pain this time. Just an air bubble to stop your heart."

"Are you crazy? No!" Anna's fist found his nose as she hit him as hard as she could. The needle flew out of his hand, and Oliver tumbled backward. Anna thrust her thumb at the seatbelt button, and it released. Falling an inch onto the roof, Anna wiggled her legs toward the door and rolled out onto the snow. Oliver was on his hands and knees beside the car, searching for the needle. He looked up as Anna scrabbled to her feet. There was blood streaming from his nose.

"No," he shouted, rising up on his knees. "You're supposed to look like you died of exposure in a car accident." He grabbed Anna's legs, and they struggled. He was stronger than Anna imagined he would be. She beat him on the head and shoulders, but still he hung on. Suddenly, he let go to reach inside his pocket. Anna fell back against the side of the car. His hand came out holding a hunting knife, the curved, black handle sticking out of its four-inch sheath.

Anna gasped and plunged into the snow in front of the car. She floundered up to her knees, her bare hands digging for a hold. With her breath rasping in and out, she struggled through the ditch back up to the road. Oliver was shouting at her to come back. She whirled and saw him clamber onto the road a short distance away. His car was parked just up ahead. Anna ran flat out toward it. Reaching the car, she grabbed the door handle and tugged. It was locked.

With a sob, Anna pushed past the car and sprinted down the road. The snow was packed and sprinkled with sand, giving her pounding feet some purchase. Clive's farm was a couple of miles up the road. She knew she couldn't run that far, but there were two houses along the way. If someone were at home, she could get help.

Seconds later, the car started up. Anna glanced over her shoulder. The lights flicked on, their two prongs catching and blinding her. The car leapt forward, and Anna shrieked. He was going to run her down.

She jumped into the ditch as he flashed by. Floundering once more, she climbed to the far side of the trough and crawled up the bank to a field. A four-foot, barbed wire fence stood in her way. Fumbling in her pockets, her hands closed on her leather gloves. They weren't very warm, but at least they would give her skin some protection against the wire. The snow wasn't as deep here. She trotted along the fence to a post. Thrusting her left foot between the strands, she grabbed the post top and hauled herself up. The wire gave some under her weight. Swinging precariously, she began to climb. She heard the car engine idling as it drew abreast of her on the road. Cursing under her breath at her slowness, Anna threw one leg over the top and pivoted. Switching hands, she swung her other leg high to clear the barbs, lost her footing, and crashed into the field on her back.

Anna lay still for a few moments to catch her breath. She was wearing polyester pants and a sweater under a parka that reached half-way down her thighs. Her lace-up boots were only ankle height, but at least they were flat and had good treads.

"Anna! Anna, this is wrong," Oliver called imploringly. "Come back here so that we can talk. I promise I won't hurt you."

Anna sat up. Oliver was peering at her from the open passenger window no more than twenty feet away.

"I should have thought this through better. I don't want to kill you. You don't deserve to die, like Julia and Latona did."

Anna sprang to her feet. Something was beginning to twig in her mind, something that Oliver had said earlier that day in his study. Rick had left the note with the box of chocolates at her office door, the letters cut from multi-coloured print. The letters on the note that Julia had received, however, had all been black-and-white. Rick and Lauren hadn't known that, but Oliver had.

"Why did you kill Julia?" Anna shouted. She waited, her breath making plumes in the frigid air. Seconds passed. The driver's door opened, and Oliver stepped out. In the moonlight, she could see that he had wiped the blood from his nose. He circled the front of the car to stand on the far side of the ditch. Only it and the wire fence stood between them now. Instinctively, Anna backed up a few feet.

"Julia was a terrible woman," Oliver said. "She broke up Robert and Sheila's marriage, using sex to lure him away. That destroyed Sheila, and left Warren a tormented, lonely child. Julia was also indifferent to Kevin. The only one she cared about, other than herself, was Rick. Then she ruined him with over-indulgence.

"Julia found out that I had a list of clients who weren't on the books. I needed the extra money to cover Bea's medical costs and to take her on winter vacations. She needs something to look forward to to keep her going. And then there's the shoplifting. Not only did I have to pay the stores back, but I had to bribe some of the managers to keep them quiet. I explained all of this to Julia and gave her the names of my secret clients, but it wasn't enough. She was going to denounce me to the press and make Kevin the president of Golden Farm. I begged her not to, for Bea's sake. I promised that I would work off the money I had taken, but she wouldn't listen. I tried to scare her with those anonymous notes, but she wouldn't budge. So I had no choice but to kill her. If I had gone to prison, who would have looked after Bea?"

"No one can figure out how Julia was poisoned," Anna called. "How did you do it?"

Oliver smiled, his face proud. "Simple misdirection. I knew how poisonous water hemlock is. My father taught us kids to be careful of it growing up on the farm because he didn't want his cows poisoned. So I helped myself to some when I visited my brother on the farm. I boiled up the root in a saucepan while Bea was out and hid it in the basement. On the night of the party, I brought some in a flask and poisoned the coffee I served Julia during our meeting. Later, when everyone was upset when she collapsed on the dance floor, I poured a little into her scotch. It wasn't difficult. Everyone was looking the other way."

Anna frowned. Julia had already been doomed by the time they had had their conversation in the ladies' room. If only she had known, Julia might have been saved.

"What about Latona? Why did she deserve to die?" Anna shouted.

Oliver scrambled into the ditch and waded slowly through the snow toward her. "She had the list of my clients on a thumb drive. Julia had hidden it in her desk. I had offered Latona a job out of the kindness of my heart, but she was going to blackmail me into a higher salary. I knew that if I didn't nip it in the bud, she'd have blackmailed me for the rest of my life.

"The boys, Jack Upton, and I got some coffee right before the press conference the Monday after Julia died. I volunteered to clean up the mess on the table as we were leaving. It was easy to hide Kevin's cup in my coat pocket. I used it to carry the poisoned coffee to my meeting with Latona."

Anna watched Oliver use his long arms and legs to crawl out of the ditch onto the field. He stopped, staring at her only a few feet away on the other side of the fence. Anna took another step back.

"You overheard me talking to Julia on the night of the Christmas party, but you didn't seem to recognize my voice," he continued. "But when I made that flub about the lettering on the anonymous note this evening, I was afraid you'd put two-and-two together. When you questioned whether Lauren or Rick had committed the murders, I thought you were toying with me. I panicked. But you're not like the others, are you? You didn't give Bea away about her shoplifting, and you came to visit her today. We can work something out, Anna. I know we can. Bea and I can disappear. Anything you like. Please, Anna. For Bea's sake." He held out his hand to her, his eyes imploring.

Anna stared into them, shivering with cold and fear. He had suffered a lot trying to look after his wife, and he had been kind when Warren needed a father. Maybe he was a decent man at heart who had been driven mad by desperation. What would she have done if her spouse had been suffering like that?

On the other hand, Julia hadn't been a terrible person, at least not to her. And he had had no right to take Latona's life, no matter how greedy she had been. She should have gone to jail, not been killed. He had murdered two people with poison, and they had died agonizing deaths. That was a monstrous crime, a sin.

"No!" Anna shouted. She turned and sprinted away.

"Anna! Anna wait!" His furious voice rang in the stillness. "All right! I tried to spare you, but you wouldn't listen. What happens next is on your head."

Anna glanced over her shoulder. Oliver was climbing the fence, coming after her. It would be a race to the death.

22

Anna gained some time while Oliver struggled to get over the fence. His long coat got in the way, snagging on the barbs on top, and he had had to stop to take it off and put on again. He must have left his house pretty quickly to follow her in his car, as well, because he was wearing shoes instead of boots. He might not have the traction she had in the snow, but his legs were longer and he was carrying a knife. She had nothing.

Anna was moving as fast as she could toward some scrub bush at the top of a hill. She didn't know what lay beyond it, but at least she would be able to see better from up there. Besides, she was too exposed in the moonlight on the snow. She needed some cover.

Stumbling over buried branches and rocks, she caught herself from falling on more than one occasion. She tried tucking fingers numb with cold under her arms, but she couldn't run like that. Panting, slowing to a walk when her lungs threatened to burst, the sound of Oliver's shouts drove her on when she wanted to drop. She had stopped looking behind her, though. Panic at how close he was getting only made her careless.

Finally, she reached the hill top and scurried into the bush. There was no path, and the treetops blocked the moonlight. Sometimes she had to squeeze between tree trunks to force her way through. After the first hurried minutes, however, she made herself slow down. She was making too much noise. Of course, it was possible that he was skirting the bush and waiting for her on the other side. Anna grimaced. What could she do? She didn't know where he was.

A twig snapped in the distance, and she froze. He was in the bush after all, maybe a few minutes behind her. Anna fought the impulse to curl into a ball on the ground and give up. Magdalena had taught her two valuable things: know that you are smarter than your adversary, and know that you are willing to kill. By letting fear make her weak in the knees, she was handing power over to Oliver. She had to stop being her own worst enemy or she wouldn't make it.

She saw a tree lying on the ground in a small clearing, its branches resting on another tree, with a pile of leaves blown up against it. Maybe she could hide beneath its branches? Dashing to the tree, she knelt and dug frantically through the leaves, pushing them aside. They were cold, but dry. There was a space big enough to hide in. Quickly wiggling backward into the gap, Anna mounded the leaves into the opening. Lying on her side, she felt a rock beside her head. It was jagged and about the size of her palm. She wrenched it free from the ground and squeezed it in her hand, its solidity reassuring. Then, she waited.

She heard a rustling sound. Oliver wasn't bothering to be silent. He didn't have to. He was the pursuer, not the pursued.

"Anna, I know you're here somewhere." His tone was different now, taunting. "You must be cold and tired, girl. You sit at a desk all day. You're not used to being outdoors. I grew up on a farm. The cold doesn't bother me, but I bet you're suffering. I bet you can't feel your toes or your fingers anymore. Come out, Anna. Let's finish this."

She heard him moving, his feet crunching through the leaves as he slowly drew nearer. She could hear his breathing as he came to within inches of her hiding place. She closed her eyes and held her breath. He moved on, and she opened her eyes with relief, her heart racing.

His knife slashed through the leaves. Anna shrieked. When it came again, she clubbed at the knife with her rock. Oliver shouted, and she burst out of hiding, scrambling through the leaves. The knife was lying on the ground at his feet while Oliver nursed his smashed fingers and cursed. Anna swung the rock at his face. As Oliver swivelled out of the way, she felt the rock connect with the side of his head. He dropped to one knee, and Anna ran. Bouncing into a tree and switching direction, she darted toward the edge of the bush where the light was brighter. She erupted from the trees and raced down the far side of the hill.

Adrenalin gave her an extra push for a few minutes. She slid in the snow, fell onto her aching knee, got up, and ran on. No longer cold, she was actually sweating. As she drew closer to the bottom, however, the snow grew deeper, making it impossible to run.

Suddenly, she heard a noise. The sound of an engine roaring in the distance. She stopped slogging through the snow to peer at the bottom of the hill. There was a driveway down there with a tractor bumping up it, its headlights rising and dipping. She recognized the driveway. This was Clive's farm.

"Clive!" she shouted, jumping and waving. Of course, he couldn't hear her. She was still a quarter-mile away, plus he'd never hear her over the roar of the tractor. It disappeared behind a stand of pine trees, and she hurried after it, stumbling down the hill again.

After a few minutes, Anna made it to the driveway. She paused to catch her breath, her hands on her knees, and glanced over her shoulder. Oliver was half-way down the hill, loping through the snow with his long legs. She hadn't stopped him; she had only gained a head start. He saw her and ran even faster. She had to hide.

She plunged into the trees that served as a windbreak for the driveway and began threading her way through them. It was tough-going, but at least she could see more than she had in the dense bush. At one point she heard Oliver's muttering and shrank behind a tree, still, waiting for him to pass. He could make much better time than she on the rutted driveway, but she didn't dare leave the safety of the trees. He might be waiting for her somewhere around a bend. She couldn't risk it.

At last Anna reached a vantage point where she could see the house. She had driven there just last week to drop off some shortbread. She knew that it would be cozy inside with a fire in the iron stove and a pot of soup simmering in the kitchen. She could smell the sharp wood smoke and had to stop herself from running forward. It was a good thing that she had because she spotted Oliver climbing the wooden steps to the front porch, illuminated by the outside light.

Oliver looked a sight. His hair was matted to his head and the back of his coat had a couple of deep slashes where it draped against his snow-crusted legs. He reached into his coat pocket and pulled out a tissue. Using it to wipe the blood from his temple, he shoved it back into his pocket. Removing one glove and tucking it under his arm, he pulled out a comb to tidy his hair. Putting his glove back on, he beat the snow from his pant legs and straightened his coat. Finally satisfied with his appearance, he knocked on the door.

Yellow light streamed past Clive's thick form in the doorway. The two men talked. Anna was too far away to hear what they said, but it didn't matter. She would wait a few more minutes until Oliver left before knocking on the door herself. That way, no one would get hurt by the hunting knife he had secreted in his pocket.

Clive took a step back, opening the door wider, but Oliver shook his head. He smiled and nodded, pointing to the driveway. Clive seemed to argue, but Oliver shook his head, still smiling. Clive shrugged, nodded, and closed the door.

Oliver's face became grim as he turned and climbed back down the stairs. He stopped in the space between the house and the barn, his head swivelling as he searched for her. He looked back at the barn and headed across the driveway toward it. He must be wondering if she were hiding there, waiting for him to leave before she ran to the house for help.

It took about ten minutes before Oliver returned to the driveway. This time he hurried past her. For all he knew, she might have doubled back through the trees and fled to one of the other houses while he was wasting time at Clive's. Or she might have headed to town; they weren't that far away from Crane here. If someone had picked her up, the police could be looking for him any minute now.

Anna made herself count to one hundred before she stepped out of the trees. Oliver had disappeared around the bend, so he wouldn't be able to see her if he looked back. She started jogging up the driveway, the house with its welcoming light getting nearer all the time. It felt like Christmas and Ben and Charlie all wrapped up in one.

She almost didn't turn in time when she heard the noise behind her. She whirled, and Oliver's knife whizzed past her right arm. Jumping back, Anna stared at him in shock. Oliver's face was fearsome. The kindly father-figure had turned into a snarling animal.

"Hold still, goddammit. You're done, Anna. You never had a chance."

But he was wrong. She'd already survived the car crash, the freezing snow, and a knife attack. She was this close to safety. If he were going to kill her, she was going to take a piece out of him first.

"Go to hell, Oliver!"

He launched himself at her and she pivoted at the last minute, grabbing his knife arm and dragging him past with all her might. Oliver took two flailing steps before slamming into the ground.

Anna jumped onto his back, grabbed his knife hand, and sank her teeth into it. He shrieked and dropped the knife. Unable to free his hand from her teeth, he managed to twist sharply and knock Anna to the ground. They struggled, Anna kicking, scratching, and biting any part of him that she could reach.

"Oliver!"

They froze. Someone rushed up behind Oliver, grabbed his arm, and dragged him to his feet. Anna stared from the ground as Oliver gazed, dumbfounded, at Warren.

"Oliver, what are you doing? Leave Anna alone."

"Warren? Where did you come from, son?" Oliver said, instinctively reverting to the fatherly-figure. Anna climbed quickly to her feet, watching both men warily.

"I got worried. You looked so uneasy this evening when we were talking about Rick and Lauren, and then you didn't come back after you said you had something to tell Anna. I called Magdalena to find out where Anna lived. I was worried about her. On the way out, I found her car flipped in a ditch, your car abandoned, and tracks leading across the snow. I've been following you."

The knife was on the ground next to Oliver. His eyes shifted to it before he glanced back at Warren.

"Did you tell Bea where you were going?"

"What? No. I told her you'd be back soon, but I had to go. What's this all about?"

"It's like this," the older man said, but then he stooped suddenly and Anna yelled, "Watch out, Warren!"

Oliver straightened, the knife arcing toward Warren. Warren caught Oliver's wrist, and they closed, shuffling and grunting. The older man had the element of surprise; Warren looked amazed as he realized Oliver was in deadly earnest.

The house door slammed open, and Anna whirled. Clive stepped out with a rifle in his hands. He pumped the lever and shouted, "Anna, move!"

She dove to the ground, and there was a 'crack.'

Anna looked up. Oliver appeared to be hugging Warren. The two men stared at each other before they both collapsed.

"Clive, help!" Anna shouted, springing up and running to them.

23

Anna sat on the back of the EMS truck with a blanket wrapped around her shoulders and a mug of hot tea in her hands. This was beginning to be a familiar part of her life, she thought ruefully. Constables from Crane's RCMP detachment strode purposely around Clive's driveway, erecting crime scene tape, taking pictures and measurements, and examining the snow. Corporal John Fox Child was arguing with Clive, who didn't want to give up his gun. A gurney went by, carried by two ambulance attendants. Oliver lay on it, swaddled in a blanket, his face grimacing. Minutes later, his ambulance departed.

A black BMW screeched up the lane and was forced to stop where the police vehicles blocked the driveway. The door flew open, and Magdalena jumped out. She dashed past the cruisers and under the tape before anyone realized what was happening. Skirting the people working in the driveway, she ran straight for the EMS trucks.

"Anna, are you all right? Did Oliver hurt you?" She grabbed Anna's shoulders and peered into her face. Anna put down her mug, half the tea dripping down the front of her blanket, to take her boss's hands.

"I'm okay, Magdalena. I'm not hurt."

"I couldn't get my car started in the cold. I had to find a neighbour with some booster cables. I was so worried.

Warren said . . . Wait, where's Warren? Did he find you? And where's Oliver?"

Steve Walker stepped up to them. "Magdalena, you can't just go running through a crime scene like that," he said.

Ignoring him, Magdalena stared at Anna with desperation in her eyes. "Anna, where's Warren?"

Anna pointed at the EMS truck parked next to hers. "He's in there. He has to go to the hospital." Magdalena blanched, her fingers loosening their grip on Anna's shoulders. Steve grasped her shoulders, as much to restrain Magdalena as to hold her up in case she fainted.

"He'll be all right," Anna hastened to say.

Magdalena took a deep breath, and the colour returned to her face. "What happened?" she demanded.

"It was Oliver who killed Julia and Latona. He told me so himself." Anna took the next few minutes to explain about the Sumpters' financial problems, the fertilizer company's secret client list, Julia's plan to expose Oliver at the press conference, and Latona's attempt to blackmail him.

"Tonight Oliver thought that I suspected him, so he followed me. He ran me off the road and was going to inject me with an air bubble so that it would look like I had frozen to death in the wreckage. But I got away and made it here to Clive's farm. Warren caught up with us just as Oliver was trying to stab me. They were struggling with the knife when Clive shot them. The bullet passed right through Oliver's shoulder and lodged in Warren's arm. You just missed Oliver being taken away, in fact. Warren will need surgery to remove the bullet, but otherwise he's okay. Although he's taking it pretty hard. I think it's broken his heart that the man who seemed like a father to him is a murderer."

Magdalena indicated the red cut on Anna's cheek. A large purple bruise was beginning to appear around it.

"Did Oliver do that?"

Anna touched her face. "This? No. My purse hit me when the car rolled."

"She agreed to have the EMS attendant check her out, but she wouldn't let them take her to Emergency," Steve said.

Anna grinned at Magdalena. "Sound familiar?"

Magdalena turned to Steve. "Can I ride in the ambulance with Warren?"

He shrugged. "I don't see why not, if it's all right with him."

Magdalena handed Anna her car key. "Here. It sounds like you'll be needing transportation home. Take my car."

"Thanks," Anna said, impressed by her boss's generosity. Her BMW. "I'll get it back to you tomorrow after I can arrange for a rental."

Magdalena slipped her arms around Anna and gently hugged her. Anna's eyes grew even wider.

"I'm just so glad that you're all right," Magdalena murmured in Anna's ear. "When Warren said he thought you might be in danger, I was afraid you might be the next victim. I'm sorry to have involved you in this."

Anna patted Magdalena's back. "I'm all right. Better than all right. I looked my demons in the face tonight, and I beat them."

Her boss leaned backward to study Anna's smiling face. "Good for you," Magdalena said approvingly. She turned to Steve and added, "Now, take me to Warren."

Anna sat on Tremaine's lap in her living room the next day. His keen grey eyes watched her face as she finished providing a detailed account of the last three weeks. The conversation had begun on the drive back from the airport.

"So, you see, the problem was that there were two sets of criminals working independently — Oliver, and Rick and Lauren — making it that much harder for Detective Soo to piece it all together."

Tremaine shook his head as he squeezed Anna in his arms. "I don't know if I should be relieved or have a heart attack because you might have died last night." He kissed her, and she nestled her uninjured cheek against his.

"I discovered how resilient I am, Charlie. No bad dreams last night, and nothing but a few aches and pains this morning to remind me of what happened. I slept in and took a sick day, but Magdalena didn't seem to mind. She didn't say a word when I handed back her key on the way to the airport."

"I should say so. She was the one who got you into this," he said angrily.

Anna didn't respond. She closed her eyes and wallowed in the magic of Charlie's arms. Now that he was here, she felt at peace. Christmas was going to be wonderful this year. She felt Charlie relax. They were quiet together with Wendy keeping watch at their feet.

"A lot of people suffered in this one," Tremaine said contemplatively. "Aside from the murder victims, I mean. Warren, Magdalena, Beatrix Sumpter, Kevin, and you." He pushed back her hair with his long fingers and traced a soft line down her throat. "What's going to happen to Mrs. Sumpter now that Oliver's been arrested?"

Anna bit his earlobe playfully. She didn't want him to think that she was an invalid requiring delicate treatment. They hadn't seen each other since October.

"Oh, she'll be okay. Warren's going to take care of her. She's been more of a mother to him than anyone else has."

"That's good." He spent several seconds kissing her throat before pushing back her collar to nip her bare shoulder. "I suppose Warren's going to remain at Westmore?"

Anna's pulse began to quicken. "Actually, he and Magdalena were talking. He's thinking about moving on." She reached down to tug Tremaine's pullover over his head, tousling his short, blond hair. He was wearing a white t-shirt underneath. Anna stroked his chest through the fabric and watched his eyes darken.

"With his reputation and experience, he shouldn't have any trouble finding another position."

Tremaine nodded. Drawing up the back of her shirt, he ran his hands underneath. There was one ticklish place between her ribs. When he found it, she laughed and squirmed away.

"Stop that." She reached behind and tugged his hands away.

"Nothing like an old-fashioned game of 'slap and tickle,'" he said with a grin.

She glanced at her watch. "Shoot. Ben's going to be home for dinner in just thirty-two minutes. I told him we wouldn't be holding our orgy until after he leaves."

Tremaine's grin became positively devilish, and Anna hopped off his lap.

"I've got something to distract you. Magdalena sent you a present."

"For me?"

"Yes, and she said it's important that you open it tonight." Anna ran to the front hall where Tremaine had ditched his suitcase and returned holding a plastic bag. She took out a box wrapped in handsome green-and-gold striped paper and tied with matching green ribbon. Handing it to

Tremaine with a curtsy, Anna dropped onto the couch beside him to watch.

Her eyes grew large when he had torn away the paper to reveal a dark purple box with silver lettering. He opened the box, folded back the tissue, and stared at the contents. One eyebrow rose elegantly.

"Are you sure this is for me?" He picked up the red lingerie by its bra straps, the white pompoms dangling from their cords. A cream-coloured card dropped from the silky material.

"Wait, there's a note. It says, 'Happy Christmas, Tremaine. Tell Anna to wear the panties.'" He dug deeper into the box. "There are panties?"

Anna squealed, and Tremaine chased her to the bedroom with the box tucked under his arm.

~ THE END ~

Hello Dolly Squares

Preheat oven to 325°F.
Grease a 9" square pan.

½ cup melted margarine
1½cups graham crumbs
¼ cup white sugar
1 cup flaked coconut
1 cup chocolate chips (Semisweet, although you may try milk chocolate, like Anna.)
1 (14 oz) can sweetened condense milk
1 cup chopped walnuts or pecans (Optional. Anna doesn't use them.)

Melt the margarine first. If you melt it in your microwave, make sure you cover the bowl first so that it doesn't spatter.

Mix the melted margarine, sugar, and graham crumbs together and press them into the pan.

Sprinkle the coconut and chocolate chips (and nuts, if desired) over the crust.

Drizzle with the sweetened condensed milk.

Bake for 25 to 30 minutes until the edges begin to brown.

Cool and cut. Enjoy!

Discover other titles by Cathy Spencer

Also in the Anna Nolan Series:

Framed for Murder, Book 1

Winner of the 2014 Bony Blithe Mystery Award. Anna Nolan discovers her ex-husband, Jack, on a deserted country road one night . . . dead, unfortunately. He could only have been in town to see Anna, unless Jack was looking for their son, Ben. At least, that's how the tall, cool Brit leading the police investigation sees it. To divert suspicion away from her son and herself, Anna delves into Jack's personal life, only to discover that the actor had been romancing three very different women on a nearby film set. With some rather unorthodox ideas on how to conduct a murder investigation, Anna sets about meeting her ex-husband's lovers, with harrowing results!

Town Haunts, Book 2

Cemetery caretaker Sherman Mason is horrified to hear his dead wife calling to him from her grave. He asks newcomer Tiernay Rae, a gorgeous witch, to hold a seance to find out what's troubling his wife's ghost. Tiernay needs a coven to focus her powers, however, so Anna Nolan and her friends volunteer to help. But with Halloween fast approaching and the seance unleashing a malicious evil in the small town, can Tiernay stop it before someone gets hurt or even killed?

Romances by Cathy Spencer

The Dating Do-Over

Elementary school teacher Viv Nowak has a sympathetic heart and abominable taste in men. She expects an engagement ring when her live-in lover of six years lands a terrific job in a new city. Instead, she gets dumped . . . on Valentine's Day! Everyone, from her best friends to her father to her estranged mother, has an opinion on how she should fix her life. Her friends even insist on a dating do-over. But will they like her choice when she finally decides what her heart wants?

The Affairs of Harriet Walters, Spinster

Harriet Walters, a twenty-six year old spinster, is evicted from her home and sent to live with a persnickety aunt. Resigned to the life of an unpaid companion, fate intervenes and Harriet becomes an heiress. Leaving her small town life for the glittering attractions of London, Harriet chooses an unconventional path to happiness and love. A sweet, old-fashioned regency.

Author Cathy Spencer is married to a singer/actor/teacher. He didn't actually say "marry me and see Canada" when he proposed, but that's practically what happened. They have lived on the west coast in Vancouver, on the east coast in St. John's, in Calgary, Alberta, and are currently living in Ontario.

Cathy writes both romance and mystery novels. *Framed for Murder*, winner of the 2014 Bony Blithe Mystery Award, is the first in the Anna Nolan series, cozy mysteries with elements of romance and humour. The second novel, *Town Haunts*, takes place at Halloween, while the third, *Tidings of Murder and Woe*, is set at Christmas. Cathy has written two romances, a contemporary comedy entitled, *The Dating Do-Over*, and a sweet regency, *The Affairs of Harriet Walters, Spinster*. She has also published two short story collections, *Tall Tales Twin-Pack, Mysteries* and *Tall Tales Twin-Pack, Science Fiction and Fantasy*.

Connect with Cathy online:
Website http://cmspencer.blogspot.com
Facebook https://www.facebook.com/CathySpencerAuthor